"Wilderness by candlelight."

Marta looked at Mac with raised eyebrows. "Who packs candles for a canoe trip?"

"Hey, *I* didn't pack this."

Suddenly Marta remembered that niggling thought she'd had about her daughter. Before she could voice her suspicions, Mac asked, "You didn't happen to notice a lot of quiet phone calls lately between your daughter and my son, did you?"

Marta groaned. Oh, no. It must be true.

Mac stood and held out his hand to Marta. He looked down at her, the puzzled expression on his face softening. His eyes held hers as he gently brushed her hair back from her cheek. "You know, I was thinking.... Maybe we *should* go together, just like they want."

"You mean, to plot our revenge?"

"Well, that wasn't quite what I had in mind...."

ABOUT THE AUTHOR

Jenna McKnight started writing stories when she was nine, as an antidote to schoolwork. Since retiring from her work in physical therapy, she's turned to writing full-time. *Eleven Year Match* is her first novel. Jenna makes her home in St. Louis, Missouri, with her husband and teenage daughter.

JENNA McKNIGHT

ELEVEN YEAR MATCH

Harlequin Books

TORONTO • NEW YORK • LONDON
AMSTERDAM • PARIS • SYDNEY • HAMBURG
STOCKHOLM • ATHENS • TOKYO • MILAN

Published February 1992

ISBN 0-373-16426-2

ELEVEN YEAR MATCH

Copyright © 1992 by Jenna McKnight. All rights reserved.
Except for use in any review, the reproduction or utilization
of this work in whole or in part in any form by any electronic,
mechanical or other means, now known or hereafter invented,
including xerography, photocopying and recording,
or in any information storage or retrieval system, is forbidden without
the permission of the publisher, Harlequin Enterprises Limited,
225 Duncan Mill Road, Don Mills, Ontario, Canada M3B 3K9.

All the characters in this book have no existence outside the
imagination of the author and have no relation whatsoever to
anyone bearing the same name or names. They are not even
distantly inspired by any individual known or unknown to the
author, and all incidents are pure invention.

® are Trademarks registered in the United States Patent and
Trademark Office and in other countries.

Printed in U.S.A.

Chapter One

Marta Howard vaulted into the passenger seat of the white and orange ambulance without a millisecond of wasted time or motion. Buckling her seat belt was as automatic as breathing. She was an experienced emergency medical technician and was used to responding to life-and-death situations on a daily basis.

John Summers, her partner of eighteen months, slid in behind the steering wheel with equally rapid ease and set the ambulance in immediate motion.

"Do you need me to check the map?" Marta asked, ready to get it if needed. But she knew by the first turn that Summers was off on another of his famous shortcuts. His knowledge of the back streets of St. Louis was phenomenal.

"Nope," Summers answered in his usual succinct style. "Chest pains, right?"

"Right."

Summers turned on the siren to warn other drivers that they were only slowing down at stop signs, and then only when necessary. A call for chest pains was a race against time. Marta used the travel time to review a mental checklist of the equipment they would need to take in with them when they arrived.

Their destination was a two-story brick apartment building in the southern section of the city, a predominantly German area. As Summers stopped the ambulance at the curb, Marta's quick glance at the scene revealed nothing unusual. It was a quiet neighborhood. The four-family building blended in with its neighbors, with its tidy lawn, neatly painted trim and hanging baskets of red geraniums.

"Where to?" Summers asked as they selected the necessary equipment without missing a beat. They quickly set the oxygen tank and jump kit on the stretcher and each took an end.

"Upstairs on the right. A Mrs. Braun called about her husband," Marta replied as they moved toward the building at a fast walk.

Once inside, appearances changed drastically. As the door closed behind them, there was barely enough daylight from the grime-encrusted transom window for them to see where they were going. The foyer tiles were blackened with dirt and covered by a poor excuse for a rug that didn't even lie flat. Summers tripped over the edge of it and came to an abrupt stop, causing Marta to do the same.

"What the—?" Summers didn't finish his expletive as he looked around for a light switch, a nearly impossible task until his eyes adjusted to the dimness.

Marta set down her end of the stretcher, frustrated with the hazardous conditions and the resulting delay. She threw the foyer rug out the door to the far side of the spotless front porch. "At least this way we won't trip over it on our way down. Too bad it's not dark out or I could throw it in the trash can," she muttered. "It'll probably just end up back on the floor."

Summers found a light switch and flicked it several times to no avail. "I doubt it. It doesn't look like anybody lifts a finger in here."

"Maybe not, but they do outside, and you can bet they won't leave that rug out there for long." Marta propped open the door for light with a paint can she found on the floor. "Let's go."

They were admitted to the second-floor apartment by a petite elderly woman, dressed very plainly in a starched house dress with a clean white apron. Her gray hair was pulled neatly back into a bun. One look at their uniforms and she gratefully stepped aside so they could enter. Marta introduced herself and her partner.

"He's right in there." Mrs. Braun gestured toward the front room. "I told them on the phone that he said his chest hurt, but he says the pain's stopped now."

An emaciated man sat limply in a vinyl recliner, looking as small as a child in an adult's chair. His right hand pressed against his chest as though to suppress pain. Lifting the fingers of his left hand from where they lay on the stuffed armrest was the extent of his effort to say hello.

Marta reached for Mr. Braun's right hand while Summers prepared to administer oxygen and check vital signs. There were several burns on the man's fingers, not all of them new. "How did you hurt your hand?"

Mr. Braun neither answered nor looked up.

"He's hard of hearing," his wife explained. "He gets shocked sometimes when he plugs in his razor, or the coffeepot."

"Where did he say the pain was exactly?" Marta asked.

Mrs. Braun answered Marta's questions as Marta opened the jump kit and pulled out the EKG leads. As soon as he saw those, Mr. Braun fumbled with the buttons on his shirt.

Marta smiled reassuringly at him, so he would know he was on the right track. "So you've done this before?" she said conversationally, even though he couldn't hear her.

"Last year," his wife answered, watching Marta put the leads on her husband's chest.

Marta continued working with Mr. Braun while Summers went into the kitchen, both to check the medications, which Mrs. Braun had indicated were kept on the counter, and to have a closer look at the electrical outlets.

Marta looked into the kitchen just as Summers jumped two feet into the air and came back down to earth with his index finger stuck in his mouth. He muttered an expletive around the injured digit.

"Have you called the apartment manager about the wiring?" Marta asked Mrs. Braun as Summers nursed his finger.

"Well, it's an old building," she answered with hesitation, wringing her hands in her apron. "With old wires and all." She obviously felt that any complaints would be considered making trouble.

"Your building manager should have an electrician fix this, ma'am. Or your building won't be old, it'll be burned down." Summers was not known for beating around the bush.

"I guess I could call him again." She sounded uncertain about it, and neither Marta nor Summers was convinced.

"Time to transport," Marta said.

Marta explained with hand gestures to Mr. Braun that they were going to lift him onto the stretcher and take him to the hospital. All the while she reassured him with confident smiles and a pat on the shoulder. They secured him to the stretcher in a semireclining position with the oxygen tank and monitor strapped on beside him. Then they carried him down the stairs, raised and locked the stretcher into position and wheeled him the rest of the way to the ambulance.

"How's your finger?" Marta asked in a spare second.

"Fine," Summers said, holding up his slightly reddened fingertip.

Marta smiled. "Nothing your girlfriend, Janie, can't kiss and make all better."

He smiled back. "That's what I thought."

After Mr. Braun was safely loaded in the rear of the ambulance, Marta noticed Summers pause briefly to study the building. "What are you looking at?" she inquired casually. Her dark-haired partner was not one to waste time looking at a flower garden when they had a cardiac patient waiting to be transported.

"Checking the address."

"Don't bother. I guarantee we came to the right place," she replied dryly.

"I was here on call last Spring. It was a nice place then. Funny how fast it's gone downhill."

"Get the number off that For Rent sign I saw in the window. I'll call the manager for Mrs. Braun. She didn't seem too enthused about the idea of calling."

Summers closed and latched the rear doors, and Marta remained in back with Mr. Braun to monitor his vital signs and overall condition. She radioed St. Andrew's Hospital to give them patient information, including data regarding oxygen and the heart monitor, and to give them an ETA of five minutes.

"Room four," directed the efficient nurse at the triage desk.

Marta and Summers had barely completed transferring Mr. Braun to the examining table before the room was swarming with staff. Debbie, a nurse Marta knew, was trying to explain to Mr. Braun what she was doing while a student took vital signs under the guidance of another nurse. A volunteer was ready to hold the door open to the main hall so that she and Summers could leave with the stretcher.

"Gee, guys," Marta said with a knowing smile. "Slow day, huh?"

"It sure makes for a long one," Debbie admitted with a sigh. "At least now we'll have something to do. Mac's on the other side twiddling his thumbs." Emergency was divided into two functioning halves, each staffed by a doctor and two nurses, whatever volunteers they were fortunate enough to get and the students who were required to be there. "I think he's about to go out and break some bones just so he'll have something to do."

Marta laughed. Dr. Lawrence "Mac" Macke seldom worked in the emergency room, but Marta knew him and most of the others on sight. As far as doctors went, Dr. Macke seemed to be less obnoxious than most.

"Tell him I'll see what I can find."

"Promises, promises," Mac said as he and the elderly Dr. Fletcher entered the room. Mac leaned against the doorframe and looked bored. This was Dr. Fletcher's half of Emergency, and he really didn't need assistance. There wasn't enough work here to keep one of them busy.

Marta turned and looked at him. "Bored, Dr. Macke?"

"To tears, Mrs. Howard." Mac tipped his head to one side to stretch a stiff muscle. He ran a hand over the back of his neck, just below where his light brown hair curled slightly over the collar of his shirt.

"You can always pray for rain during rush hour. That's always good for a few broken bones."

"Too late. I'll be done by then."

Marta shrugged. Short of going out and running over someone, there was nothing she could do for him.

"At this point I wouldn't even care if you brought me someone with a rash."

"If anybody calls us for a rash, I'll be sure to bring them here," Marta promised on her way out the door. She made it a point not to hang around after the handoff and get drawn into conversations with doctors. She disliked the way they always stuck together when one of their own made a mistake.

"Will it help if I beg?" he called out just as the door swung shut behind her.

Marta had never seen a doctor beg for anything, and she wasn't about to hold her breath this time. Ordering was their usual style. It was taught in medical school. Ordering 101.

"She's always in a hurry, isn't she?" Mac asked the room in general.

"She's busy," Debbie said.

"She doesn't like doctors." Fletcher spoke slowly as he worked, imparting the wisdom of his years, relishing his audience. "She doesn't know I know, but I know."

Mac's curiosity was aroused. "You think so?"

"I work Emergency more than you do, Mac. She's turned down every intern, every resident and every doctor who's ever asked her for a date." He emphasized each *every* for effect. "And, I might add, that number adds up into double digits. So, if you're thinking what I think you're thinking, forget it."

"Don't be ridiculous. I'm too busy to date."

"Mmm-hmm," Fletcher replied.

MARTA SAT in the lounge at the scarred wooden table, filling out yet another emergency report. She propped up her feet on an empty chair, muttering unkind things about the cigarette smoke in the room and how EMTs ought to know better. Summers was stretched out supine on the orange vinyl couch, his face buried in a newspaper.

Johnson and Hawkings, the other EMT team who shared the lounge, sat at the table with Marta. Their chipped mugs of coffee were in front of them, and their cigarettes spiraled smoke up toward the yellowed ceiling tiles. They were each holding ten cards. Gin was their favorite on-duty pastime. Off duty, Hawk was a dedicated, middle-aged family man, and Johnson was a dedicated skirt chaser.

"Howard." The nonurgent call came from the supervisor's office. Marta had given up on him ever calling her by her first name. For a month after she'd started work she'd kept trying to get him to call her Marta. And he'd kept telling her everything was more professional if everyone called everyone else by their surname. Summers had explained it with one word: *Army*.

Marta thrust her pen and report form into Summers's hands on her way to the super's office just off the lounge, knowing that the report would be finished by the time she returned. Summers was the best partner she had ever had. He was strong, conscientious, honest, reliable. And he was helpful. Not the "Oh, you're a woman, let me get the door for you" type helpful. But he *would* get the door if her hands were full, just as she would get it for him. They looked out for each other.

"Yes?" She stopped just inside the doorway.

The supervisor was a middle-aged, balding, "retired" paramedic. With the advent of a back injury two years ago, and unable to lift anything heavier than a phone book, he had accepted this desk job. While his experience was invaluable, his attitude was brisk, efficient, all business and no play.

"The Boy Scouts need a substitute teacher for their first-aid class tomorrow after school. You volunteered."

A slow smile spread across Marta's face. "Did anyone else volunteer with me?"

"You want Hawkings? You can take him. I can't turn Johnson loose with a bunch of eleven-year-old boys—he'd have them using rubbers for tourniquets. And Summers is just too damn quiet."

"He's also dying of smoke inhalation out there."

"Take Hawkings. You both have kids. You'll know how to communicate with them."

Marta and Hawk spent the next hour searching through the shelves in the storeroom for the items they would need to instruct a group of preteen boys in basic first aid. Summers and Johnson took the next call that came in.

"What school are we going to?" Hawk asked while Marta piled his arms full of stretch bandages, gauze and triangle slings.

"Lewis School in Webster. Where are the safety pins?"

"Behind you. Isn't that where Sherri goes?"

"Yeah. Some of these boys will probably be from her class. You've got three sons, Hawk. Do you have any helpful hints on how to talk to eleven-year-old boys?" Marta climbed up on a stool and searched the top shelves.

"Oh, sure. Talk gory."

"Gory?" Marta paused and looked down at Hawk for verification.

"Well, yeah. You can't talk to them like you do to Sherri. She's a girl. She takes gymnastics. When she and her best friend are together, you probably talk tumbling, twirling and trampoline. Am I right?"

Marta nodded, somewhat distressed that she was so predictable, and somewhat relieved that Hawk understood.

"And the main topic for the past two weeks has been the uneven parallel bars." Marta grimaced. "You know, the ones where the high bar is over her head and someone has to lift her up to get her started?"

Hawk chuckled. "I'll bet you were about to bite your nails off when you saw that."

Marta stepped off the stool and piled more stretch gauze onto Hawk. "Actually I was pretty impressed with the instructor. She spots the girls really carefully, even when she's sure they know what they're doing. And that's saying something, since all eleven-year-old girls think they know what they're doing."

"Boys, too. They think they know all about bike racing. You know, that motor-cross stuff. But when you listen to them, they talk about wipeouts, skids and road burns. Real blood-and-guts stuff." Hawk shook his head. "And that's not to mention the movies they like to watch. Last time I took the twins to the show, I almost had to leave when they had this close-up of the eyes of the victim and the guy's hands—"

"I get the point," Marta interrupted as quickly as possible, wondering why he let his kids see movies like that. "Boys like gore, gore and more gore."

"Right!"

"Maybe we should take a bottle of ketchup along for dramatic effects."

Hawk smiled. "Then you would be 'The Awesome Mrs. Howard.'"

"WHEW!" Summers said with a big smile on his face later that afternoon. "I thought you were going to get to deliver that one in the back."

"Thanks to your driving, that's one more baby who gets to be born in the hospital."

"Too bad we didn't have time to get them to St. Andrew's," Marta lamented as they approached the exit, their stretcher between them. "They were so bored this morning when we handed off Mr. Braun, even a normal delivery would have been welcome."

"Mac said to bring him a rash, not a mother ready to drop a baby in his lap."

"Not exactly the same thing, huh?"

"Not quite."

"Howard! Wait up!"

Marta and Summers heard Hawk's call and turned as they were just about to exit through the automatic doors at the Emergency entrance. Hawk and Johnson approached quickly.

"How was yours?" Marta asked conversationally. They had been sent out at the same time, and both had been directed to bring their patients to this hospital's ER.

"Uh, look, I just talked to the super and he says there's someone over at St. Andrew's who wants to see you." Hawk stumbled over his words, clearly nervous.

"Who?"

"I'm sure she's okay. It's probably nothing major or anything." He licked his lips, and Marta was more worried about this tower of strength crumbling in front of her than what he was gibbering about.

"Yeah, it happens to all kids," Johnson added.

"What happens to all kids?"

"Well, you know, they fall. Out of trees, off bikes, down stairs, off roofs," Johnson was running his phrases together as usual.

"Who fell?" A kid? At the hospital? Fell? Images were flashing through Marta's mind of every kind of accident that could befall a child, when her brain suddenly switched from work mode to motherly nightmares. "Did Sherri fall?"

Before anyone had time to answer, Marta could feel her hair suddenly stand on end. She broke out in a sweat, and her stomach felt as heavy as if she'd eaten a pound of lead.

"Geez, Johnson, you're scaring her," Hawk admonished as Marta went pale. "I'm sure she's okay, really." Now that Hawk had gotten the hard part out of the way—relaying the bad news—his nervousness disappeared and his mind started ticking off ways to handle a frantic mother, which Marta was quickly in danger of becoming.

"She fell?" What was today? Tuesday. Open gym at gymnastics, which meant less supervision! "Did she fall off the high bar? How bad is it? Where is she?"

Summers put a comforting hand on her shoulder. "Easy, Howard. They're not explaining this very well, but they did say she's okay."

"How do they know? Did they see her?" she asked Summers sharply, then turned back to the other two men. "Did you see her?" she demanded, knowing they hadn't. "I knew I never should have let her take gymnastics!"

Marta stormed out the hospital door with Summers right behind her. She didn't remember loading the stretcher, getting into the van, buckling her seat belt or any of the siren-screaming ride to her daughter's side.

They were supposed to return the ambulance immediately after their last run of the day. Go directly home. Do not stop. Do not pass go. There were other rules, too. Like do not exceed the speed limit. Do not use the siren needlessly. Summers broke every rule in order to get Marta to St. Andrew's as quickly as possible.

When Sherri had first asked to take gymnastics with her best friend Laurie, Marta had almost panicked. Would the teachers be qualified? What safety measures would be taken? Were the teachers not only qualified to teach the dangerous maneuvers, but were they also up-to-date on emergency procedures?

They had visited three gymnastics centers. One was very rigorous, and the teacher made the girls do push-ups for every infraction. No one was going to bully Marta Howard's daughter into doing tricky stunts!

The second center had seemed okay in all respects, but at the third one Sherri had just seemed to click with the very qualified teachers. They had allowed Marta to watch them take Sherri through a trial hour of instruction. One of the first things they'd stressed was the right way to fall. And an added bonus was that the hospital was right across the highway.

Should she have let Sherri engage in an activity where accidents were bound to occur? Should she have made sure that she, Marta, was in the gym during the whole two hours, just in case? After all, who could cope better with an emergency than an EMT?

Sherri had pointed out that accidents occurred everywhere. And who knew that better than Marta? Hadn't she told Sherri about many of the odd accidents that happened to people in their own homes? About people who had gone out for a nice, safe hour of fun, like bowling, just to get their toes broken when the guy in the next lane let a ball slip? Sherri had quoted a dozen incidents of accidents that happened in "safe" places, using carefully selected newspaper articles to back up her case.

In the end Marta had given in. She'd told herself how Sherri would improve her balance, muscle tone and coordination. How she would learn responsibility for her own body, stretching out and cooling down gradually. How she and Laurie would grow more self-assured together, instead of growing apart, pursuing different interests.

Now Marta's baby was in the hospital. She asked Summers what he knew about the message. Who had called? Had they said what was broken? Was Sherri conscious? Was she brought in by a trained crew, or did someone just pick up her broken body and put her in the back seat for the ride to the emergency room?

Summers was unable to answer any of those questions, and the thought that an inexperienced, untrained person may have picked up her injured child was almost enough to make Marta scream. Finally they pulled into the ambulance court.

Once in the hospital, confronted with all that was routine, Marta bypassed reception and made a beeline for a familiar face.

"Hi, Debbie, where's my daughter?" she asked in a rush, anxious to find Sherri and assess her condition for herself. At Debbie's blank look, Marta continued. "Sherri Howard, eleven years old, fell in gymnastics—"

"She's your daughter? Oh, Marta, I'm sorry. Mac treated her on the other side."

Sorry! Marta didn't wait for any more *sorrys*. She ran down to the other end of the hall and started looking in the examining rooms.

Chapter Two

Marta's check of the examining rooms came up empty. Knowing Sherri probably had been admitted, might even be on her way to surgery, Marta looked around for someone who would know about her daughter's whereabouts.

"Joan!" she said, recognizing the nurse coming out of room ten. "Where's Sherri Howard?"

"Oh, hi, Marta." Joan took a closer look and frowned. "Are you okay?"

Marta gripped Joan's arm. "Sherri's my daughter. I just got word that she was brought here from gymnastics."

Joan tried to steer Marta toward a quiet examining room and some privacy. "Calm down, Marta. You'll get her all upset."

Marta balked at the door. "I already looked in there. Where is she?"

Joan looked at her watch. "She should be—"

"Mom!" A volunteer pushed a very relieved-looking Sherri around the corner in a wheelchair. "I thought you couldn't come."

"Sherri." Marta breathed a sigh of relief, her hand going to her chest as though to still her pounding heart.

Sherri's right arm was in a cast and sling. Only her arm. Marta took another deep breath and tried to relax.

As Sherri started to get up, Marta quickly kicked the chair's footrests out of the way before they tripped her little girl, then enveloped her in a hug.

"Ow, that hurts my arm," Sherri protested.

"I'm sorry." Marta settled for holding Sherri's good hand. "Are you all right, sweetie?"

"Sure, Mom. I just slipped off the low beam. Look at the picture on my cast."

Marta was taken aback by Sherri's casual attitude. "Are you sure you didn't hit your head?" she asked and disguised her physical assessment of Sherri's cranium with a loving pat on the head.

"Mo-om," Sherri complained, not fooled for a minute. She tried unsuccessfully to hold up her cast. "Just my arm."

Marta's neighbor Linda appeared around the corner. She was Laurie's mother. "Marta! I'm glad you could make it. Did Sherri tell you what happened?"

"Something about the low beam."

"Low is right. She only fell about eighteen inches. The doctor says it's not a bad break. There he is, if you want to talk to him." Linda indicated Mac, farther down the hall.

"He's neat, Mom."

"I can take her with me to go back and get Laurie," Linda offered.

Marta looked at her little girl standing there, dried traces of tears on her cheeks in spite of her casual attitude, not much color in her face, putting on a brave front, and knew she had to keep her nearby.

"How would you like a ride in an ambulance?"

Sherri's eyes lit up. "Can I turn on the siren?"

"No, you can't turn on the siren."

"Come on, Sherri," Summers said, holding out his hand. "I'll show you where it is. Sometimes I bump it by accident." He winked at Marta over Sherri's head as she followed him willingly.

"Are you sure it's okay?" Linda asked.

"I'll make it okay," Marta assured her. "I'm off duty as soon as I get back to the office, anyway." She stopped and placed her hand on the other woman's arm. "Thanks."

"Nothing to it," Linda said with a wave of her hand, and gave Marta a brown plastic bottle. "Here're the pain pills the doctor prescribed. And the woman in the pay window would really like your insurance number."

"I'll take care of it after I talk to the doctor."

"Oh, speaking of which," Linda warned with a twinkle in her eye and a lowered voice, "I think Sherri may have done just a little matchmaking while she was getting her cast."

Marta frowned, then dismissed the thought. "She knows how I feel about doctors in general. She wouldn't do that."

"Well, maybe. But when I came back from getting her a cup of water, I know I heard her say you were single."

"I'm sure it was just for Medical Records. They're snoopy that way," Marta said with a quiet laugh. And she was sure Sherri wanted to live long enough to see her twelfth birthday.

"Dr. Macke?" Marta was too impatient to wait until he finished his notations.

"Yes?" When Mac looked up from the chart and noticed it was Marta, he snapped to attention. "Hey! I knew you would come through. What did you bring me?"

"Nothing this trip," she replied with a slightly forced smile. "I'm Sherri's mother. You just finished casting her arm."

"You're Sherri's mom? Gee, you didn't have to do that. You could have brought me just anyone off the street."

Marta was speechless. Arrogant doctor or not, she couldn't believe this man would joke about her little girl's painful broken arm.

"How come I never see you at the PTA meetings?" he asked.

"Excuse me?"

"Sherri and my son Rob go to the same school."

Marta didn't remember seeing him at school meetings, either, not that she had enough energy left over after work to attend each and every meeting. She summoned forth great amounts of tact. "Oh, I guess I just look like every other mom there. Look, I really wanted to ask you about Sherri's fracture."

"Let's see if her X rays are still out." He led the way into the casting room and needlessly pointed out the fractured bone with the end of his pen. "Nice and clean. I don't expect any problems, and you know what to watch for. Just bring her into the office in six weeks."

"What about capillary return?" Marta stared at the film, wanting to crawl inside of it for a closer look, to be absolutely certain they hadn't missed anything.

"Normal."

"Distal sensation?"

"Normal, really. A text-book clean break without complications."

Mac reached out to turn off the view box and noticed just how intently Marta was still staring at the films. While it was true he hadn't seen her at any PTA meetings, he certainly had noticed her in the emergency room from time to time. For the first time she looked vulnerable.

He knew Marta was a woman who took pride in her profession. She was quick, efficient and conscientious. If ever his son had to be brought into the ER, he would trust her to do it right.

He flipped the switch, and when the light went off she looked up at him briefly with worried blue eyes. "Hey, she'll be fine," he said softly. "I know how it is." He searched for the words. Both of them saw broken bones every day. "It's different when it's your own kid, isn't it?"

Marta nodded and was mortified to feel something suspiciously close to tears forming as he uttered the kind words. She'd expected a curt assurance that her kid was no different from any of his other patients. And the fact that he actually had something akin to a caring bedside manner played havoc with her already-strung-out emotions.

Mac noticed Marta's struggle to maintain her composure, and it was almost his undoing. Until now, he had always thought she was just another pretty worker, a slender brunette with an easy-care hair-style, like the ones so many nurses at the hospital wore—the ones with homes and families and a full-time job, and little time for elaborate hairdos. Shorter than he, about five-seven, she looked as though she worked out regularly.

Unlike the other women at the hospital, though, she seldom had more than business words for him. She always called him Doctor, and had never even mentioned that she had a daughter. Yet he could see that her neglect to mention Sherri hadn't been because she didn't love her daughter. It was as Dr. Fletcher had said: she just didn't like doctors.

"Look, I'm sorry about that crack I made." He smiled a little, tentatively, wanting to comfort this woman who had suddenly and inexplicably become more to him than just another coworker in the space of five minutes.

Marta looked up into his eyes, and he saw her confusion.

"You know, the one about breaking Sherri's arm just so I'd have something to do this afternoon."

"Oh, never mind." His wisecrack had been no less than she'd expected. And, since then, she had received so much more from him.

"She'll be all right, really."

"I know." Marta glanced back at the dark film.

Mac wasn't convinced, and he felt compelled to put his arm around her shoulders and give her a reassuring squeeze on their way out of the casting room. As Marta neatly stepped away from him in the expanse of the central corridor, an idea struck him.

"Here's my home number." He wrote it on a prescription pad. "I want you to call me anytime if there's a problem, or a question." Mac didn't anticipate either event, but other than extending this small concession, he didn't know how else to reassure her.

Marta was embarrassed, and she accepted the number with a shaky hand. What else could she do? Refuse his offer? The fact that she was taken aback by his unexpected compassion was no reason to be rude. She stuck the paper in her pocket, then stared at her hand. "Who would believe a simple broken arm would reduce me to this?" She tried to laugh it off.

Mac saw her eyes moisten again and knew the only comfort Marta would accept right now was to spend time with Sherri. He wondered at his own sudden inclination to be the one reassuring her. He had seen vulnerable women before, and he had seen strong women before. He tended to prefer the latter. He hadn't known Marta could be both.

"It's okay. It happens to the best of us. Call me if you need me. All right?"

Marta nodded. "Thank you, Dr. Macke." She started to turn away. Sherri was waiting. Summers was waiting. Her supervisor was going to be furious. Obviously her brain was starting to function again.

"Just 'Mac,'" he said.

"What?" she asked, turning back. Now that her worries about Sherri had been laid safely to rest, she could notice the man standing there. Really notice him. Sherri had called him neat, but different words quickly came to her mind. Handsome, caring, concerned. Sexy.

"My name is Mac."

Unfortunately the word *doctor* also came to mind. "Thanks, Dr. Macke. See you in six weeks."

Marta remembered to see the cashier and give her her medical insurance number. But her mind was on the person she loved the most and the man who had kindly put the broken pieces back together again. By the time the cashier was satisfied, however, Marta had only Sherri on her mind, and she hurried out to the waiting ambulance, climbing in and closing the door.

"Ready," she told Summers. "Buckle up, Sherri," she said automatically.

"Mo-om," Sherri whined as she rolled her eyes and held up her casted arm as evidence that she was incapacitated.

Summers reached over and buckled her in, then started the engine and pulled out, "bumping" the siren for a couple of short bleeps when they were on the street.

"Awesome!" was Sherri's comment. "Wait until I tell Laurie about this. She will be so-o-o jealous."

Marta smiled to herself. Sherri had always been a realistic child and was handling this injury with aplomb. She had always handled medical things without any fuss. From the time she was very little, she had never refused to open her mouth for the icky-tasting cough syrup. When she turned six and could reach the first aid box, she started patching up her own cuts and scrapes with peroxide and Band-Aids.

Sherri was well-known at the office, and before Marta could finish gathering her things there was a cast-signing in the lounge. Besides the four men on Marta's shift, the next shift coming in also took part with various colored markers.

"Who drew the picture?" someone asked.

"Dr. Macke," Sherri replied. "Isn't it radical?"

Marta lifted her eyebrows at her daughter's speech and made a mental note to check out the "radical" picture after dinner, and after she called her sister Kelly about the upcoming Labor Day float trip, which would have to be canceled.

"What's for dinner?" Sherri asked on the way home.

"What would you like?"

"You mean I get to choose? Awesome!"

"YOU'D BETTER NOT be calling to try to weasel out of the canoe trip," were the first words out of Kelly's mouth after "hello." Marta would rather have discussed this in person, but there wasn't time for them to get together right now.

"Look, Kelly, something's—"

"You promised," Kelly wailed. "Not only me, but you promised Sherri, too. Come on, Marta, it's not like those other singles groups. These people are fun. You like my husband, don't you?"

Marta sighed. It was an old argument. "Yes, Kelly, I like Ron. But that doesn't mean there're any more where you found him."

"Sure there are." Kelly's voice softened as she added, "Be sure to talk to Dave while you're on the river."

Marta could afford to be a little more patient than usual with Kelly's badgering, because she knew in the long run that Kelly would feel guilty about hounding her when she discovered that the cause of Marta's call was Sherri getting hurt.

"Look, Kelly, it's about Sherri—"

"Don't use her for an excuse, Marta. She really wants you to go."

"Only because you convinced her it would be to her benefit."

"Well, it will. If you had someone else in your life to worry about, you wouldn't have the time to overprotect her so much, Marta. All that nagging about vitamins and seat belts and looking both ways before she crosses the street. She's eleven years old, for heaven's sake."

"So? You're twice that and you could still use some good advice."

Kelly laughed. "I bet I know just the big sister who's ready to give me some, too. Come on, Marta, stick with our deal. You go on the Labor Day trip, give it a fair try, and I'll never, ever harass you again about being single."

"But Sherri—"

"Sherri will be fine with me. I love Sherri. It'll be like one, big, long slumber party. We'll pig out on caramel popcorn and chocolate bars."

Marta groaned and Kelly laughed. "I'll take good care of her, I promise."

"Broken arm and all?"

"What?"

"She fell in gymnastics today and broke her arm."

"Gosh, Marta, I'm sorry she's hurt. She'll be okay, won't she? I never would have accused you of trying to weasel out of this trip if I'd known. And you don't really overprotect her. Well, maybe a little bit, but not too much. Would you say something?"

"Why? You're doing a fine job of groveling."

"You're really enjoying this, aren't you?"

"Yes, but you don't sound quite guilty enough yet."

"You're the one backing out. Why should I feel guilty?"

"For trying to use my daughter, that's why."

Kelly sighed. "Tell Sherri I feel badly for her, and I'll come visit this weekend. And I hope she'll feel up to doing something with me by then."

"Sure, as long as you don't make her feel guilty for breaking her arm and making me miss this trip."

"Marta! That hurts. I would never—"

"Would, too."

"Would not!"

Marta hung up the phone with a smile on her face. She had been dreading the singles' group canoe trip, but she hadn't realized just how much until now. She felt as if a half-ton weight had just been lifted from her.

MAC ARRIVED HOME late, tired after a long, boring day, and wondered how people could survive jobs that didn't offer any challenge. He thrived on activity, even in the emergency room, where the time flew on a busy day.

He'd enjoyed treating Sherri and talking to Marta. In spite of the fact that not many words had been exchanged, he felt they had really communicated. He knew more about Marta now than anyone else who worked in the ER. He had seen her vulnerability and her love for her daughter.

He also had a feeling that Marta wouldn't appreciate ever being reminded that he had been kind to her, put his arm around her shoulders and offered her his home phone number. Knowing how she had been and knowing what Dr. Fletcher had told him about what she thought of doctors, he imagined that she might barely speak to him again when they met in the hospital the next time. He hoped he was wrong.

And, just in case she needed him tonight, Mac turned up the ringer volume on his phone while he took his shower.

WEDNESDAY MORNING was dreary and drizzly. Sherri had had difficulty sleeping, and Marta had let her sleep in late that morning. Linda agreed to keep an eye on her during the day and to call Marta immediately at work if needed.

The thin layer of oil on the streets transformed rush hour into crush hour, and more than one ambulance company was busier than it wanted to be. Johnson and Hawk had gotten tied up at an accident involving a tractor-trailer and several cars, and Summers and Marta had made three runs to three different accidents themselves, before finding time to buy a quick lunch and take it back to the lounge.

Marta carefully extracted herself from her fluorescent-orange uniform slicker, trying in vain to keep her damp clothing as dry as possible. She hung the slicker up next to the others, and they dripped in an uneven cadence while the two teams ate their lunches and filled out reports around the table.

"You know what I feel like doing on a day like today?" Johnson asked no one in particular as they all continued writing. "Start a tow truck business."

"Geez, Johnson, can't you do better than that?" Hawk's response didn't even break his stride writing his report. "You'd still be getting all wet."

"Yeah, but sometimes I'd get to rescue a damsel in distress."

"We did that this morning," Marta reminded him.

"I'm talking able-bodied ones. You know, standing by the roadside, lifting the hem on their skirt to catch my attention because they have a flat tire."

Marta shook her head in exasperation. "You're hopeless. Hawk, why doesn't your wife fix him up?"

"Uh-uh," Johnson objected vehemently. "It has been my misfortune to discover that when a married woman fixes me up, she fixes me up with a woman who wants to get married."

"You're not married, Howard. You fix him up," Hawk retaliated.

"Howard!" the supervisor called. "Phone call on line two."

Marta took her lunch with her to the phone, knowing that it was probably Sherri wanting to talk, and not knowing when the next emergency call would come in. She didn't want to miss what might be her only chance for a meal.

"Hi, Mom." Sherri sounded lonely and bored and in need of some TLC.

"Hi, sweetie. How's the arm?"

"It hurts, Mom."

"I know, honey. You can watch cartoons if you want."

"I did. The chipmunks were doing cartwheels. Mom, it'll be forever before I can do cartwheels again," she whined.

"Hold on a minute, Sherri." Marta put her hand over the receiver. "Hawk, would you mind if we took Sherri to the first aid class with us? She's really down."

"Sure. She can be our demo."

Marta shot Hawk a grateful smile as she returned her attention to Sherri and extended the invitation.

"Really, Mom? I can go while you're working?"

Sherri was ecstatic and almost hung up on Marta before saying goodbye because she was already engrossed in deciding what to wear. By the time they picked her up three hours later, her room was a collage of clothes strewn about—tried on and discarded.

Since the rain had stopped and the boys had just spent eight hours in classes prior to their arrival, Marta moved them out onto a dry section of the playground for her very short, very basic lecture, followed by a practice session with bandages.

"Okay, guys, divide up into groups of three or four, and we'll practice some of the things I just talked about. There are four stations, and I want you to spend about ten minutes at each one. Sherri will be at the sling station, and you can practice on her if you go easy. Hawk and I'll rotate around. Call us if you need us."

The boys scrambled to their spots and started bandaging and slinging each other as if they had all just run up against a child Rambo. Questions flew from every direction.

"Is this right, Hawk?"

"Shouldn't he do it like this, Marta?"

"Hey, Hawk, what do I do if he doesn't have an arm anymore?"

"Marta, this bandage won't stay on his tongue."

Hawk passed behind Marta as he changed stations. "Did I mention gore?" he asked with a laugh.

"How do you live with three of them?" she retorted.

"I work all day."

Marta soon noticed that besides herself and Hawk, one of the boys was helping the others, and he, at least, didn't think he was training to be a wartime medic.

"That's very good," Marta praised him as she watched over his shoulder. "Have you done this before?"

"My dad's a doctor," he said proudly. "He says everyone should know first aid."

"He's right ... Rob," she read his name off the tag on his shirt. "You never know when it might come in handy. At home, or on camping trips."

"You'd like my dad," he continued, glancing at her ringless left hand.

Marta was aware of the look and plastered a benign smile on her face. "Would you excuse me? I think Hawk needs some help over at the splinting station. Coming, Hawk," she called out as she moved away, before the kid asked for her phone number.

Hawk chuckled at her predicament when they found a free minute to stand aside and watch the boys. "You can't avoid him that way. His kind are persistent. By the way, the scoutmaster says he's never seen the kids quite this way before. Whatever that means." He added, "I was afraid to ask."

"Mom! Mom! Guess what?" Sherri came running over with Rob in tow. "This is Rob Macke. His dad is Dr. Macke." She held up her cast as though Marta needed a reminder.

"Oh, Rob. Yes, I remember you said your father is a doctor."

"And he did my cast," Sherri reminded her. "He says his dad sprays neat cartoons like mine on casts all the time."

"Sprays them?" Marta asked curiously.

"Yeah. Show her." Rob urged Sherri as she fumbled to remove her latest sling. "He's got a little portable air brush that uses canisters. He keeps it in his briefcase."

"Yes, well, he was having a rather slow day that day," Marta thought out loud. "I guess they're lucky he didn't start painting the treatment room walls."

Sherri held up her cast to proudly display the picture Marta had heard about, but forgotten to check out.

"That's really good." Marta admired the two-colored drawing of a red gymnast falling off a blue beam and cracking the floor with her arm. "Quite a talent."

"Do you know my dad?" Rob asked with a curious look in his eye.

"We've met. In the emergency room," she stressed, hinting that their relationship was solely a professional one.

"Did you like him?"

Marta couldn't believe his brashness. Whatever happened to timid little boys? "I don't really know him, Rob. We just work together sometimes. Not very often."

"I think you'd like him."

"He seems nice," was the most noncommittal thing she could think of to reply, mostly because she was concentrating on how to get away from this kid before she had to hurt his feelings. "What were you going to show me, Hawk?"

"Hmm?"

"Something over there at the snake-bite station, I think. Excuse us, kids." Marta grabbed Hawk by the arm and moved away quickly.

GETTING OUT OF THE HOUSE perked Sherri up considerably. She was talkative on the way home in the car.

"He's really cute, Mom. And funny."

"He seems like a nice boy, I guess."

"Mo-om."

"What?"

Sherri sighed. "I'm talking about Dr. Mac."

"Oh. I'm glad you like him, honey."

"He's awesome! You'd like him."

Marta glanced sideways at her daughter, careful to get her eyes back on the road quickly. "Did Rob put you up to this?"

"He thinks you're cool."

"No." Marta's voice was firm.

"No what?"

"No to whatever you two have cooked up. You know how I feel about doctors."

"He's not like that. He told me if the cast itched I could use an ice bag to stop it. Did you know that?"

"No, I didn't. Try it and see if it works. If it does, I'm sure I can pass the information along somewhere."

"If it works will you reconsider?"

"No."

"Mo-om."

"Lock your door, honey."

SHERRI ANSWERED the phone when it rang during dinner that evening, and carried on a quieter conversation than usual.

"It's dinnertime," Marta called to her after three minutes.

"It's Rob, Mom."

"You can call him back after you do your homework." When Sherri returned to the table, Marta added,

"But the answer is no to anything he wants to set up that involves your parent 'meeting' his parent."

Sherri finished her dinner in a glum silence, then rushed off to do the homework that Laurie had brought her from school.

"Mom, I've been thinking."

Marta wasn't surprised. Didn't children always have something to talk about at bedtime? "What, dear?"

"Well, about that canoe trip you're going on."

"I'm not going, remember?" Marta tucked her in and sat beside her on the bed. "We can spend the whole weekend together."

"But I want you to go."

Marta's heart dropped into her stomach. "What?"

"Well, you made plans and everything."

"I don't mind..."

"And Aunt Kelly was looking forward to my staying with her..."

"There'll be other times..."

"And if you don't go, Aunt Kelly will start bugging you about dating again."

Marta had no comeback for that one. It had been the one thing that had convinced her to agree to the trip in the first place. Kelly had been mentioning that newly divorced sales rep at work lately, and while Marta knew and understood it was just a threat to get her out with the singles group, it had worked.

Marta sighed. "What about your arm?"

"Go ahead and go, Mom. My arm feels fine. If I need anything, Aunt Kelly can take me to another doctor."

"Another doctor?" Marta frowned.

"I meant Dr. Mac again. I'm sleepy now, Mom. Good night."

Marta's eyebrows raised at that dismissal, but she knew a good thing when she heard it, so she kissed Sherri goodnight and turned out the light as she left the bedroom.

She hadn't gotten around to calling the people in charge of the trip and formally canceling, so instead she went and found the packing list Kelly had given her. It was right there in the trash can, right where she had tossed it that morning after grabbing it off the refrigerator and crumpling it up into a tiny little ball. She had made it on the first try, too.

BY SATURDAY MORNING, Marta had all her gear assembled in the living room. Not that there was much of it. A sleeping bag, some T-shirts and cutoffs, spare shoes, clean underwear, toiletries and a few other necessities of life: a bottle of vitamins and a first aid kit.

"Mo-om! Hurry up! Aunt Kelly's here."

Sherri was unusually energetic for six in the morning. She not only had dressed and had gotten Marta out of bed at the crack of dawn, but now she helped toss her mother's gear into waterproof trash bags, as Kelly had advised. Then she watched Marta tie them securely shut and ushered her out the front door to Kelly's waiting car.

"We're ready!" Sherri announced to her aunt, who was waiting patiently behind the wheel.

Marta crawled sleepily into the back seat and grumbled.

"Did you call him?" Kelly whispered to Sherri.

She whispered back, "It's all taken care of. He'll be there."

MARTA WAS the first one off the bus, dragging her two trash bags with her onto the beach, which was crowded with gray canoes lying side by side like an offering to a higher being. Anything was better than riding on a bus with fifty strangers who were busy smoking and drinking beer at 10:00 a.m. and partying like there was no tomorrow. Surely they had acquired a newer, wilder bunch of singles since Kelly had met her husband here.

Was it possible they would be short one canoe and she could skip the float trip and return home? She said a quick prayer.

Perhaps there was an odd number of passengers and she wouldn't have a partner and could leave.

No, she realized that wasn't a likely possibility as she watched three women strip down to their very skimpy bikinis and toss their outerwear into one canoe. Obviously this was a two- or a three-person sport.

Trying to go unnoticed, she packed and repacked her gear until she was down to one double bag and one large plastic Tupperware container. Her sister had participated in this annual holiday ritual for the past two years and had passed along several hints: put everything in trash bags to keep it dry when the canoe tips; wear old tennis shoes; wear your swimming suit under your clothes, a two-piece for pit stops; pack insect repellent, sun block and toilet paper.

The gravel beach at Baptist Camp was becoming less crowded; canoes were departing. Some only went a few yards before tipping. Voices were loud as warm bodies came in contact with sixty-five-degree water.

Confusion was rampant. Beers and sodas were lost overboard when canoes swamped. Flotation cushions were floating downriver, paddles were following. People were splashing around in the icy cold water, righting the canoes, tossing items back in. Other canoeists had reached out to help and had also tipped, spilling more gear into the river.

Marta let her breath out in a sigh that waved her feathered bangs. She didn't want to get into an unstable canoe with an amateur partner already guzzling beer. She looked around desperately for a sober partner.

"Really, Mrs. Howard," a frighteningly familiar masculine voice spoke from somewhere in the crowd of people running around like little ants packing their goodies away for later. "We could have met somewhere a lot closer to home."

Mac stepped out of the crowd, a fishing pole in one hand and a friendly grin on his face that took the sting out of his words. Marta wanted to severely maim him.

Chapter Three

Yes, she had been feeling sorry for herself. Yes, she had silently prayed that there might be one, just one, sober person here with whom she might be able to spend the weekend, someone who could talk intelligently and say something other than "Where's the beer?"

But did it have to be Mac? A doctor? Someone she had to see at work? She looked upward and silently asked why.

"Pretty day, huh?" Mac asked, oblivious to her inner turmoil, turning his gaze to the sky to see what was occupying her attention. "Nice white clouds, blue sky. No rain in sight."

Marta looked at him, obviously comfortable in his cutoffs, old T-shirt and khaki fishing vest, standing there with his hand on his dog's head and smiling as if he was enjoying this. Why not? He hadn't just endured three hours with the group of morons on the bus.

Mac hadn't seen so much beer since a fraternity bash, and he was glad Rob hadn't come. When Rob had presented him with a three-day fishing trip, he had naturally assumed it would be for the two of them and Dixie, the dog. That was the way they usually went fishing.

He had packed food elaborately, knowing how Rob loved to see other people's faces as they canoed by and saw campers dining on the beach on crab dip and lamb chops, with a real table cloth and real candles. He had also thrown in his sketch pad, remembering the caricatures he had done on past trips and what fond memories they evoked. He and Rob had had more fun looking at the drawings than at photographs.

Rob hadn't told him until last night that Mac had misunderstood, that this weekend was his opportunity to get away from everything: his son, his medical office and patients and his apartment buildings. Mac didn't need to get away from Rob, but the boy's enthusiasm was genuine, and in the end he had accepted gracefully.

Rob had explained to his dad that with the busy Labor Day weekend, he had had to sign him up with a group, and that in order to take Dixie, Mac would have to drive to the river in his own car. After all that, Mac wondered just how much longer he could be graceful about this fiasco. After Rob went to bed, Mac had tossed the lamb chops and half the other food back into the freezer and unpacked the candles.

Now Mac was faced with a real fiasco head-on. A sneaking suspicion about Rob and Sherri drove Mac to walk over to his cooler, open it and declare loudly, "Ah-ha!"

Marta stared at him. He had appeared sober, but now he was poking around in a cooler, probably looking for beer like everyone else. She hadn't known he was a member of the singles group. Kelly had never mentioned it. Sherri had never mentioned it. Sherri...

Mac was holding up two candles.

"Candles?" Marta asked with raised eyebrows.

"Candles," Mac confirmed. "I didn't pack candles." He said it as though he was proving a point, and Marta remembered that little niggling thought she had just had about Sherri. And Rob. And all those hushed phone calls.

She refused to believe it. "What else is in there that you didn't pack?"

Mac poked around some more, then stood back up with a wry grin. "Lamb chops and crab dip for starters."

"Gee, can I hire your packer next time?"

"I think you already did. You didn't happen to notice our kids making a lot of rather quiet phone calls lately, did you?"

Marta groaned under the weight of the evidence. So, Mac thought their kids were guilty, too. It must be true.

"And to think I told Sherri she could have a big birthday party this year," Marta said quietly. She would be lucky to live so long.

"Yeah, well, Rob's going to be grounded until his next birthday."

"Surf's up!" someone roared, and when Marta turned to look she almost collided with a naked chest, covered solely by a beer hanging in an insulated holder from the man's neck.

"Come on, honey." He belched. "The sooner we get movin', the sooner we get movin'." He wiggled suggestively, roared in laughter at his own play on words and clamped a large meaty hand on her buttock.

Marta quickly sidestepped.

"Hey, pal, she's with me," Mac said quietly and firmly.

Marta was about to object to Mac's attitude when she realized how stupid that would be. The man laughed and then stumbled over to join his friends in their two canoes.

"Bye!" the others called as they pulled out. "See you at the campsite!" The man who had been suggestive to her on the beach then tried to stand up in the canoe and execute his bumps and grinds, tipping himself, his partner and the entire contents of their canoe into the cold water.

"Not if we see you first," Mac spoke quietly as he shook his head at the scene in the river, then turned to Marta. "I hope you didn't mind my saying you were with me."

Marta smiled. "Not under the circumstances."

"Good, because I think we should go together."

Marta's grin matched his. "And spend the weekend plotting revenge?"

Mac briefly looked as though that hadn't been quite the answer he was expecting. "You bet." He bowed and extended his arm toward the canoe. "M'lady?"

"Mmm." Marta resisted the urge to laugh at his antics. "You do know how to work this thing, don't you?" she asked, indicating the canoe with a kick of her toe. "I would like to get home in one piece." Without a concussion, hypothermia or multiple fractures.

"Guaranteed." He shook his head again at the drunk in the river.

"He might not make it at all."

"Oh, he'll make it, all right. They always do. Some just remember it better than others." He looked at her. "Are these people friends of yours?"

"No way! They're my sister's old friends. She's convinced I'll meet the man of my dreams if I just give them half a chance. That's why I'm here."

"Husband hunting?"

Marta laughed at the stunned expression on his face. "Don't worry, you're safe." She looked at the departing canoes. "So are they. I'm here to get my sister off my back. Nothing more."

"I planned on fishing a lot and staying away from them, but, under the circumstances, I guess you won't mind that. Let's load up before the next group gets here."

Marta dropped her bag into the canoe, and Mac's gear soon joined hers. The tent and food promised by the club would be at Cedar Grove.

"What's in the bucket?"

"Personal stuff. And don't ever let my sister hear you call her Tupperware a bucket."

"Your sister sounds like one tough cookie."

"Not really. She just thinks married women are obligated to help the rest of us get that way."

Marta knew Kelly had planned this trip weeks ago, but she wondered if Kelly knew about Sherri's and Rob's matchmaking plans. Sherri had probably told her, and Kelly had probably helped. Marta added Kelly's name to her revenge list.

"Welcome aboard, Marta. First stop is twenty minutes downriver." Mac announced graciously as he waved her into the canoe.

"Great! Where do I sit?"

Mac threw a yellow flotation cushion down in the center bottom, next to an empty onion bag which he explained would be the litter bag. "You'll be safe there."

"There?" Her confusion was evident. All the other canoes had a rider on each seat.

"Mutiny already?"

"All right, all right. I suppose your dog has dibs on the front seat?"

He nodded. "Dixie and I make a great team, and this way you won't have to do any work. If you like, I'll teach you to canoe when we get somewhere quiet."

Marta helped him push the canoe into the river and got in and sat down when he told her to. The golden retriever was busy sniffing around the beach, in doggie heaven.

"What about Dixie?"

"She'll jump in when she's ready."

The canoe bottom scraped noisily over the gravel, then suddenly all was quiet. They were afloat. Mac let them drift out to the center of the river, picked up his paddle and let it drag, steering them slowly. This was it, his first moment of freedom on the river. He loved it. He looked forward to it. He needed it.

The sight of Marta's slender back in front of him wasn't bad, either. She was a light packer and hadn't brought along a lot of unnecessary junk. From the look of her freshly scrubbed face, he would wager that she hadn't brought any makeup. Refreshing.

Marta leaned back against the thwart. Maybe this would be all right after all, she thought hopefully. Mac didn't seem to be having trouble maneuvering the canoe in the water the way a lot of the others had. He wasn't half loaded. He hadn't grabbed her, made lewd comments or otherwise disgusted her.

She took a deep breath of fresh air and sighed. Maybe Sherri was right. Maybe she needed to get away. Maybe she would just stretch out, lay her head back on the cooler, look up at the blue sky, imagine animal shapes in the clouds...

Loud splashes abruptly broke the silence, and a golden mass hurled itself at them, landing in the bow of the canoe and sprinkling Marta with buckets of water in the process.

"What—!" she sputtered, wiping water off her face so she could open her eyes and glare at the newcomer.

Dixie stood in front of the seat, two paws up on the bow of the canoe, looking ahead, drenching Marta with every wag of her strawberry blond tail.

"Meet Dixie."

"I'd love to," she replied just a bit sarcastically. "Does she turn around, or do I just shake her tail?"

"Now, now, we're here to have fun, remember?"

Marta decided a wet dog was preferable to a drunk as a companion, and she gave in gracefully. "Welcome aboard, Dixie."

Her only reply was a faster tail wag which sprayed Marta with more ice-cold water.

The Current River at Baptist Camp was thirty feet wide and extremely cold, being only a few miles from the spring-fed source at Montauk. It flowed slowly, and up ahead in the distance Marta could hear the other canoeists. Side-bangers Mac called the amateurs who couldn't keep the paddle from banging against the side of the canoe with each stroke.

As they drifted slowly downriver, blue buses rumbled down the gravel road to discharge more people, coolers, beer and canoes. This stretch of river would be heavily traveled over the holiday, which traditionally marked the end of summer vacation.

The thought crossed Marta's mind that she could jump out and beg a ride back on one of the buses, but she looked up at the clouds and promptly squelched that idea. She would stay, and Kelly would just have to keep her mouth shut forever after. A deal was a deal. And, as far as Sherri went, revenge would be sweet. She and Mac would come up with something suitable to teach their two meddlesome eleven-year-olds a lesson.

Dixie leaned heavily over to the side to watch someone's puppy frolic on the gravel, and Marta quickly grabbed the sides of the canoe as if she could right it by sheer willpower.

"Relax," Mac said soothingly. "We've been doing this for years."

They slid over an underwater log, and Marta could feel its pressure through the bottom of the canoe. The large dog changed directions and again tipped the canoe to what Marta thought to be a precarious angle.

They glided past fallen trees and around large boulders. Marta looked ahead to where a half dozen canoes and their occupants were grouped, apparently waiting on a canoe jam ahead of them. Mac held way back.

Loud male voices carried back to them, and paddles were lifted between two canoes as if in a sword fight.

"I can't believe we have to share a campground with them," Marta complained.

"I brought my own tent and sleeping bag," Mac replied. "What about you?"

"I've got a sleeping bag." Marta was afraid to turn around for fear she would tip the canoe, but she did manage to twist her head around enough to frown at Mac. "Are you thinking what I think you're thinking?"

Mac smiled. "I have plenty of food for the weekend, thanks to you-know-who. We could do a lot more brainstorming with peace and quiet. Think about it."

The waiting canoes moved forward when the jam disappeared. The river narrowed, quickened, snaked to the left, then back again to the right. Canoe one snaked too far to the left and got hung up on a fallen tree. Canoe two hit them, bounced off and continued downriver. Canoe three ended up on the far side of number one, and both were hit by four and five.

Women could be heard yelling, "Paddle harder! Harder!" "To the right! To the right!" "Look out!"

Men were standing in the waist-deep water yelling, "Push off!" as they attempted to straighten out the mess.

Marta gritted her teeth in frustration, waiting for someone to get seriously hurt, run over by a canoe, hit by a paddle or pinned under a log. She didn't want anyone to get hurt, but if they did she would have to be ready to provide emergency medical care. This was no way to relax.

"Where does Dixie sleep on these float trips you take?" Marta asked noncommittally.

"In the tent."

"Good. She can sleep between us."

Fortunately the crash pile cleared out of their way without injuries, and Mac started slowly forward. Marta debated on whether to cover her eyes as they approached the fallen tree, but Dixie stood there bravely, so she just called back to see if Mac wanted her to paddle, too.

"Not necessary," was the calm reply.

Before she could argue with him about being too proud to let her help, they glided safely past all obstacles with two yards to spare. Marta released the breath she had been holding. No wonder the dog trusted him.

As the river widened back to thirty feet, Mac stowed his paddle and lifted his fishing rod. Marta soon saw his line float out to her right and drift downriver. Dixie, totally unconcerned about tipping, proceeded to stand with her front paws up on the side of the canoe, leaning toward the water, studying the river and whining. Very loudly.

"What does she want?" Marta asked as she shifted her weight to the left to compensate for the dog leaning right.

"Now you're getting the hang of it," Mac's voice drifted forward. "She's waiting for the fish."

Marta looked around at the woods. Trees grew to the river's edge on the left, forming a dense jungle-type growth which permitted only limited vision into the interior. A gray-colored bluff was on the right, with trees growing directly out of its stony and sometimes moss-covered surface. Birds could be heard calling to each other, but only insects buzzed near the canoe.

The river ahead of them eventually cleared of other canoeists, and Mac kept fishing. Marta leaned back and breathed deeply, determined to start relaxing. Five blissful minutes passed before side-bangers were heard from behind, the drumlike noise traveling for long distances on the water. Mac put down his rod and took up his paddle.

Fifteen minutes later he intentionally ran the canoe up onto a gravel beach, just a few feet past a quick bend in the river with a partially submerged tree trunk. Dixie jumped out and ran around the beach sniffing and playing while Mac started unloading the bags.

"We're camping already?" Marta asked.

"Absolutely. The rental companies will be putting canoes in all weekend. The more upriver we are, the sooner they all pass us, and we can have some peace and quiet."

The last thing he needed was drunks and showoffs scaring all the fish away. Forget the fish, the last thing he needed was drunks and showoffs scaring him and Marta away.

"Unless you've changed your mind? I promise Dixie's a great chaperon."

"Really?" Marta asked skeptically. "I'll hold you to it." She smiled and pitched in to help unload cushions, bags of gear and the cooler, which they lifted together.

"We'll have a lot more fun here." When the canoe was empty, Mac dug into his vest pocket for a small jar, from which he extracted a cheesy substance which he proceeded to pack around the hook on his fishing line.

Marta wrinkled her nose. "Gross! What is that smell?"

"Gross?" Mac repeated with a laugh. "You think this is gross? Gosh, I haven't heard that word used that way in years. I always liked it though. It's one of those words that means what it sounds like. Like gross anatomy."

"How about pee-yugh? What is that stuff, anyway?" Marta rubbed her nose, trying to get rid of the bad odor.

"Trout bait." He cast his line into the river, rested his rod against the canoe, then rinsed his hands in the water. "Let's get the tent up."

Marta watched as he untied a trash bag and extracted a maroon and gray bundle. He tossed it onto the gravel and began unrolling it until it lay on the ground like a big deflated beach ball. Then he began snapping some skinny tent poles together.

Great, Marta thought. Not only was the only sober person on the river a doctor and an associate, she'd agreed to share a tent with him, too. Sherri was in deep trouble and getting in deeper and deeper by the minute.

"It's a big tent," Mac said conversationally, seeming to read her thoughts. "Rob and I sometimes camp out from one weekend to another, and with all our gear and Dixie, we need lots of room." He ran the poles through the casings, and after several pushes and grunts he stood before a dome-shaped tent. "It sleeps four," he said to emphasize its size.

Dixie began barking. The canoes they had heard following them rounded the bend and began piling up on the submerged tree. The air resounded with banging canoes, men's shouts and general bawdiness.

"Of course, you could probably hitchhike down to Cedar Grove and meet up with the rest of your group. I'll help you flag one down, if you like."

Marta watched the canoeists right themselves, swig their beers and move on.

"Right," she said sarcastically.

MAC TOSSED HER a fifteen-foot length of rope. "Can you hang this for our clothesline?"

Marta quickly examined the undergrowth by the trees. "Are you kidding? There's enough poison ivy around here to make me itch just looking at it."

"What? Mutiny already?" he roared in his best swashbuckler voice as he closed one brown eye, pretending to have a patch over it, and drew an imaginary sword. "Walk the plank, woman!"

She couldn't help herself; she giggled. "Gosh, I can't imagine why your son thinks he has to fix you up. I wonder if he'll grow up to be a pirate, too."

"No doubt," he said agreeably. Then abruptly he exclaimed, "Oh! My line!" and dashed down the slight hill to where his rod was moving to and fro from the pull on the line.

He reeled in an empty hook, rebaited it and set it up again.

"You do all this packing just to fish like that?" Marta asked.

"No, just till camp is set up. Later I'll do some serious fishing. Now, about that clothesline," he said as he took it from her gently and proceeded to walk through the weeds to tie it between two trees.

"Mac! I wasn't kidding about the poison ivy!"

Mac turned from what he was doing to smile at her. "I'm not bothered by the stuff myself."

He finished tying the line, then picked an orange flower off a wispy three-foot-tall plant growing nearby. "See this?" he asked as he held the bell-shaped flower out for her to examine. "It's called a touch-me-not."

She snatched her hand back. "Something else to be allergic to?"

"No," he assured her with a smile. "As a matter of fact, it's supposed to be nature's remedy for poison ivy. Supposedly, if you break open the stem and leaves and rub them on your skin after exposure, it's a cure."

"Really?" She didn't know whether to believe him. None of her herb literature had covered that. "You're into natural remedies?" If so, Marta would have to give some serious reevaluation to judging this book by its cover.

"Some." Mac calmly continued to set up camp and, with Marta's help, leveled off a six-foot diameter circle in an area that was more sand than river rock. Marta watched in astonishment as he then picked up the tent and set it down where he wanted it.

"What kind of tent is that?"

"A dome tent. I can put it up in a few minutes by myself, it weighs next to nothing, and if I don't like where I put it, I move it." He held out his arms as though he had just performed a magic feat. "One drawback, though," he cautioned. "If we don't put our gear in it, it can blow away."

He pulled the sleeping bags out of their separate trash bags and tossed them into the tent, followed by another trash bag which probably held his clothes. Marta set her Tupperware container inside the tent door before he zipped it closed.

Mac made sure the cooler was in the shade, set the water jug in the river to keep cool and called her attention to the path by the clothesline.

"This is our shovel," he pointed out needlessly as he stuck the short Army shovel into the soft earth next to the path. "And this is our toilet paper." He slipped the roll over the shovel handle.

Marta groaned. "No outhouse?"

"Be thankful. They are notoriously filthy."

"But usually free of poison ivy." She would prefer a few germs to four weeks of the gosh-awful itchy rash. Most people got contact dermatitis for ten to fourteen days. For some reason it always stayed with her twice as long. Vitamins or no vitamins.

Mac dug into a bag and tossed her a small plastic bottle with a flip top. "Maybe you'd like some of this. It's really good stuff. I swear by it for mosquitoes and it's supposed to work on poison ivy, too."

Marta read the label and chuckled over the fine print. Apparently this was a biodegradable all-purpose cleaner, used for dishes, bodies, et cetera, and it swore to not only prevent poison ivy, but to keep the insects away, too.

"I know it sounds impossible, but just try it," he offered again.

"Well, I take enough B vitamins to keep all the insects away, but I will try anything if it prevents poison ivy. I don't want to use up all your stuff, though."

"Don't worry," he said with a smile. "There's plenty, and if you go home covered with poison ivy and mosquito bites you'll be too weak to carry out our revenge on the kids."

They could hear more canoes coming. Mac tossed his single folding lawn chair out of the canoe, handed Marta his fishing rod and dragged the canoe partway up the slight incline until it rested upside down and flat enough to serve as their table.

She handed the rod back. "I believe I have to have a fishing license to hold this."

"You didn't buy one?"

"No. Kelly never mentioned fishing. I brought along a book to read."

Mac smiled down at her. "If it was Kelly's intention to match you up this weekend, I doubt she told you to bring along a book."

"Well, what Kelly doesn't know won't hurt her." Marta smiled impishly. "I only agreed to come here. Nothing more, nothing less."

Dixie was intently studying the river where Mac's line disappeared below the surface of the water, wagging her tail, occasionally whining. Every time Mac reeled his line in and cast it out again, she danced in circles around him, constantly eyeing the bait, snapping at it when in reach.

"Won't she get that hook in her?" Marta worried aloud, wondering whether the tackle box contained the right equipment for hook extraction.

"Hasn't stopped her yet," Mac replied nonchalantly as he cast his line again. "If you don't mind, I'd like to get some fishing in before we discuss what we're going to do to the kids. It's my way of winding down."

Marta nodded. "Sure, I need the time to cool off, anyway. Right now I think grounding's too easy. We can come up with something more creative later."

Mac walked across the river where it was thigh-deep in the middle and climbed a large fallen tree trunk that formed a natural bridge from the water to the high bank on the other side of the river.

While the tent and cooler were in the shade, very little of the rest of the small gravel beach was. But if Marta guessed right, the over-hanging trees would provide shade by early afternoon. She noticed some dead limbs hanging down, just about the right height to cause an eye injury. She snapped them off and tossed the twigs toward the fire pit.

Then she stripped off her T-shirt, revealing a modest blue-and-white-striped bikini top from an old suit she had found stuffed in a box in the hall closet. She had skipped the bikini bottoms and decided on cutoffs. The whole world didn't have to know she had cellulite. She slathered on a generous coat of sunscreen.

From across the river, Marta could hear the clicks and whirs of Mac's rod and reel, sounding to her like a camera button being pushed, followed by an automatically advancing film. The only other sounds at the moment were the ones she had been hearing continually since getting off the bus: water gently lapping over the rocks, birds singing and insects in the woods rubbing their wings or their legs together, or doing whatever made that constant hum. A country girl she wasn't.

It was hot and Marta moved the lawn chair down the incline so she could sit with her feet in the cold water. Another group of canoeists was starting through this bend. Several men, the ones who were good enough to make it through without tipping, asked Mac about his fishing luck as they drifted by, but the more common "tippers" commented to Marta about her great vantage point to watch all the people crash.

Marta wondered how she could ever relax if she was going to be constantly subjected to watching one accident following another. Her glance across the thirty feet of beach didn't turn up one piece of driftwood she could use as a splint. It made her nervous to watch people reach out between canoes that were about to crash broadside. Somehow, time after time, their reflexes were fast enough to escape without even a scratched finger.

MAC OBSERVED Marta from his position across the river. She was trying to read a novel she had brought along, but spent more time gripping the arms of the lawn chair every

Eleven Year Match

time two canoes collided. He imagined her knuckles were white from the strain.

Even so, he enjoyed watching Marta. But he would enjoy it more if he could find a way to help her to relax.

When he first started medical school, Mac used to picture himself doing all sorts of spectacular first aid rescues while camping on the river. The most he'd ever been called on to practice, though, was to pour hydrogen peroxide on some guy's scraped elbow and knee, and to loan out his peppermint soap to the owners of a dog sprayed by a skunk. All in all, since he really came here to fish, the low accident rate was a good thing.

MAC RETURNED for lunch when the sun had moved westward just enough to place their canoe table and half the beach in shade. Canoes were still passing by regularly, and Marta was beginning to see the amusing side of amateur canoeists trying to negotiate the "rapids" of the upper Current River, some while under the influence of several beers.

"What's for lunch?" Marta asked as Mac opened the cooler.

"Well, let's see what the little guy packed."

He handed her cheese, salami, ham, buns and hard-boiled eggs, which she laid out on the red-and-white-checkered tablecloth lying across the flat bottom of the overturned canoe. Mac poured two mugs of iced tea from a large thermos jug and tossed two flotation cushions down for seats.

Marta retrieved her vitamins from the tent, poured out six different tablets onto the tablecloth and recapped the bottle. When she was thirsty, she popped a tablet into her mouth before sipping her tea.

"Don't you think that's an awful lot of vitamins?" Mac asked as he sprinkled salt all over his hard-boiled egg.

"Don't knock it. I haven't had to go see a doctor since I started this two years ago." She wondered if he could say the same about his blood pressure, given the amount of salt he ate.

Mac thought that provided him with a good opening to pursue the subject on his mind. "I take it you don't like doctors?"

"Some," she admitted, and Mac smiled. "But in general, no."

Mac's smile quickly disappeared. "Why not?"

Marta took a deep breath while she stacked more deli meat on the bun.

"Oh, little things. Like how come they kept treating Sherri for ear infections for years, and never once did they tell me how to prevent swimmer's ear with vinegar? I had to read about it on my own. The books I bought on home remedies and the vitamins they recommended cost less than one trip to the doctor's office, and saved Sherri a lot of pain."

Mac didn't have an answer for her. He knew it happened. It wasn't fair to think it happened only in the medical profession, but he didn't want to start a three-day weekend together with an all-out battle. He would work on her slowly.

"Any ideas on what to do with our kids?" he asked instead.

"Well," Marta said with a sigh, "after eating this great lunch that Rob packed, I'm less inclined to have him drawn and quartered."

Mac almost choked. "I hadn't thought of anything quite so drastic, myself."

"So, you're going easy on him, hmm?"

"Probably. I only thought of things like having him clean the attic and the basement and the garage, rake leaves and wax the car. I figured if I kept him busy he couldn't interfere in my life."

"Wouldn't you have to follow him around and be sure he did all that stuff?"

"Yeah, you're right, it'd just be more headaches for me. Drawing and quartering is fine."

"Well, maybe we could compromise," Marta suggested.

"I'll give it some more thought. Meanwhile, want to go downriver and help me catch minnows for bait? It's about a five-minute walk."

They waded down to Ashley Creek, a source of warmer water emptying into the Current. Dixie was told to stay where Mac left her in the shallow stream, and Marta was coached on how to hold her end of the minnow net.

"Now, watch this." Mac called to Dixie.

The golden retriever bounded toward them, happy to be allowed to move again, and in her enthusiasm she scared scores of minnows towards the net.

"Lift it now," Mac ordered and they lifted the net together.

"Oh, look at all of them!" Marta was fascinated by the silvery bodies flipping around in the net, and Mac efficiently scooped them up with his fingers and dropped them into the waiting minnow bucket.

They were unable to wade back upriver immediately due to another parade of canoes. They sat on the beach together with their feet in the water and watched another round of crashing, tipping and dunking.

"I know!" Mac said suddenly. "We could pretend everything was all right with us and the kids, take them to

Six Flags, put them on the scariest ride there, and bribe someone to let it run for about an hour."

"Sherri loves Six Flags."

Mac sighed. "Rob, too."

"But you're getting better."

Mac stood up and held out his hand to help Marta. She took it without thinking, until she rose next to him and he didn't let go immediately.

"Mac..." She was sure it meant nothing. She wouldn't let it mean anything.

"Yes?" He looked down at her, his eyes holding hers as he gently reached over and brushed her hair back from her cheek.

Marta dropped her eyes, realizing that was probably a mistake as she stared at his broad chest. His T-shirt stretched tightly across his pectorals. "I don't hear any more canoes."

Mac gave her hand a quick squeeze before he dropped it. Her prejudice against doctors was standing as strong as a brick wall between them, and he could feel it. He wouldn't push. Maybe over the weekend he could change her mind. "That's hopefully the end of them. Now we'll have peace and quiet the rest of the day."

"We're really alone out here, aren't we?" Marta looked around at the miles and miles of woods surrounding them.

"Not as alone as you might think." Mac strove to lighten her mood, to get the conversation back onto a friendly footing. "The buzzards are starting to join us."

"Buzzards?" Marta noticed Mac looking up and did the same.

Four large birds were circling overhead, high up, coasting on very large outstretched wings.

"Turkey buzzards," he confirmed. "You can tell by the head carriage and the shape of the wings."

"Buzzards?" she repeated. She'd seen the TV Westerns when she was a child. Buzzards meant dead people over the next hill.

Mac seemed oblivious to the stricken look on her face. "They roost in trees for the night, just northwest of here."

In the short period of time they were discussing the birds, several more joined the circling foursome.

"Are they aggressive? I mean, should we light a fire or something?"

Mac smiled. "No, you can read your book in safety. You'll go blind before you're attacked by a buzzard. I'm going to fish down here for a while. What about you?"

"I'll see you back at the campsite." Marta waded upriver, keeping an eye out for an errant bird. They made no sound at all to add to the song of the river and the insects. She felt truly alone and wondered if she liked it.

She was hardly ever alone. She worked full-time, she ran her errands, and after dark Sherri didn't like being left home alone, so they were usually together.

She sat and listened to the water and the insects, studying the trees, the flowers and the white puffy clouds moving across the very blue sky. She decided she liked being alone. There were no sirens here, no flashing lights, no shortwave radios.

Several people she had worked with two years ago had already left the field of emergency medicine. *Burnout,* they called it. She understood it. But if they weren't there to do the job right, who would do it? She was trained to do it, and it was important to her.

She finally had enough hours logged to go on for paramedic training. That was her next goal. When school let out next summer, if she could find a class to fit her available hours, she would enroll.

The rhythm of the water running over the rocks, the breeze gently blowing her hair and the warmth of the day began to lull her into peaceful thoughts. She forgot work for a while, and tried to turn her thoughts to plotting her revenge on Kelly and Sherri. But revenge wasn't as sweet as the peace and quiet she was enjoying so much.

Chapter Four

Marta and Mac sat on cushions and leaned back against the canoe after eating the dinner they had cooked together, watching as evening darkened into night. Stars studded the sky like nothing Marta had ever seen before, and Mac pointed out the density of the Milky Way. The buzzards had disappeared northwest as promised.

"So, we agree that sending them both to boarding school in Switzerland is too harsh," Mac said.

"And too expensive. Besides, I have to teach Kelly a lesson, too, and I can't send her away."

"I think your sister will be the easy one. What's her goal for you?"

Marta rolled her eyes. "To marry a doctor. Can you believe that?"

"Knowing how you're prejudiced against us, no. Okay, so you tell her...you fell in love with... Hmm, let's see." Mac looked up at the stars for ideas. "I know! One of these good ol' boys down here that rents canoes out for a living."

Marta laughed. "You're nuts."

Mac smiled and continued, undaunted by her critique. "Think how upset she'll be when you tell her you're quitting your job, hiring a moving company, taking Sherri out of school—"

"Boy, you must have told Rob great bedtime stories when he was little. That's good, I admit, but I need something that lasts longer. I mean, as soon as she sees I'm not moving, it's all over, you know?"

"Well, we'll work on it."

Mac stretched and yawned and dropped his arm along the length of the canoe behind her shoulders. Marta wasn't sure whether to chide him for that old trick, or assume he really was innocent.

Instead she yawned and rose to her feet. "Well, I got up early this morning, and it's getting cold out here. I think I'll turn in."

"I've got a sweat suit you can slip on if you want to stay up awhile longer."

"No, thanks. Come on, Dixie," she called the dog. She wanted to be sure to put Dixie between the two sleeping bags. She ducked quickly into the tent.

"I'll help you get set up," Mac offered as he hurried in behind her.

Marta turned around and found herself standing in a very small space next to Mac, who had to bend over somewhat since she was occupying the tallest spot in the dome. It was dark in the tent, too dark to notice the color of his eyes or hair. But not too dark to notice his lean body, his muscled forearms, his strong back bending in front of her. The darkness made him seem closer. She could hear him breathing. She could smell his peppermint soap.

Mac moved and his arm brushed against her in the dark. "Sorry."

She quickly knelt down and untied the nearest sleeping bag.

Mac crouched next to her. "You know, since you're chilly, we could zip these bags together for more warmth. They're big enough we could still put Dixie between us—she usually ends up on top of somebody anyway."

Marta quickly tried to figure a way to refuse graciously. There was no other tent for her to share with anyone else and no way she could canoe downriver in the dark. She hadn't seen any campfires or heard anyone else's voice through the woods.

"Or I could get out of here and give you some privacy," he offered with a smile, knowing that it would probably be okay for some men to tease her with such a suggestion, but coming from a man who was also a doctor, as well as one who was still nearly a stranger, it was probably the worst thing he could do.

Marta looked up at him, kneeling only a foot from her. "That one sounds good," she answered honestly and gratefully.

Mac nodded and quickly ducked out through the tent flaps, congratulating himself for thinking fast enough to salvage the situation.

"Mac?"

"Yes?" His voice came from just the other side of the nylon.

"Thanks."

DAWN BROUGHT sounds of Mac and Dixie out fishing. The fishing wasn't very noisy, but Dixie whined a lot when she saw one, and Mac had to crab at her several times to leave his hook alone.

Marta rolled over and went back to sleep, lulled by the rushing water into what seemed to be the deepest sleep she had had in years, but it was only minutes before Mac was shaking her foot through the soft thickness of her sleeping bag.

"What?" She jumped up, immediately alert, looking for the emergency.

"Gosh!" Mac backed off, both hands raised in surrender as he sat on the floor of the tent. "I just wanted to wake you for breakfast, not sound the alarm."

"Where am I?" Marta crawled out of her bag, fully dressed in her shorts and T-shirt and peeked out the tent flaps. She hadn't awakened anywhere but her own bed in years.

Sunshine had set a glow to the surrounding wilderness; a crisp breeze blew across the water and teased her hair. Smoke from the campfire drifted lazily upward.

"Oh, now I remember." She groaned as she crashed onto her stomach and lay her head back down.

"Want some coffee?" Mac inquired, letting his eyes wander over the long length of her shapely legs stretched out in front of him, almost touching his bare knees.

She shook her head. "How are you fixed for a hot shower?"

"I could arrange for a cold bath."

"No, thanks." She wasn't into sixty-five-degree river baths.

He got up to move back out through the tent flaps, putting forth a great effort to keep his hands all to himself. "Breakfast in ten minutes," he said as he left.

Marta used her allotted time to change into clean underwear and a fresh T-shirt and to run a brush through her hair. She had fallen asleep almost immediately the night before, probably due to all the fresh air and the lulling gurgle of the river passing by just twenty feet away. She had never even heard Mac come back into the tent, and she made up her mind to forget his offer to "keep her warm" and to continue to treat him like the friend he had become during their easy time together yesterday.

Two fishermen in hip boots waded through the shallow part of the river by the campsite as Marta and Mac cooked breakfast. They exchanged quiet greetings with Mac, not pausing for a second in their fishing, not even glancing at her. Marta watched them catch three fish in a short period of time, then release them immediately.

"Why do they keep throwing those fish back?"

"They're too small. This is trophy trout area. You can't keep anything under fifteen inches long."

"They sure are catching a lot," she pointed out as the fishermen released two more. "How many did you catch yesterday?"

"My fair share, smarty-pants. Think you can watch the bacon?"

"Sure." Marta crouched down beside the fire and had to change positions several times to avoid the smoke. "Boy, I'll never complain about my gas bill again."

SIDE-BANGERS could be heard coming down the river, and Mac rummaged through the tent for a few minutes before settling down on a cushion next to Marta with a drawing pad and pencil. As people started piling up their canoes on the submerged tree again, Mac began drawing with brisk strokes.

Marta watched in amazement as the jumble of people in front of her began showing up humorously on paper. Nothing was drawn to scale. Mac emphasized what was funny.

One caricature after another emerged, exaggerating canoes bent in half, people covering their eyes in fear at the obstacles in the river or shaking enlarged fists at their dates. Extra large supplies of beer flowed over the sides of one canoe.

They watched, fascinated, as a loud argument between two young teenagers ended with a mutual decision to go back upriver and try again. This time, it was decided that the girl would sit in the back while her brother could see how he liked "rushing to be the first one to hit that tree at ninety miles an hour."

Mac turned to a new page and caricaturized two little people pulling a yacht-sized canoe upriver behind them while he and Marta waited for their return.

It was obviously the girl's intention that they race through the bend by the tree so fast that they wouldn't have time to get caught. They stopped very quickly. The girl put out an arm for balance, and the next thing the kids knew, they were in for a dunking.

Mac paid no attention to the screaming duo. He tried not to notice Marta's knuckles turning white as she gripped the chair arms, obviously certain that there would be a severe injury to treat in the next few seconds. He concentrated instead on drawing a very large paddle in the hands of an irate girl, drenched to the skin, hair hanging wet and limp to her shoulders. She was advancing on a rather small laughing boy, who was waving a white flag and pointing to the canoe floating away downstream.

They took off running for the canoe, their differences momentarily forgotten as their only transportation drifted away.

Mac made a final drawing of the kids in juvenile court, the canoe divided equally between them, their faces exaggerating their sibling rivalry, while the canoe wore a silly smile and chalked up another mark on its side.

Marta was so amused by the drawings that Mac tore out the one of the fight on the beach and handed it to her. The longer she studied it, the more she chuckled. She folded it and placed it in her book to keep.

"After watching that, I'm not sure if I want to learn to canoe," Marta said.

"There's no time like the present." Mac stood and held out his hand again.

Marta looked up at him for a moment, studying his face against the blue sky. How could a man who looked so at home in a hospital emergency room look equally at ease on the river? There was no nurse here to do his bidding, no patient looking to him for answers, no one to stroke his ego. Just Marta, she thought to herself with a laugh, and she wasn't likely to do any of the above.

"What's funny?"

She reached up and accepted his hand. "Do you feel you're being punished for something?"

"No. Should I? Oh, you mean the kids? We ought to come up with a workable plan by lunch tomorrow."

"We'd better start now, then."

"First, your lesson."

MARTA DIDN'T LIKE being in the back of the canoe. It was difficult to understand what Mac was saying. "The what stroke?"

"The J stroke. Like this," he said patiently as he demonstrated. "Just go slow. The reason all those people crash is because they panic and try to get through it as fast as possible."

She soon adjusted to steering down the river, and together they were strong enough to paddle back up the slow section so she could practice some more. Then Dixie decided she'd had enough of being left out.

"Dixie, no!" Mac yelled too late.

Eighty pounds when dry, who knew how much when wet, Dixie took a flying leap into the center of the canoe, landing safely... for a few seconds. Marta was unused to dealing with the shift in weight, and with Mac in front of Dixie where he couldn't see her every move, he couldn't make the usual adjustment.

Marta wanted to scream when she surfaced. She couldn't believe how cold sixty-five-degree water felt, and the shock robbed her of her voice at first.

"You okay?" Mac asked. Somehow he'd been able to right the canoe before it swamped.

Marta's answer was somewhere between "Yes" and "Yikes!"

He laughed. "Cold, huh? Yeah, this spring-fed water sure is great."

Giving him a dunking would have been nice, but he was bigger than she, so Marta settled for splashing him. Dixie barked and joined in the splashing free-for-all, swimming back and forth between the two, biting at the sprays.

"Oh, stop," Marta declared with a gasp. "I'm laughing so hard I can't see where you are."

"Right here," he answered as he picked her up and threatened to drop her again.

Marta was accustomed to the water temperature now, but she preferred to relax in his arms rather than continue the fight.

"You done?" he asked. He walked up on the beach and set her down on the two flotation cushions.

"Gosh, I haven't played that hard in years," she answered when she'd caught her breath.

"Me, neither." Mac sat on the gravel beside her, shoving his wet hair back off his face.

"Do you think I can canoe well enough to bring Sherri out here for a weekend?"

"People do it all the time, but personally I'd like to see you have a little more practice first. Maybe next time you can come with Rob and me, and he can handle the kids' canoe until you get more experience. But I promise I won't tell anyone at work," he said with amusement.

She laughed ruefully. "Yeah, that might be kind of hard to live down."

MAC INSISTED on preparing dinner alone that evening as a treat for Marta and sent her off to find two rocks that would make good candle holders for the table. When she had finally found two to his exact specifications, she took a last rinse in the river to wash away any poison ivy she might have gotten off Dixie's fur, then changed into dry clothes.

Mac paused from setting the meal on the table. "It's our last dinner together on the river," he said. "We have to leave in the morning."

Marta sat on the yellow flotation cushion on the side of the canoe away from the smoking campfire. Mac served her cheese-covered potatoes, fresh green beans and a lamb chop.

She stared at the lamb chop and the candles. "My, Rob really packs creatively, doesn't he?"

Mac smiled. "Believe it or not, this is the way Rob and I usually pack. We like to spoil ourselves on the river, and then we laugh about it later."

"Maybe he'll grow up to be a chef."

"Oh, no, he's already decided to be a real estate tycoon." Mac placed great emphasis on the last three words, and Marta could almost hear Rob dreaming out loud.

"Tycoon's good. Why real estate?"

"I inherited some rental property from my dad when he died a few years back. Rob has a computer class in school, and he had to do an independent project on it. So he got some facts and figures from me on the properties, did some long-range projections and concluded that *tycoon* is definitely within his reach." Mac laughed to remember how enthused Rob had been with his projections.

"How nice."

Mac figuratively kicked himself. He didn't want to sound as though he was bragging about his possessions. His son, yes, but his real estate, no.

"Sure, it would be nice, but it's inaccurate. He didn't know the whole story, see? For instance, as property values increase over the years, so do expenses, materials, repairs, et cetera. I found that all my free time was taken up with maintenance, and I had trouble getting the renovations done that my dad had scheduled before he died. You know, calling plumbers, electricians, carpenters, and keeping an eye on what they were doing. So, I hired a full-time manager a couple of years ago. And I'm sure he's going to want cost-of-living raises."

"Is he worth it?" Marta didn't have much sympathy for a guy who had to hire someone else to make his living for him. As far as landlords went, there were good ones and there were bad ones. She wanted to believe Mac was the former. After all, he had provided the lamb chop she was busy devouring, along with all her other meals this weekend.

"I'm here. He's working. I haven't had any complaints since I hired the guy. No more broken water heaters, stuck windows, leaky pipes, wobbly railings and so on. He handles it all. Collects the rent, everything. I always hated that."

"What?" Hated collecting money? An unusual landlord, to say the least.

"Collecting the rent from people who get behind. A lot of my tenants are the same ones who rented from my dad. They stayed on after he died." Mac spoke slowly, as if reminiscing. "Some of them knew me when I was a kid. They were on a first-name basis with my dad, and they all call me 'Rob's son.' How can I demand payment when some elderly lady looks up at me and reminds me I'm Rob's son?

"Actually, my medical office manager talked me into getting an apartment manager. She said she was tired of seeing me all bleary-eyed several mornings each week. So I interviewed several, and I hired the one with the most experience in dealing with the public, because I didn't want to alienate any of Dad's old tenants. I just needed a middleman.... And, thanks to him, I have a free weekend."

"And, thanks to our kids, you got saddled with me."

"Oh, it hasn't been so bad."

They laughed together.

"Are you divorced?" he asked quietly.

"Yes. Several years ago." She had no difficulty in voicing her situation. "Tom lives in St. Louis, has new baby twins. I don't hear from him much, except about the rare occasions he has Sherri come spend the weekend."

"Don't they get along?"

Marta shrugged. "Sherri says he's more like an uncle. She likes him, but they don't have much in common. She says she wants her own complete family under one roof—father, mother, Sherri. Apparently it doesn't have to be her biological father. What about you?"

"Oh, yeah. Me, too. My ex-wife is a regular social butterfly. Last I heard she was over in Europe somewhere. She sends Rob postcards."

"No wonder they want new parents."

"Rob's maternal grandmother's closer to him than his mother. He spends some weekends with her, has a great time, gets lots of love over there."

"Does that bother you?" Marta asked cautiously.

"Oh, no," he assured her. "I think it's great. Just because his mom's irresponsible doesn't mean he can't love his grandma. I'm perfectly comfortable around her, but that's probably because neither one of us understands her daughter."

"Were you thinking of joining that singles group?" he asked suddenly.

"No. I came only because Kelly twisted my arm and took Sherri home to visit with her."

"Blackmail?"

Marta smiled. "No. Bribery. She promised never to nag me again about being single if I gave in just this one time. And if that wasn't enough, she proceeded to tell me how a certain daughter, namely mine, needed a break from an overprotective parent once in a while in order to grow up nonneurotic."

"And are you overprotective?"

"Sure. My last words to my daughter when she saw me off Saturday morning were 'Be sure to wear your seat belt.'"

"What's wrong with that?"

"Take your pick—she already had it on, and I was boarding a bus which, by the way, doesn't provide them."

"I see."

"Mac, this dinner is just outstanding. I'm sure Rob can't wait for you to get back." If he did this well over an open fire, she would love to see how he cooked at home.

Mac didn't want to think about their departure just yet. He wanted to spend some more time on the river with Marta before letting the reality of their everyday lives swallow them up. He was a doctor for heaven's sake. His time wasn't always his own.

And even if he had all the time in the world, she had already indicated that doctors were not her favorite breed of people. He thought that was kind of funny considering how many women had tried to catch him as a husband. Even some of his female patients came on to him. Doctors might have trouble keeping wives, but not many had trouble finding them.

He decided to be sure the subject was changed. "We've got chocolate pudding for dessert."

"Great!" Marta couldn't believe how hungry she was, nor how much she ate, and quickly swallowed her last vitamin before accepting the prepackaged plastic container of pudding.

Mac let the candles continue burning as darkness fell, removed the grill and fed the campfire some more wood. They cleaned up the dishes, suspended the trash bag from a tree branch and settled back down by the fire as the night grew chilly.

"Here." Mac stuffed a cushion between her spine and the canoe for comfort.

She didn't move away when he draped his arm across her shoulders this time. They sat side by side, the candles burning on the canoe behind them, the fire warming their legs.

"I've had a nice weekend with you here," Mac stated some time later. His arm tightened around her.

"Me, too," Marta admitted. As he pulled her closer to snuggle under his arm, her thoughts quickly flew to the fact that she really was out of practice in intimate conversations with men. She would have preferred to begin that practice on a lighted front doorstep where society imposed certain limits.

"Do you bring friends here often?" she asked. Nothing like hinting about a girlfriend to cool a man's advances.

"No. I don't get out here very often, and if Rob doesn't come, I'm alone." He slowly closed the distance between them.

His lips, when they met hers, were warm and irresistible. They closed over hers gently, mesmerizing and drawing her closer. She felt his hand on her shoulder, turning her toward him until she could feel his chest against the fullness of her breasts, and then his muscular arm enfolded her snugly against him.

Marta ignored the rush of cold air on her skin as Mac slipped his hand under her T-shirt and pressed his warm palm against the skin on her back, massaging gently, soothingly.

Marta let the comfort from Mac's firm body against hers surround her, envelop her, entice her to want more. Unable to put her arms around his neck without pulling away, she slipped them around his rock-hard torso.

Their lips parted and met again as Marta murmured her pleasure down low in her throat. Mac wanted to hear her make that little throaty sound of pleasure again.

The moment was shattered as Dixie, feeling left out, came over to kiss them both at the same time, letting her wet tongue lap out across both their faces.

"Dixie," Mac complained hoarsely as they sprang apart. "Go away, dog."

As Mac pushed the retriever away, Dixie turned her attention to Marta, aiming for her face again. Marta laughed at the dog's antics and silently praised her good timing.

"You were right, Mac, she is a great chaperon. And I guess it's my bedtime. Thanks for the lovely dinner." She

Eleven Year Match

ducked around Dixie and gave Mac a light kiss, then headed quickly for the tent.

"Then I guess this is good-night," he called after her. He turned and scowled at Dixie. "Next dog I get is going to be male."

Dixie turned and followed Marta to bed.

Mac was left with warm thoughts of Marta, and he smiled to himself. He'd like to see her again in St. Louis, and the only connection he could think of to maintain ties was their kids. The only question was how could he use them, realistically, to get Marta back into his arms?

AFTER BREAKFAST the next morning they packed the canoe before the sun got hot and set out for Cedar Grove. Marta settled herself in the center of the canoe with one cushion for a seat and another for her back and let Mac handle all the navigation without any of the incidents she had been witnessing for the past two days on the river. No crashes, no advice from her on how to do his job, no fights.

She let her head rest back on the cooler while she studied the sky through the overhead canopy of trees. At times there were just glimpses of blue, at others she saw a wide expanse of sky broken by a few white clouds. She relaxed enough to enjoy the flowers blooming along the shore: brown-eyed Susans, more of the touch-me-nots, elderberry and a couple of groups of unidentified purple flowers growing in shady areas.

They'd left early enough to have the river to themselves, with the exception of a few walking fishermen. Marta let her mind wander, daydreaming about how what she was seeing was probably unchanged from when only American Indians inhabited the region. There was no evidence of civilization as she knew it—no electric wires, houses, traffic or sirens in the distance.

Sirens. Marta would go back to work tomorrow, and the siren she would hear would be riding with her, going wherever she was needed, to help whomever needed help. Like that stupid individual she saw up ahead, standing on a bluff, obviously trying to get up the nerve to jump off the thirty-foot-high ledge into the water below.

Quickly Marta looked around. There was a dirt access road on the left side of the river. An old beat-up pickup truck of indistinguishable color was parked there next to a dirty white van. Two men in brightly colored shorts were on the beach, shouting encouragement to the man up on the ledge. They were dripping wet, and from their calls Marta deduced that they had just completed the stunt themselves.

Marta swiftly assessed the situation. In case of an emergency, like the diving individual cracking his head open on a submerged rock, one vehicle could leave to call for medical transport. In the meantime, she and Mac were qualified to get the injured party out of the water and onto the beach without inflicting any further spinal injury, give CPR if necessary, stop any bleeding and try to prevent shock. If there were no blankets in either of the two vehicles parked by the road, they could utilize her sleeping bag.

The individual in question indicated that he would wait until the canoe passed by before jumping, so Marta didn't have to worry about watching the fool kill himself. She was still afraid of tipping the canoe by turning around. She heard the splash shortly after they passed the ledge and asked Mac if the guy came up all right.

"No rescue today," he answered calmly.

Eleven Year Match   77

Marta let her head rest on the cooler again, closing her eyes and letting out the breath she had been holding. An accident in these primitive surroundings, hours from a proper emergency room, would stack the odds against any victim. She knew. She frequently raced against the clock. Minutes could matter. Seconds even.

She concentrated on regulating her breathing, forcing herself to relax.

Mac let the canoe drift slowly in the quiet stretches of the river, even pausing to fish for a while, enjoying the quiet time before his three-hour drive to St. Louis. First thing tomorrow he was due back in the office he shared with two other orthopedic surgeons.

He also thought it was a doubly good thing the man hadn't been injured diving into the river. If the man had been hurt, Marta would have been faced squarely with the fact that Mac was a doctor when he'd taken control of the emergency situation. Oh, he knew she knew. It was never far from her thoughts. But she had managed to put her prejudices aside for most of the weekend, and that was a big first step.

That thought was Mac's first realization that he was thinking of the future with Marta, and he didn't even know if she would give him her phone number.

"About our kids..." he said. "I've been thinking."

Marta smiled. "I've been trying not to. Honestly, everything I come up with is so far-fetched I'm almost embarrassed."

"Yeah, your idea about the body cast.... You remember? Yesterday afternoon?"

Marta groaned. "I remember."

"Well, I didn't mean to laugh so hard."

"You?" Marta started laughing again at the impression Mac had done of a person attempting to walk around on the beach in a stiff body cast, arms and legs sticking out at all angles. "I thought I was going to be permanently damaged."

"It was a better idea than grounding them forever. That's too hard on us."

"But Sherri meddled where she was told not to, and I have to do something."

Mac had gone over several ideas before entering the tent late last night, long after Marta had dropped off to sleep. She might not like doctors per se, but she was definitely warming up to him as an individual. If he didn't pursue this now, it might be too late. Marta would return to work, meet up with one doctor she didn't like and refuse to ever see Mac again. Guilt by association.

"Rob, too. So let's teach them a lesson they'll never forget."

"You've come up with something?" Marta was very interested in hearing a viable solution and was comfortable enough now to turn partway around so they could talk face to face.

"They wanted us to go out. Let's go out."

"You mean like on a date?" Marta was flabbergasted.

"More than just *a* date."

Marta thought he must have lost his mind. "You got too much sun this weekend, Mac. I don't know about Rob, but Sherri's objective is to get me seriously involved in a relationship so I won't have time to be such a mother hen."

Mac's grin was growing wider. "Then let's do it."

"How does that teach her a lesson? Besides which, I don't get involved with doctors."

His grin didn't waver as he brushed her objection aside. "I know that. But if you want to teach her a lesson more effective than breaking her other arm or grounding her for a month, then this is the way to go. We'll go out a couple times, then we'll tell the kids we're moving in together and scare the hell out of them."

Marta couldn't help herself. One look at Mac's expression and she started chuckling over the idea. "Can't you just see their faces when we tell them that?" she asked.

"Rob will wonder if he has to get rid of his snakes."

"Sherri will ask if she has to move away from her best friend next door."

"Rob will complain that he can't run around the house in his underwear anymore."

"And I'll be sure to tell Sherri that she'll have twice as many dishes to help me with after dinner. What a great idea, Mac! Let's do it. How long should we make them suffer?"

He shrugged. He didn't want to limit himself. "A couple of weeks? I don't know. We'll cross that bridge when we come to it."

Marta wasn't sure this was the best method of punishment for the children, but seeing Mac again suddenly sounded like more fun than not seeing Mac again. And if Mac started showing his true colors later, acting like a typical doctor, she could back out easily.

"You don't think it's too crazy, do you?" Marta asked.

"Just crazy enough to work," he suggested. "Why don't you ride back to St. Louis with me and we can talk?"

"Good idea. Then we can go over the ground rules."

Mac nearly groaned. He should have known that with Marta there would be ground rules.

Chapter Five

"Sherri! I'm home!" Marta called out as she let herself in the front door, then held it open for Mac who was playing the gallant gentleman and carrying almost everything.

"Hi, Mom." Sherri barreled around the corner, then stopped dead in her tracks near the wall. "Oh, hi, Dr. Mac."

"Don't I get a hug?" Marta held her arms open.

"Uh, sure, Mom." Sherri kept a wary eye on Mac as she hugged her mother.

"Well, I'd better get going," Mac said. They had agreed he would only make a brief appearance, for shock value. They knew that even though the kids had set them up, they wouldn't have thought far enough ahead to know how to react if confronted with the consequences so soon and so directly. "Where should I put this stuff?"

"Just set it down." Marta slipped her arm around Mac's waist as she walked him to the door, and he draped his naturally across her shoulder. "I had a great time, Mac."

"I could tell that you really tried to relax, after you bent the arms on my lawn chair."

Eleven Year Match 81

"What?" she asked with a laugh and gave him a light punch in the biceps with her free hand.

"We call that the white-knuckle disease."

"She's good at that," Sherri chimed in.

"I hear it's symptomatic of an overprotective mother."

Marta tilted her head to say something, and Mac stopped her with a kiss. Their lips met, not too briefly. Long enough for Sherri to go tearing down the hall toward the bedroom phone.

"That was for show," he whispered. "This is for you." Mac circled her with both arms, engulfing her willing body in his warm embrace, and his lips met hers with tenderness.

Marta wanted to let her body melt into Mac's. His embrace felt so naturally right that for a moment she just let herself go. She enjoyed it. She wanted to feel it again. Dating Mac might be fun.

Sherri charged back into the room and stared.

Marta jumped. This had never come up before: her kissing a man in front of her daughter. They broke apart. "See you," he said to Marta, then tossed Sherri a wink and left.

Marta stood at the door and waved to Mac as he got into his car, biding her time, letting Sherri stew a little longer, maybe wondering just how much trouble she might be in.

"You don't look so good, sweetie. Do you feel all right?"

Sherri chewed her lip. Marta knew Sherri was trying to decide what she could safely say or not say without actually owning up to the truth or lying.

"I'm fine, Mom. You look like you had a good time," she began tentatively.

82   *Eleven Year Match*

"Oh, I did. Who would've ever thought I'd fall for a doctor?"

Sherri brightened considerably. "Does that mean you're not mad?"

"Why should I be mad?"

Sherri fidgeted.

"Oh, you mean because your plan worked? Because you meddled in my life? Because you conspired with Rob and Kelly to get Mac and me together?"

A barely perceptible nod was the only answer Sherri gave.

"Well, I would be very upset if you gloated or anything, because what you did and how you went about it was wrong. But..." Marta didn't want Sherri to get off the hook too fast. "I'm thirsty. Would you like to split a soda while we discuss this?"

"Sure." She didn't look too sure, but she followed Marta into the kitchen.

"Well, as I was saying, I kind of fell for Mac."

"Really, Mom?" Sherri was all ears now and quickly sat down at the table, apparently waiting for juicy details.

Marta wondered what an eleven-year-old would consider juicy.

"Oh, Sherri, he is such a gentleman. And so nice. He taught me how to canoe and invited us to go with him and Rob sometime. He's a great cook. He asked me out. He has a great dog, too, named Dixie. You'll love her."

"I will?" Sherri was almost bouncing in her seat she was so happy. "You're really going to go out with him?"

Marta smiled and nodded. "He's quite a guy." Her enthusiasm surprised even her. Saying all those nice things about Mac was amazingly easy!

Eleven Year Match

"HEY, HOWARD'S BACK in one piece."

"What? Hey, Howard, no broken bones?"

"Forget the broken bones. No hangover?"

Marta was welcomed back to work early Tuesday morning. Her dreaded canoe trip with the fifty strangers in the singles' group had been no secret. She had been griping about it for weeks.

Summers was stretched out on the couch. He lowered his newspaper momentarily to welcome her back. Johnson and Hawk were, as usual, playing gin, fortified with their chipped mugs of coffee and their cigarettes.

Hawk stubbed out his cigarette and pushed his wire-rimmed glasses up further on his nose. "So, how was the dreaded singles' group?"

"Unbelievably noisy."

"Couldn't have been too bad. You don't look stressed out."

"Well, I sort of camped out upriver from them."

"Camped out upriver, huh?" Johnson queried. "All by your lonesome, out in the woods, made your own campfire, cooked your own food, paddled your own canoe?" He snorted his disbelief. "Come on, Howard. Give."

She chose her words carefully. "Well, I met this other single person who didn't want to camp out with the group, either, so we set up our own camp."

Marta couldn't believe she hadn't thought about what she'd tell her coworkers. It had sounded like such a good plan when she and Mac were on the river. Too good to be true, obviously. She wondered how many other fine points she had overlooked. Hawk's wife and Kelly worked together and could conceivably compare notes later.

Johnson noticed Marta's pause, then hooted and slapped the table, sending several cigarettes rolling. Marta winced. Hawk quickly grabbed and saved his stash.

"So, what's the guy's name?" Johnson asked as he shuffled the deck and dealt another hand.

Marta suddenly knew there was only one way to keep Johnson from teasing her to death. She told the truth. "Mac."

"Yeah? Mac who?"

When Marta didn't answer, they all knew Mac who. There was silence as they each waited for someone else to mention the obvious, and each knew they'd better let the subject drop if they were planning to live through the day. Ribbing Marta for spending the weekend with a doctor could be hazardous to their health. Summers returned to his newspaper.

"Gin," Hawk announced with a big smile.

"SO, I HEAR your weekend went well," Kelly gloated over the phone.

Marta had known this was going to happen. She knew Kelly would gloat for all it was worth, but she also knew that she would get even with her later. In about a week she was going to tell her sister that she was moving in with Mac, and then she was going to keep her in suspense. Kelly would go absolutely crazy.

"Yes. Thank you for talking me into going." This was making her nauseous.

"Well, I don't like to say it, but I told you so."

"Yes, you certainly did," Marta said with a light laugh. "I don't know how I can ever repay you." She knew, all right. She had it all planned. She just couldn't do it yet.

"Make me your matron of honor."

"I wouldn't have it any other way."

"ARE YOU GOING to bed early tonight, Mom?" Sherri asked as they cleaned up the kitchen after dinner.

"I thought I might catch up on my reading. Why?"

"Can I lie in your bed for a while?" Marta's bed was Sherri's favorite place for serious mother-daughter conversations.

"Okay."

Sherri curled up in bed with Marta shortly before her bedtime. "I thought you might want to tell me about your weekend," she prompted.

"Really? You want to hear about the fishing or the cooking?"

Sherri sighed loudly. "Mo-om. Aunt Kelly said you would have a romantic weekend." Ordinarily Sherri thought nothing about romance, other than hoping her mother would meet an irresistible man some day soon, and Marta recognized Kelly's influence immediately.

"Maybe you should tell me what you want to know."

"Do you think he's a hunk?"

"I wish you wouldn't talk like Kelly."

"But do you?" Sherri crawled under the covers and confiscated one of the pillows.

"Yes, he is." There was no sense lying to the child. Mac was a hunk, and any female in her right mind would admit it.

"How much?"

"How much what?"

"On a scale of one to ten. You know."

"Yes, I know. Remind me to have a chat with Kelly, though, will you?"

"Sure, Mom. Is he a ten? Aunt Kelly says there're no tens in St. Louis."

"Really? How does she rate her husband?"

"She says he's an eight, and so is Daddy."

"Well, if they're both eights, and there are no tens, then Mac must be a nine." Personally, after that last kiss Mac had given her, she thought ten was closer to the mark, but eleven-year-olds didn't have to have the complete truth.

"That's nice. How can you tell?" she asked very seriously.

"Lots of ways. You'll know when you're older."

"Do you think Daddy's an eight?"

Marta was caught off guard. How could she tell Sherri that her very own dad was on the minus side in all the intangibles? "Maybe in looks," she said.

The phone rang and Marta ignored it. She cherished these moments with Sherri, knowing someday her daughter would think she was too big to climb into Marta's bed and talk about personal things.

"Aren't you going to answer it?" Sherri sounded as though the world would end if Marta didn't.

"No, let's talk."

"But, Mom, it might be Dr. Mac!"

"If it's important, he'll call back."

Sherri quickly climbed over her and answered the phone, and Marta turned away to hide a smile. Obviously Sherri didn't want all her hard work to go to waste.

"See, I told you," Sherri whispered as she shoved the receiver at Marta.

"Hi, Mac."

While Mac was returning the greeting, Sherri was asking if she should leave.

"Oh, no, sweetie. We won't be long. You can stay here." She knew Mac would catch that hint.

"I've missed you, sweetheart," he said.

Marta thought Rob must be within earshot also. "I've missed you, too," she replied for Sherri's benefit, and she was surprised at how easily she thought of the right words.

"Are we still on for Friday night?"

Eleven Year Match 87

"Friday night? I wouldn't miss it, Mac." Marta had to turn to see the delighted looks crossing Sherri's face. Revenge was going to be so sweet.

"Dinner?"

"Sounds wonderful." Her voice was husky.

"I'll pick you up at six, okay?"

"I'll be waiting." Marta thought she was beginning to sound like a very bad actress, but Sherri apparently didn't think it was too much.

"I miss you."

"You, too, Mac. Will you call me tomorrow?"

"I'll call you every night."

Marta couldn't believe it. If someone had told her ten days ago that she would be sitting on her bed talking to a doctor socially on the phone and actually enjoying it, she would have taken their temperature and checked them out for signs of brain damage. She hoped that the kids wouldn't be around tomorrow night, because she would like to have a real conversation with Mac.

"Where's he taking you?" Sherri asked before Marta had the receiver recradled.

"Oh. I forgot to ask, but he's going to call me again tomorrow night, and I'll find out then. Guess I'm out of practice, huh?" she asked Sherri with a smile.

Sherri laughed. "Guess so, Mom. But you're smart. You'll catch on in no time."

"GEE, DAD, you didn't talk long," Rob criticized.

"She was in the middle of something with Sherri."

"You didn't even tell her where you're taking her Friday night."

Mac sighed, ran a hand through his hair and stared his son down. "I thought you were going to butt out now that you got things started. I know how to go on a date, for heaven's sake."

"I know, Dad. But Marta's kind of different."

Mac sat down at the table where Rob was enjoying cookies and milk. "I know. But you're only eleven. How do you know?"

"I'm not a little kid or anything. I could tell she doesn't like doctors. And Sherri told me, too. You've got to handle her special, Dad."

Mac smiled inside. He had to handle precocious little adolescents "special," too. He was liking his plan better all the time.

"MOM, AREN'T YOU going to wear any makeup?" Sherri had been hanging around since school let out, watching Marta select her dress and shoes, brush her hair, stuff her purse with tissues, nail file and emergency money. Sherri felt free to offer criticism frequently.

"Yes, of course. I just haven't gotten to it yet." Makeup, she thought. She must have some around somewhere, and she should have thought of it sooner. Deception obviously was something one had to practice. "Are you sure this dress is okay?"

"It's fine. I'm glad you're going to wear makeup." The kid had a one-track mind. "Mac's a doctor. He's probably used to young nurses falling all over him trying to get a date."

Marta's eyebrows arched, and she peered closely into the mirror to see if she was in such desperate need of makeup as Sherri seemed to think. "Is that right?"

"Sure. Trust me, Mom. You wouldn't need much. You're pretty, anyway."

Marta was amused by her daughter's continued matchmaking as she went into the bathroom to lightly apply mascara and lipstick. She could afford to be amused instead of perturbed, because she knew who was going to have the last laugh.

"I can't seem to get my hair quite right," Marta said more to herself than Sherri.

"Here. Give me your brush." Sherri quickly made some adjustments in back, and then reached for the side.

"No!" Marta said in time to stop her. "I like that side. It's the other one."

"Don't get in such a tizzy, Mom. It'll be perfect as soon as I just poof this out a little."

Marta realized Sherri was right; she was in a tizzy. This wasn't a real date, and she was only supposed to be pretending it was. Wasn't she? At this rate, a real date with Mac probably would make her heart stop.

The doorbell rang and Sherri announced that she would let Mac in. But upon leaving the bathroom to greet her guest, Marta was attacked by a wet spray of perfume, compliments of her daughter.

"Sherri!" she whispered threateningly. "I already had enough on."

Sherri whispered back, "Go on, Mom. He's waiting."

Marta floated into the living room, and Mac rose from his position on the couch.

"You look lovely," he said with a smile, dropping a chaste kiss on her lips. "And you smell good, too."

"Not medicinal, you mean?" she replied with a light laugh.

"Definitely not medicinal. We have reservations for six-thirty at Russeli's. What about Sherri?"

"Her best friend is coming over at seven."

Marta turned to say goodbye, expecting the usual sour look Sherri gave whenever she got left behind. Instead, the eleven-year-old matchmaker was ushering them toward the door with a big smile on her face. Mac's kiss had obviously been a brilliant addition to their charade.

"Bye, sweetie. I'll be back in a couple of hours. Call Laurie's mom if you need anything. Okay?"

"Sure, Mom. Have a good time. You, too, Dr. Mac." Sherri hugged her mother with her good arm without embarrassment. "Don't rush. I'll be fine. And wear your seat belt," she called as the two adults went out the front door.

"Like mother, like daughter." Mac took Marta's arm as they descended the front porch steps and kept the gentle contact as they went down the walk to where his car waited at the curb.

Marta's arm continued to tingle after Mac had tucked her into his sports car, and she rubbed it briskly with her other hand, trying to banish the feeling. They were on this date in order to teach their children a lesson, and she wondered if she should be enjoying it so much already. She automatically locked the car door with a punch of her elbow and buckled her seat belt.

"Nice car." The leather still smelled new.

"Thank you. The other one's the family car. I like this little two-seater for running around town."

When they reached the restaurant and Mac went around to open Marta's door, he had to tap on the window and point to the door lock. She mumbled an apology behind the window as she turned and pulled up the button.

Russeli's was located on a quiet street in Kirkwood, and was well patronized in spite of the fact that there was no sign outside. Candlelight glowed on each small table, and the mood created was one which was elegant and intimate. She was glad she had made the extra fuss with her hair.

Eleven Year Match

The maître d' held Marta's chair for her, then snapped out her dark linen napkin and lay it across her lap. They were suddenly surrounded by quiet people removing extra place settings, pouring ice water, putting plates of bread and butter on the snowy white tablecloth, offering tall leather menus and waiting to take their cocktail order.

When all was quiet again, and they were conspicuously alone at the table, Marta became self-conscious. Everything had been so spontaneous on the river, from the way she'd ended up sharing his canoe, to the time he'd dropped her off at home. Now, she wasn't sure whether to remain silent or talk about the weather.

Mac broke the silence. "This is quite a bit different from campfire smoke and using the bottom of the canoe for a table, isn't it?"

"Well, we still have the candlelight and tablecloth."

"Good. I'm glad you don't think this is all bad."

Marta laughed. "Mac, it's lovely. I've never been here before."

"Your dates don't like candlelight and tablecloths?"

"We won't go into my dates, if you don't mind. We're here because of our children."

Marta's dates had been few and far between. Her job pretty well limited her to meeting emergency personnel, firemen, policemen, doctors and the fathers of her daughter's friends. The fathers were almost always married, doctors had always been off-limits, and she'd decided she couldn't take the strain of developing a relationship with a policeman. More than half the remainder were already married, and she found most of the single ones about as desirable as Johnson.

She'd decided that when she found a man to fall in love with, he would be single, faithful, kind, loving, supportive of her career and patient with her daughter. She was surprised to find herself counting how many of those qualities applied to Mac.

"Let's forget our children while we're here, okay?" Mac suggested. "We did just fine on the river, and it wasn't because I was thinking of Rob."

"We can't forget them completely. After all, they're why we're here."

Mac smiled. "Partly."

Marta covered up her nervousness by fiddling with her silverware.

"How late should we stay out tonight?" she finally asked.

"Well, if we really want to set the stage, I guess we should get in about dawn." Mac had never had such a comfortable first date, if this could be considered in that light. After all, he reminded himself, it was really all just a prank on their busybody kids, even if he was having a good time. "Then, when we tell them next week that I asked you to move in, they won't find it suspicious."

The cocktails that they'd ordered had been set so quietly on the table that Marta hadn't even noticed at first. She reached for hers as she tried to think of a response.

"On the other hand," she said, toying with the skinny straw in her wine spritzer, "I can't keep my eyes open past ten o'clock, and just think how much more shocked the kids will be if they don't see it coming."

"I'm sure we can compromise on a time somewhere between ten and dawn. Didn't you bring your vitamins?" Mac asked when she neglected to pour out her regular six to take with her drink.

"Don't be a nerd," she said, imitating Sherri's speech. "I'm not a fanatic, for heaven's sake."

Eleven Year Match

"No, of course not. That's why I had to knock on your car door before I could open it."

She couldn't help but respond to his light tone, and shrugged, deciding to relax and enjoy it. "I already admitted I'm a mother hen, long ago. What about you?"

"No, I'm not a mother hen."

"But you're a landlord."

Mac set down his drink as the crab rangoon and rumaki were set before them. "Forgive me if I don't make the connection."

"Insurance. You must pay terribly high premiums, and the only way to keep them from going even higher is to install all the safety features you possibly can."

"Here, try this rumaki," he said as he lifted one with a fork and put it on her plate. "Tell me, what safety features would a mother hen install in her rental property?"

Marta finished the rumaki and stole another from him. "Adequate locks and chains, for one. More smoke and fire alarms than are presently required. Safety lighting. Regular maintenance on things like railings, hinges, gas appliances. Oh, and ground fault interrupters on any outlets by sinks."

He broke in before she could continue. "Do you have ground fault interrupters in your bathroom?"

She smirked triumphantly. "I certainly do. How can you raise a kid with a blow dryer in the bathroom and not worry?"

"You educate them as to the hazards of mixing electricity with water. And pray," he added. He was beginning to suspect she was more of a fanatic than he had thought at first.

"Is your property manager a mother hen?"

"I haven't had any complaints."

She thought about the apartments she had made runs to lately. "Maybe you ought to check."

Mac didn't want to talk business. He received regular written reports from his manager, detailing what had been repaired, costs involved, and projections for future maintenance. There had been no more calls from his tenants after he had explained to them that all calls were to go directly to the new man. He was satisfied that everything was going well.

The remainder of the dinner was spent discussing all the pros and cons of the different ideas they each suggested for teaching their children not to meddle in the lives of others. Grounding was out, they both agreed. If the kids were stuck at home they would just have more opportunity to drive their parents nuts. On the other hand, Mac and Marta agreed that it would be good for the children to learn to be careful about what they wished for. They might just get it, or so they would think.

In the end they decided to compromise. Tonight Mac would deliver Marta to her door at the respectable hour of 11:00 p.m., and next Friday they would stay out all night and drop the bomb on Saturday.

"I had a lovely evening, Mac. Thank you."

They were on Marta's porch, and they could hear the TV in the living room.

"I think you have a welcoming committee."

Marta looked over at the window and saw the curtain move slightly. "Looks that way. Wait till she's out on a date."

Mac laughed. "You'll be lucky if she's in plain sight the way we are."

"Oh, please, don't mention it. I won't be able to stand it when she goes out with a boy. I won't have any control over his driving or whether he drinks or—"

"Stop." Mac placed two fingers softly on her lips. "I can feel your blood pressure going up from here."

Marta's lips tingled where he had touched her. His fingers moved down to the side of her neck, under her hair. His thumb moved gently back and forth, stirring something vague inside her. She would agree that her blood pressure was on the rise, but it wasn't from thinking about whatever it was they had been discussing.

"Mac?"

Gentle pressure on her neck drew her closer to him. Her hands rested on the smooth front of his suit coat. As he pulled her slowly closer to his chest, her hands slid around to his back. Her eyes focused on his lowered eyelids before she closed hers. His lips, when they met hers, were gentle, warm, inquisitive.

Marta started to step back after a moment, and Mac's kiss became more compelling. He wrapped his strong arms completely around her, pulling her against the warmth of his hard chest. His lips became more demanding, drawing her up onto her toes.

Her arms slid down his torso, her hands found their way under his coat to feel the hard cords of his back muscles.

When Mac had kissed her on the river, Marta had been glad Dixie had sent them flying apart. The dog had been as effective as a cold dunking in the river would have been. But this time Dixie wasn't here, and Marta was beginning to think that was rather a nice thing.

Mac knew the girls were probably peeking through the curtains again, but he didn't bother to look. He wondered whether Marta was only returning his kisses for the kids' benefit—to teach them their lesson. And he had absolutely no doubt Sherri would tell Rob.

One of Mac's hands was in Marta's hair. The other lay on her back, in plain sight. But with a slight pressure he was pushing her yielding body into contact with his pelvis, letting her know the effect she was having on him.

"The girls..." Marta muttered as she broke contact with his lips and stepped back slightly. It was one thing to kiss Mac to teach Sherri a lesson. It had even been enjoyable, but she wasn't going to let it go any further. "We have an audience."

"I'm not used to this," Mac admitted as he ran his hand through his short brown hair.

"Neither am I." Marta wasn't used to being kissed at all. "But somehow I think you mean it differently."

Mac stuffed his hands into his pants pockets before he was tempted to pull her into his arms again.

"Next Friday again? Six o'clock?"

"I can hardly wait." She thought that sounded too eager. "I mean, to teach the kids a lesson and all."

"Right. The kids," he agreed, nodding his head.

Had he been wrong? No, she hadn't been kissing him good-night like that just to put on an act. She obviously felt something for him, too.

He opened the door for her and checked to see that it was safely locked after she disappeared inside, telling himself that made him a gentleman, not a mother hen.

Chapter Six

Marta remembered their common goal—teach the kids a lesson—and plastered a dreamy look on her face as she went inside. She was soon yanked back to reality. The two girls had trashed the place.

She could understand the sleeping bags on the living room floor in front of the TV and the pretzels and sodas on the coffee table. What she couldn't understand was all the clothes strewn about on the couch and matching chair, across the carpet and both sleeping bags. Not to mention the purses, scarves, shoes, hats and jewelry.

"We'll clean it up!" Sherri spoke quickly while Marta stood there with her mouth open, speechless. Sherri moved very slowly, however, though Laurie scooped up an armful frantically, not sure how loud Marta could yell.

"Is that my black bag?" Marta asked. "And my silver earrings?"

"I'll put them away. Trust me, Mom."

"Trust you? I'll trust you to be grounded the first time I can't find something I want." That threat would probably take care of Marta's belongings at least. Sherri's possessions were another matter entirely.

Marta knew she would find articles of Sherri's clothing weeks later in unlikely places. Undoubtedly there would be purses in the underwear drawer, clean scarves in the dirty laundry and jewelry in the Kleenex box. Knowing that no amount of warning now would help items find their proper places, Marta left the two girls to it. Perhaps Sherri would learn her lesson someday when she couldn't find an accessory she wanted ten minutes before some big dance or party.

Marta was snuggled in bed, recalling how nice it had been to kiss Mac, when the phone rang thirty minutes later. Giving herself a pat on the back for having had their one phone installed in her bedroom instead of the kitchen, she leaned over and lifted the receiver off the nightstand.

"Did you get the third degree?"

Marta laughed quietly as she snuggled down deeper. "Hello to you, too, Mac. No, I didn't get the third degree. My living room was such a disaster area that the subject didn't come up."

"Well, I just called to warn you. It will. My son followed me into the bathroom, for pity's sake. I finally had to race him to my bedroom and lock myself in."

Marta tried to picture Mac in his bedroom and wondered whether he was dressed. The thought of seeing the muscles she had felt through his shirt produced a sudden warmth deep inside her.

"Are you still there, Marta?"

She nodded, then realized he couldn't see her. She cleared her throat. "Yes."

"I was saying that I called you as soon as I locked him out, so that I could tie up the phone. Otherwise, he'd be calling Sherri right now to cook up something else for us."

"I'll be sure to answer the phone first, then."

"Are you teaching first aid again Tuesday?"

"No, they have a field trip planned."

"Are you in bed?"

Eleven Year Match

She didn't want to say yes and sound provocative, but she had told him she retired early, so lying would be hard to carry off. "Yes."

"Then I called to say good-night, too."

"Good night, Mac. Unplug your phones so Rob can't call here and wake me up."

He laughed lightly. "He'd just plug them back in."

"I'll do mine then. Good night."

As he pulled back the covers on his king-size water-bed, he thought of Marta. Her dark hair would look lovely fanned on his silver-gray pillow slip. Maybe when they were done teaching the kids a lesson, if he thought it wouldn't be bad for Rob, maybe he would continue to see Marta. If she wanted to see him. He slid between the silky sheets and folded a pillow double under his head, flicking on the TV with a remote switch. It would be a while before he could sleep.

"I'LL GET IT," Sherri yelled when the doorbell rang.

"Two minutes till dinner," Marta said, warning her not to run off and play.

A large bouquet of roses entered the kitchen, almost overwhelming Sherri, who carried them.

"Good heavens!" Marta exclaimed at the sight of the huge yellow arrangement.

"They're for you, Mom." Sherri set them on the table and beamed. "I think he likes you."

Marta thought so, too, at least until she remembered this was all a prank. What a great idea Mac had, sending such a visible sign of affection. "Think so?" she asked.

"Mo-om."

Marta knew Sherri wouldn't buy a gushy reaction to this display. She smiled a secretive sort of smile for her benefit. "Well, I kind of like him, too."

She was rewarded with a huge smile on her daughter's face before she ran out of the kitchen, yelling as she went, "I'm going to call Aunt Kelly."

"Dinner's—" She let it drop. This would be good for Kelly, too. Rub it in. Build her up for the fall. She put the dinner on simmer to keep warm.

"Mom, she wants to talk to you," Sherri said, returning to the kitchen where Marta waited patiently. "Can I start?"

"May I," she corrected as she went to get the phone. "Hi, Kelly. Did Sherri tell you about my flowers?"

"Yes, she—"

"They're gorgeous! There must be a dozen or two and baby's breath and ribbons." Play it up, she told herself.

"Marta—"

"They just arrived. He had them delivered."

"Marta—"

"And they smell so-o-o good. I won't even be able to taste my dinner—all I smell is roses."

"Marta!"

"What?"

"Do I have your attention now?"

"Sure, Kelly. What do you mean? I'm right here," she said innocently.

"Uh-huh. Sort of. Are you going to send him something?"

"You're kidding! Send something to a man?"

"This is the nineties, honey. How about a boutonniere that he can wear at the office?"

"When's the last time you went to see a doctor and he was wearing flowers?"

"Then you think of something."

Marta smiled to herself. "How about balloons?"

"Great idea!"

As she thought more about it, Marta decided it *was* a great idea. She could send them to Mac's house where Rob would get to see them, too. She'd send them the next day.

MARTA SPENT Thursday night picking out her dress and accessories for the following night. She also did a little planning so that Friday after work all she would need to do would be to run home, shower, dress, put on a little makeup and answer the door when Mac arrived.

"The dishes are done," Sherri said as she entered Marta's bedroom, hoping to supervise. "Good grief, you have flowers in here, too?"

Marta paused and fingered one of the soft white rose petals. "Here, smell," she said as she picked them up and offered them to Sherri. "Aren't they lovely?"

Sherri backed off. "I don't have to sniff them—the whole house smells like roses. Yellow in the kitchen, red in the living room, white in here."

Marta returned the vase of flowers to her dresser and gave them an appreciative sniff herself, even though Sherri wasn't interested. "Enjoy them. I'm going to go take a shower and wash my hair."

Sherri didn't waste any time. Now was her chance to use the phone in private.

"Rob, it's me. I can't believe it. He sent another dozen roses. White ones this time," she said excitedly. This was better than she could have hoped.

Rob was equally enthusiastic. "I know. And your mom sent balloons. Dad never got balloons from anybody before. You should have seen his face! He was like a little kid at a birthday party."

"I helped her pick them out. Isn't this neat?"

"I'm trying to talk Dad into a barbecue this weekend. Then you can come over and see my dog."

"Gosh, it'll almost be like we're related or something."

"I never dreamed it would go this great," Rob said. "Dad's never been like this, sending flowers every day and stuff."

"My mom's never sent anything to a man before. Maybe they'll have a good time Friday night, then I'll see you at the barbecue."

MARTA AND SUMMERS were sent to an auto accident late Friday afternoon, during the beginning of rush hour.

"We've got a fractured femur, possible fractured pelvis and he's disoriented," Summers called to Marta from his crouched position next to the man they had found lying on the pavement. In his confusion following the accident, the middle-aged man had gotten out of his car and fallen where he now lay.

Marta radioed the hospital for permission to apply MAST trousers which would both stabilize the fractures and help reverse shock.

Traffic was bad, with one lane blocked, bystanders were always a potential problem, and Marta was grateful there were enough police on the scene to control both. People usually meant well, but having seen medical shows on TV made some of them ask questions that, on the surface, sounded rather more like giving advice. Like "Shouldn't you start an IV?"

Once permission had been received, they removed the man's shoes, socks and pants and velcroed the MAST trousers onto him. They inflated the MAST trousers, then transferred him into the ambulance on a long backboard. Marta stayed with him to monitor vital signs during the ride to the emergency room.

When they arrived, Marta immediately recognized the tense atmosphere in the large ER. Code Blue. Maybe more than one.

In times of cardiac arrest, personnel on one side would do what was needed to help the other—either lend a hand or handle all the other emergency patients. In addition to all the emergency room staff, the Respiratory Therapy team also was summoned. Everyone moved at top speed.

Today there were no students in the hall. The waiting room was overflowing with lesser emergency cases. The nurse normally stationed at the triage desk was gone.

"What's going on?" Summers looked around quickly, this way and that.

"I'll check. Cross your fingers." Marta disappeared at top speed through the electric doors with the words "Authorized Personnel Only" printed across them.

Sounds emanating from the Code room clued Marta in before she looked through the open door. A Code Blue was in progress. She stepped in and stood out of the way next to a nursing student who was awaiting orders.

"Is there a Code on the other side, too?" she asked, afraid to hear the answer, but having to ask. She had a seriously injured patient in the hall, who could also easily arrest at any minute.

The student nodded.

"Damn!" she cursed quietly.

Marta knew the situation on the other side would be just as busy, if not more so. One Code Blue was enough to tie up the ER and back up the waiting room to the overflowing point. Two was unrealistic. Even so, she checked the situation on the other side. It was not almost over.

Marta knew she had to return to her patient quickly. He had shown signs of shock when they had arrived on the scene. No higher authority was available to make any decisions or take over. No one was available to order or start an IV. Now it was up to her and Summers to do all they could to keep him alive until the necessary personnel were available.

As she pushed the wall button and started through the electric doors, she saw her partner bending over their patient.

"We've got trouble!"

Summers was very competent at his job; if he said they had trouble, Marta knew it was bad.

"Respiratory arrest!"

Marta couldn't believe it. What next?

"All the rooms are full." She looked around. The whole waiting room was staring their way. Some were even edging toward them and would get in the way. "Let's move into the work lane."

Summers pushed, Marta pulled. It only took seconds for them to get into the hall where they'd be closer to all available equipment.

"Damn," Summers said, realizing the hall was empty of personnel.

"Double damn. There're two Codes." Marta quickly searched the rolling shelves for the equipment she required.

Summers had inserted an airway in the patient when he had lost consciousness by the triage desk. Now that they were in the ER and had access to more equipment, Marta selected a different airway from the cart and began to prepare it for insertion.

"What are you doing?" Summers asked, continuing to monitor the patient's vital signs. "We can't use that."

"We most certainly can. We can eliminate gastric distention with this. Who knows how long it'll be before this guy gets a doctor? If I'd had one of these in the ambulance and I were in the same predicament, I'd use it. We might as well still be in the ambulance."

Marta was used to emergencies. She was well trained and had years of experience. She was not, however, at all pleased with this situation. She had lost patients before, but not because of a stupid lack of personnel.

"Howard, we can't use that. We can get by with this."

"But this will be better." Anything to help. She had to help.

"I know. That isn't the problem—"

"I got licensed for this last summer." Marta had not hesitated in her preparations during the discussion. She had tested the cuff and lubricated the tube.

He cut her off. "I don't remember that."

"You forgot," she said without thinking about him. Marta set the syringe and lay it where it would be handy. Her brain was reviewing the preparations and procedures for inserting the device.

"Howard..."

"You're making me nervous. Look, there's a phone right over there. See it?"

Summers looked over his shoulder. "Yes."

"Go use it. Somewhere in this hospital there must be a doctor who can come down here and lend a hand. This guy could use an IV for starters. If we don't get help soon we're going to lose him."

"Damn, Howard."

"I don't know how, but somebody usually gets this kind of patient into surgery." Marta removed the original airway and deftly inserted the new one. She tested its position with a blow of oxygen. "Just find somebody, Summers, okay?"

Five steps took him to the phone. She had no idea who he called or what he said. She finished inflating the device and attached it to the ventilator, then started looking around for a suction machine, just in case.

A doctor stepped out of the Code room. He took one quick look at Marta's patient. "Fractures?"

"Femur and possibly pelvis."

"Those have to be deflated specially, don't they?" He pointed to the MAST trousers, which indeed had to be deflated under certain very definite procedures.

"Yes, sir."

He turned to the nurse behind him. "Get that paramedic student in the Code room to start an IV." He glanced quickly at his watch. "And page Dr. Macke and see if he's still in the hospital. Maybe he'll lend us a hand and take this one right into surgery. And notify X-ray." The nurse rushed off to do his bidding.

He turned back to Marta. "As soon as that IV is started, you monitor his BP and start deflation. Don't rush it. We'll send Respiratory Therapy to you as soon as we can. Holler if you get into trouble." He paused and looked at her closely. "Can you handle it?"

"If you come when I yell," she said.

With that he was gone, unavailable for any questions or comments. Marta was on her own again, but this time with some possibility of assistance.

"I sure hope we won't need to yell," Summers commented.

"Can you find a suction machine?"

He nodded briskly and proceeded to hook one up.

The paramedic student had just finished getting the IV in place and started when a technician with a portable X-ray machine showed up and did her job. Marta kept an eye on the patient's respiratory condition while she began deflating the abdominal chamber of the MAST trousers. Summers monitored blood pressure.

She heard Mac coming before she saw him. He was asking someone what room the orthopedic patient was in.

"Over here, Doc," Summers called, not looking up.

"X rays are there," he said as he pointed to the view box. "What are vitals?" He was all business.

Summers repeated them. Marta's attention was on her deflation procedure.

"All right!" Respiratory Therapy arrived on the scene asking, "Who's the nice guy who put that in for us?"

"I did," she answered. She felt more than saw Mac pivot her way.

"Makes my job easier," the therapist said happily. He looked tired.

A doctor was on the scene, and Marta was greatly relieved. She and Summers had stabilized a dangerously injured patient, gotten him to the hospital and maintained all systems without any oxygen deprivation. She could afford to relax ever so slightly.

She looked at her watch and smiled wryly. "You're going to be late for dinner, Doctor."

Mac assessed the patient to be well stabilized, and lucky to be so, considering the fact that the ER was shorthanded.

"I was going to be up all night, anyway. I'll eat later.

"Tell me," he continued, "I've never dealt with these trousers before, but I know they can't just be removed. Can you come along and finish in the OR?"

Mac's situation was not unique. MAST trousers were not carried in all ambulances, and not everybody who worked in the ER could be familiar with everything. Just knowing what he couldn't do with the trousers was one step in the right direction. A big step. Admitting his ignorance was an even bigger one, and Marta recognized that.

"Under the circumstances, I wouldn't let him out of my sight. Lead on."

Marta and Summers slowly continued deflation in the OR, after being swathed in sterile gowns and masks.

"You're welcome to stay and watch," Mac offered to both of them.

Summers declined. "We've got to get the ambulance back for the next shift."

"I'd like to stay for a while," Marta accepted quietly.

Mac winked at her and turned to the job at hand.

"Could I see you outside for a minute, please?" Summers asked.

In the hall Marta pulled her mask aside for fresh air, and Summers began taking off his sterile coverings.

"You don't mind taking the ambulance back alone, do you?" Marta asked uncomfortably. "I mean, we are off duty."

Summers was quiet until he had tossed all the OR greens into the hamper. He faced her with his hands spread on his hips. "I don't get it. First you don't like doctors, then you date doctors, then you want to stay and make goo-goo eyes during surgery."

Marta laughed. She wanted to sag with relief against the wall at the break in tension, but she needed to stay as sterile as possible. "Goo-goo eyes? Summers, you amaze me. I have a date with Mac tonight at six o'clock. At this point neither one of us is going to be on time, so I might as well wait for him here."

"Oh. Well, I guess that makes sense. I talked to the office earlier, and they were going to call home for you to let

Sherri know you'll be late." He started to walk away, then turned back and smiled wickedly. "Better find a chair and get some rest. I heard your date say he planned on being up all night." He winked and walked away.

AT TEN O'CLOCK that night Marta's stomach was growling for food. She had left the operating room an hour into surgery and crashed on the emergency room personnel lounge couch. Her purse was at work, and after calling Sherri, she had too little change in her pocket to buy any food.

She had been fascinated watching Mac perform surgery. The femoral artery had been injured in the accident and had to be repaired. Without the MAST trousers, the man would have bled to death before surgery had even begun.

Mac's commands in the OR were concise, quick. His hands were nimble, versatile. He had worked with Marta, following her guidance in MAST trouser procedures. He treated all the staff in the OR with respect. Marta continued to be impressed.

"Marta?" Mac opened the door a crack and peeked in. "I'm starving. Ready?"

"You won't need to ask twice," she said as she bounded off the couch and through the door. "Have you been in surgery all this time?"

"No, but one thing leads to another. Let's get out of here."

"Mac!" The doctor Marta had met earlier outside the Code room called from just down the hall.

"Uh-oh, too late," Mac muttered.

"I just wanted to thank you for lending a hand like you did," Dr. Nelson said as he walked quickly up to them. "I was going to say I owe you one, but," he looked at Marta, "if this lovely, more-than-competent EMT is your consolation date for dinner, I guess you owe me."

"Now how do you figure that?" Mac asked.

"I brought you together, Mac. You wouldn't have met if it weren't for me."

"On the contrary, if it weren't for you, we wouldn't both be late for the six-o'clock dinner date we had previously arranged."

"Oops. Well, look at it this way. If it weren't for me, a doctor would have had to wait while his woman was tied up in the ER. Kind of a new twist on an old story, hmm?"

"So, you owe me one," Mac told him as he took hold of Marta's hand. "And I'm going to get some food into this lovely lady."

"Thank you, Miss Howard," Dr. Nelson said as he turned to her. "It's too bad you couldn't have brought my Code Blue in. He started with a fractured femur, too, but he didn't make it."

Marta knew the dangers that lay in a fractured femur. If the artery was damaged, a patient could lose two liters of blood internally in a matter of minutes in the affected extremity alone. MAST trousers could make all the difference, but not all ambulances carried them.

"I'm sorry."

"Yes, we all are. But aside from that, you did a remarkable job coming in here and finding the staff tied up like you did and handling the case on your own. I know you're trained to get them here in the best condition you can and then leave them to us. I'm very grateful that you could extend your expertise."

"You sure got swamped, Charlie," Mac commiserated.

"It happens. Fletch couldn't make it at the last minute, and by the time I got here things were already starting to escalate—not that it made any difference in patient care, mind you,'' he added carefully.

"Is Fletch all right?" Mac really wanted to go, but Fletch was a friend and, to the best of Mac's knowledge, he had never missed work except when his dad passed away several years ago.

Dr. Nelson glanced at Marta, just enough for her to get the feeling he was watching what he said. "Yeah, I think so. Why don't you call him tomorrow and see?" With that he bade them a good evening and returned to finish his shift.

"Where to?" Mac asked as they walked out into the fresh night air, still holding hands.

"Back to work, I guess. I need a shower, and I have a change of clothes there."

Mac held the car door for her, and they buckled their seat belts. "No wonder you have a thing about safety. You get to the accidents long before I see them, before they're cleaned up and prepped for surgery. Before they're anesthetized." A tired sigh escaped his lips. "Lock your door."

Marta was tired, too. "About staying out all night, Mac—"

"I've got a better idea," Mac stated as he exited the hospital parking lot. "My housekeeper left a jar of split pea soup in the refrigerator, and I'm pretty good at grilled ham and cheese sandwiches on the side."

"And my shower and clean clothes?" she reminded him.

"I've got a shower, a robe or sweat suit you can wear, a washer and dryer. You can be clean, fed and get a nap if you want before we surprise the kids at dawn. Rob's at his grandmother's."

"I'm really too tired and cruddy feeling to think of anything better," she admitted. She had to make decisions twenty-four hours of every day, week in and week out. Working a full-time job and raising a child alone saw to that. Tonight it felt good to let someone else decide for her.

"There is one thing I don't have that you'll need."

Marta roused herself from her thoughts enough to lift her head off the headrest and ask, "What's that?"

"Vitamins," he teased. "I know you say you're not a fanatic, but I noticed how healthy you are, and I wouldn't want to be responsible for your missing too many."

Healthy, indeed. *Trim, shapely, sexy, pretty.* The words came to mind unbidden. *Strong,* too. To be an EMT, he realized, she had to hold up her end of the lifting, so to speak. Energetic, good stamina. She'd never gotten worn out on the river and had helped load and unload everything with ease.

And she would be in his shower tonight. And afterward, wearing his clothes or robe. Maybe enjoying a nap on his sheets. He remembered his fantasy from last week and every night since, seeing her hair fanned out over his silver-gray sheets. The housekeeper had changed them, though. They were red this week. Bright, passionate, fiery red.

"Mac!" Marta exclaimed as she stomped an imaginary brake pedal and found nothing but foot space on her side of the car.

Mac's attention returned fully to the traffic, and he deftly changed lanes to avoid the car in front of them.

"I'm sorry. Riding in a small car makes me nervous sometimes," she apologized.

"No problem. My mind was wandering a bit."

Mac lived in Webster Park. They drove down the private street for a half mile before turning between two stone pillars into a narrow driveway lined with oak trees. He parked in back and led Marta across the flagstone patio to the lighted back entrance.

The kitchen had high ceilings, tall oak cabinets with etched-glass fronts, sparkling clean in the light from the old-fashioned gas-type ceiling fixture. The floor was tiled in gray and white to match the tiled counters. Strawberries grew profusely on the walls in the form of wallpaper.

The dining alcove to the right was as large as Marta's bedroom at home and furnished with an antique oak dining set. Pots of Boston ferns hung in front of the bay windows.

"Mac, this is beautiful," she said with admiration. "How did you ever find it?"

"I inherited it, along with most of the furnishings. My dad had it built. And if it was good enough for Rob, it's good enough for Rob's son, as my mother used to say."

"Don't you like it?"

"I love it. But it's far too big for the two of us. Sometimes I worry that Rob won't learn how to share, because there're six rooms for each of us, plus two bathrooms each. It's not normal for two people to have so much room."

"Tell me about it," she said dryly.

"You can use my shower while I cook," he said as he beckoned her to follow him.

He led her through rooms filled with a mixture of comfortable-looking furniture and antiques that Marta longed to admire later. His room was upstairs, in the front of the house, with a bathroom off it that she estimated to be the size of Sherri's bedroom.

"Clean towels are in the closet. You'll find shampoo and anything else you need, and there's a robe on the back of the door. Laundry is downstairs. I'll show you after we eat, in—" he studied his watch "—say, twenty minutes?"

Marta imagined this must be how bathrooms were in the finest resorts—king-size tub with whirlpool jets, plants, towel warmer rack, heat lamps. A hot whirlpool bath with lots of bubbles would be heavenly, but not an efficient use of her allotted twenty minutes. She opted for her usual shower and shampoo.

"Mac..." she began as she entered the kitchen. Her damp hair hung to her shoulders, where she'd draped a towel to protect his royal-blue velvety robe from any wetness.

"Perfect timing," he said, placing bowls of steaming split pea soup on the table next to their plates of grilled sandwiches. "Milk? Wine?"

"Whatever you're having."

"Sit, sit, make yourself comfortable."

She sat. "Mac, do you realize I'm sitting here in your robe—?"

"Do I ever." He waggled his eyebrows and gave an exaggerated leer. "And I doubt if you borrowed any of my underwear."

Marta dropped her eyes. She couldn't help it.

"You're blushing!" He was astonished. She was in her thirties, a mother, divorced. He couldn't believe she was nervous.

"I am not."

"You are, too. You're as red as can be."

"It's the steam from the soup." She raised her eyes and glared at him.

"Marta, please. I am a doctor, and I know a little steam from soup does not produce those results. Let me enjoy it. I made you blush. I haven't made a girl blush since high school."

"Oh, all right. Now, may I continue?"

"Does it get better? Please do."

"Anyway, I'm sitting here...in your kitchen...I've used your shower—"

"Mmm-hmm!"

"Don't say it!" she interrupted. "What I'm trying to get at, and I'll do it very quickly now, thanks to your vivid imagination, is that I don't even know your first name."

"Oh," he sounded disappointed. "Lawrence. But don't use it. I don't like it."

"What's wrong with Larry?"

He shrugged. "I like Mac. It feels right. Comfortable, you know?"

"Oh" seemed inadequate, but it was all she could think of to say until she remembered to compliment his cooking.

Mac let Marta off the hook for a while and tried very hard to keep to himself what he imagined. She was here, in his kitchen, in his robe. They bantered fabulously. He loved it. He wanted more of it. If he could have a wish right now, it would be that she enjoyed it as much as he did and wasn't going along with this just to teach the kids a lesson.

He wondered if he suggested that she move in with him for real, whether she would agree. That would have an even greater impact on the kids. Dinner passed too quickly and tasted like ambrosia.

"I'd love to discuss what we're going to do to the kids, but I'm exhausted," Marta said as she pushed back her chair and carried her dishes to the sink.

"You go curl up in a bed. I'll throw your clothes in the washer and catch some shut-eye myself."

Mac wanted to offer her *his* bed. But she looked half-dead on her feet already, and when and if he got her into his bed, he wanted her wide awake and in the mood. Timing could be everything with a woman, and he was already cooking up ideas about how to get her in his house again, when she wasn't tired and they had hours to learn to enjoy each other.

"Do you have a T-shirt I could sleep in?"

"You bet."

Marta was almost too tired to feel nervous, following Mac up the stairs and around the hall into his bedroom. Almost, but not quite. She couldn't help but think that under different circumstances this could be quite wonderful. She was enjoying Mac's company, but knew that for him this was all just part of their plan to teach the kids a lesson.

Mac's selection of a large T-shirt for her to sleep in seemed so personal, especially since he didn't grab the first one he saw, but seemed to be looking for a special one.

"Ah, here," Mac said, pulling out a long shirt that would cover her modestly. It was old and soft, and bore his college football numbers on the back. It was his favorite shirt. "You can wear this," he said simply, wanting to see her in it.

"Thanks, Mac." She accepted the shirt and held it tightly to her chest, as though it would protect her and keep her thoughts from straying where they didn't belong tonight. "Is the bedroom across the hall okay?"

Mac glanced out the door to the other room. It was close, but suddenly seemed too far. He nodded, and when she left he followed.

Chapter Seven

Marta sensed Mac was following her and turned at the door to her room to face him. "Dinner was great, Mac. Just what I needed. Thanks."

"Marta..." He stood only inches away, close enough to appreciate the fresh scent left by her shampoo.

"Yes?" The hall was dimly lit. They were in the house alone together. They had slept in the same tent on the river, almost side by side. Today they had worked together to save a man's life. She knew Mac was a good man.

"I just wanted to say good-night."

Marta's smile was soft, and she shifted up on her toes to touch her lips to his. "Good night, Mac," she whispered.

Mac was torturing himself and he knew it, but he had to have more. He dipped his head so Marta would be more comfortable, gathered her into a gentle bear hug and prolonged his sweet agony. He could feel her knuckles against his chest where she clutched the T-shirt, and he knew when they relaxed against him. He knew when he could take no more.

"Sweet dreams," he said before turning and going downstairs.

MAC'S DREAMS were sweet, but he wasn't necessarily asleep. He had visions of Marta not only telling Sherri they were moving in, but actually doing it.

He could see her in the evening when they both got home. Eager to be with him again, sharing dinner. Sometimes it would be he who got home first and cooked dinner.

They would go to PTA meetings together in the evening, hug the kids good-night, tuck them in their beds. Not at first, though. At first, Mac suspected, the kids would be a little hostile. They really did need to learn a lesson.

Somehow Mac needed to find a way to talk Marta into extending the kids' lesson a couple of weeks on his turf. And, he realized, maybe it wasn't totally just to teach the kids not to meddle anymore.

MARTA OPENED HER EYES at her usual 6:30 a.m., in spite of the previous late night. Mac's door was wide open, his bed unmade. She wandered in to use his bathroom since it was handy, borrowed his comb and used her finger for a toothbrush. By the time she made her way down to breakfast, she was eager to see him.

"Good morning," he greeted in a cheery mood. "I heard you moving around upstairs, so I started breakfast. I hope you like scrambled eggs?" He scooped a large spoonful onto the plate in front of her.

"Mac, if you keep spoiling me like this, I'll think I'm on vacation."

Mac laughed. "I think you're a workaholic. When's the last time you and Sherri took a vacation?"

"We went to the zoo last summer."

Eleven Year Match

"A vacation, Marta. You know, pack your suitcases, drive away, no cooking, that sort of thing." He paused and waited expectantly, but she didn't answer. "Ever?"

"Not since I got divorced. Years. The three of us drove out to Yellowstone. But we camped, and I still cooked. Does that count?"

"Not totally, but that's not all bad. How did you like my bathroom last night?"

Marta set down her fork and smiled as if she'd won the lottery. "I know. You're going to offer me your house and housekeeper for a vacation."

"How did you—?"

"And you and Rob are going to move into my house for your vacation, so he can get used to sharing a bathroom with you and grow up normal, like you were talking about before. Mac, what a wonderful idea!"

Mac rested his elbow on the table and his chin on his hand as he studied her across the table. "Why is it I think you're going to shoot down my idea before it's even presented?"

Marta tried to look suitably chastised. "We can't move in with you just to teach the kids a lesson."

"Why not? It's perfect, if you'll just hear me out. Okay?"

She nodded. "I always liked fairy tales."

"Okay. Here goes. We decided that to really scare them we would have to pretend to decide to move in together or pretend to start planning a wedding."

"Right. Pretend."

"Hush. We laughed about Rob's snakes and running around in his underwear and Sherri missing her best friend next door, I believe.

"So, if we pop in on Sherri this morning and tell her you two are moving in, and just pack enough to last until the movers arrive, and then Rob comes home and finds Sherri in one bedroom and you in another, think how really distressed those two kids will be."

"I'd get my own room? What about your bathroom? I believe that's how you started to bribe me to go along with this whole vacation scheme."

"You can have my room. I'll sleep next door in my office."

"Excuse me, but two eleven-year-olds know that people 'living together' do not sleep in separate rooms. It'll never convince them."

He pretended to make a big sacrifice. "Oh, okay, you can share my room."

"That is not what I was getting at and you know it." She slapped at his hand resting on the table.

"Ow." He pulled his hand back. "I was teasing."

"About the whole idea, I hope."

"No, not everything. My office connects to my bedroom through my bathroom. We'll lock the bedroom door, I'll cut through the bathroom, and no one's the wiser. You get a semivacation out of it—I know you still have to work. The kids each lose some of their freedom. And I...I have to work, too."

Marta thought about it while Mac got up to refill his coffee. She knew he was trustworthy. He had made a couple of passes, but so what? She would have been insulted if he hadn't. And he'd taken no for an answer.

After the good-night kisses they had shared recently, she wouldn't mind spending a little more time with Mac to see if they could fit into each other's lives.

He was good with kids, seemed to take more interest in his patients than most doctors she'd dealt with on a personal level, was respected by his OR staff—and staff always knew who the good ones were—didn't resent her profession, and she could go on and on but he was waiting for her answer.

How many women got a trial run and a whole week or two to make up their minds without having to worry about how to move out if it didn't work? She and Sherri could move in, she and Mac could have a little privacy to get to know each other, and when the time was up, she and Sherri could go back to their little house...if they wanted to. Which they probably would. Mac was doing this as a lesson for the kids and a vacation of sorts for her. Nothing more. She would be wise to remember that.

Sherri wouldn't be upset. She would be relieved that it had all been a trick. Same with Rob. Mac certainly wouldn't be upset if it didn't work out. Neither would she. She'd be relieved, too. Sounded great all around.

And if it did work out, they'd all know it. They wouldn't be two single parents tap dancing around how to introduce their kids to each other without one killing off the other the first day.

"All right."

"All right?" Mac slowly sat back down across from her, afraid he was hearing things because he wanted it so much. "All right?" She nodded. "All right!"

"Don't sound so happy about deceiving these wonderfully bright children of ours, Mac. I might get the wrong idea."

Mac smiled to himself. He should be so lucky. He knew they should decide on how long her "vacation" should last, but couldn't bring himself to set a time limit for fear it would be too short. He was falling for her, but he wasn't sure whether this was all still just a lesson for the kids to her. He didn't want to rush her. He'd let her get to know him better first.

"We should actually tell them we're moving in next weekend, right?" Marta asked.

"Rob's expecting me to ask you to a barbecue this weekend. Let's ruin it for him."

"This weekend!?"

"Pack today, move tomorrow?"

"You sound like a commercial for a moving company. I'll tell you what. We'll tell Sherri this morning that we're moving in together, but we won't say just when. Then, if she's too happy about the whole situation, we'll move tomorrow. I can't see letting her be happy for a whole week when the purpose of all this is to teach her a lesson."

Mac conceded gracefully. Pushing was out of the question. "I'll wait to talk to Rob until I see what you're doing. He'll be home from his grandmother's tomorrow afternoon. Wouldn't it be great if he came home expecting a barbecue and found you guys already moved in?"

"WHERE'S SHERRI?" Mac asked as they entered the house.

"Next door." They heard the back door slam. "Correction. She's home."

Sherri came flying into the living room, all smiles. "Hi, Mom."

"Hi, sweetie," Marta said as she gave her a hug and kiss.

"Hi, Dr. Mac."

"Hi, Sherri. Why don't you call me Mac?" he offered.

"Really?"

Mac looked at Marta. "Really," he prompted. "Since we'll be spending more time together."

"Really! Are we having a barbecue?"

"Not just a barbecue," Marta answered, trying to match Sherri's excitement. She stepped closer to Mac and hugged him. "Breakfast and dinner every day. Lunches, too, on weekends."

"Sounds great, doesn't it?" Mac returned her hug and added a kiss.

"I'll say." Marta gazed into Mac's eyes, wishing she knew how much was role playing and how much was for real. On both their parts.

"How can we do that?" Sherri asked.

"Why, sweetie, we'll move in with them."

At first Marta couldn't tell what Sherri's reaction was. Her smile got bigger. Then her mouth dropped open in a big O. Finally a genuine smile returned. "Dr. Mac..."

"Just Mac, Sherri. We're going to be family, now."

Marta could tell Sherri was just tickled with that.

"Okay, Mac. Do you have a dishwasher?"

"Sure I do."

Sherri screamed in delight as only little girls can scream.

"That does it," Marta muttered to Mac, knowing Sherri couldn't hear her. With all that screaming, she didn't even know if Mac heard her.

"Done?" she asked when Sherri settled down.

"There's more good news?"

"Why, yes, sweetie."

"I don't know if I can stand it!" She was hopping up and down, unable to contain herself. "What? What?"

"Since Mac and I both have such busy schedules, we're packing today and moving tomorrow."

"Yes! Can I go tell Laurie? Can I? Please? Please?"

Marta was counting to ten.

"That sounds like a good idea," Mac said. "But be back in thirty minutes so you can start packing."

"Nine...ten," Marta finished as the door slammed behind Sherri.

"Did I do okay?" Mac asked. "I didn't want you blowing up at her."

"She's not only not upset, she's ecstatic!"

Mac shrugged. "I noticed. What did you expect? As soon as you calm down, you'll remember she's only eleven, and shortsighted."

Marta sighed. "Yes. Yes, that's true. I'm glad you told her to be back in thirty minutes. If it hasn't sunk in by then, I'll be sure to find plenty of jobs for her to do."

"That's the way."

"It's a shame she won't be able to take all her stuffed animals," Marta said, smiling wickedly.

Mac laughed. "Now you've got it. I'd better be going. I'll call you tonight to see how it's going."

"Mo-om." Sherri was dragging out the title as long as possible. She had come home nearly in tears, apparently having wised up to the fact that she was going to miss her best friend.

"Want to help me pack, then I'll help you?" Marta asked innocently. "That way, we can be sure we'll get just the right stuff for the next week or so until the movers can be arranged. And I'll make a list of all the other things that need to be done. You can help me do them later. Let's see now... post office... school records..."

"Mo-om. We can't do this."

"Telephone..." Marta stopped and looked seriously at her daughter. "Why not, sweetie?"

"You didn't ask me or anything. It's my life, too, you know. Laurie's my best friend." She was struggling to hold back the tears.

"She can come and visit." Marta had to remind herself to be strong about this. If she caved in now, Sherri would never learn her lesson. Preaching did not penetrate children's brains. Experience might have a chance of crossing the barrier. "Come pick out your clothes, or I can do it for you."

Never was there a worse threat to a preteen daughter. Sherri moved toward her room, slowly, resentfully.

"Just take what you can fit in one carload," Marta said as she followed her. "And leave some room for my stuff."

Sherri stood in her room and stared at her belongings. "What about my desk?"

"We can't take that. Just what we can carry. The movers will bring the rest in a week or two. I'm not sure how much notice they need to move a whole household."

"But, Mo-om. I helped paint it myself." The tears started.

"Oh, sweetie, don't cry. Your desk'll come later. This is a change for the better, you'll see." Marta put her arm around Sherri for comfort. Her goal was to teach Sherri a lesson, not make her feel unloved. "Isn't this what you wanted?"

Sherri sniffed. "I want my desk. It took me weeks to find it, and I picked out the colors and the pretty knobs."

Marta knew this wasn't just about a desk. It was about change. If she thought Sherri would learn a lesson about meddling from just this much anguish alone, Marta would have told her the truth now. She didn't know when or how she was going to tell Sherri about the plot against her and Rob. She might wait until Sherri was twenty-one, rather than going through all this again. But kids bounce back so quickly, and Marta knew better. She rummaged through the closet and pulled out Sherri's favorite outfit first.

"I don't want that."

"Okay." Marta hung it back in the closet. "I'll go downstairs and get the suitcases. You start picking out your clothes."

Marta smiled as she left the room, proud of maintaining her own calm.

"ARE YOU SURE this is right?" she asked Mac on the phone that night. Sherri had slammed the door to her own room an hour ago.

He let out the breath he had been holding. He had been half afraid Marta would call and cancel the whole plan. "Couldn't be better. She's scared. Let's let it sink in."

"You're right, of course. It's just so difficult to watch her cry."

"I know. I think this might be harder on her than Rob. She has to give up her home and her best friend, but he doesn't. Help me think of something special for him."

"He'll have to learn to share."

"Share what? This house is huge."

"Games, pets, space. Maybe Sherri'll want the furniture in her bedroom switched with some of the stuff in other rooms."

"If Rob's going to share his pets, I hope Sherri likes snakes."

GETTING SHERRI into the car early the next afternoon was an exercise in perseverance.

"Why can't I take Brownie?" Brownie was only about her hundredth favorite stuffed animal.

"You can take Brownie, sweetie. I didn't say you couldn't. But then you'll have to put something else back. Our car is full."

"Why can't we come back for more?"

"We have enough to last one week. Maybe next weekend we'll have time to get more."

"Why can't I take my bike?"

"And put it where? Okay, I give in. Take out all your stuffed animals and we'll see if the bike fits."

Sherri turned her back on her mother and got into the car in a very huffy manner. She buckled her seat belt without a word. She had tried to call Rob last night, but he wasn't home, and she was feeling very alone and lost.

"THIS IS YOUR ROOM, Sherri." Mac walked into the room Marta had slept in the previous night, carrying Sherri's two suitcases. She hadn't said one word since arriving a few minutes before.

Sherri followed slowly, her arms full of brightly colored stuffed animals, and sat quietly on the bed. Her tear-stained face was buried in the rainbow of plush fur.

"I hope you like it. Feel free to look through the house. My housekeeper always leaves cookies in the cookie jar in the kitchen, and I think I smelled brownies yesterday when I came home." He spoke softly to the child, and Marta was reassured that he really felt for her.

They left her alone in her new room to work out her misery in private, though Marta came close to calling the whole thing off. It was tough to see her daughter suffer needlessly, but then she remembered it wasn't exactly needlessly. The meddling had to stop.

Mac felt badly as they left Sherri. He wanted to scare the kids, but not badly enough to have to spend the entire week worrying about their mental condition. Well, they'd play it by ear. Rob wouldn't take it so hard, and Sherri would follow his example when she'd had time to think about it.

"Dad! Dad, I'm home! What time's the—" Rob stopped his ascent on the stairs leading to the second floor. "Hi, Mrs. Howard. Did you bring Sherri, too?"

A car horn sounded in the driveway. Mac tousled Rob's hair on his way down the stairs to throw open the front door and wave. He had to let Grandma Vicky know Rob got in safely or she would be at the door checking, then inside asking questions.

"Oh, yes, I brought Sherri, too. Why don't you call me Marta?" she offered.

"Okay." Rob was in a good humor. He had wanted his father and Marta to like each other, and here she was. While they were busy barbecuing, he and Sherri could make more plans to keep them seeing each other.

Rob was knocked aside as Dixie charged through the front door and bounded up the steps to check out the visitor. When she recognized Marta she whined in her desire to get petted. Finally Marta sat on the stairs and hugged the bundle of golden fur.

"Hey, she likes you a lot."

"Oh, Marta has a way with animals," Mac explained.

"She has a way with me, too, Rob."

"Yeah, Dad?" Rob looked up happily.

"Yes. I asked her and Sherri to move in with us."

Rob looked from one to the other and settled on his father. "Really, Dad? When?" His expression was guarded. Marta knew he thought his plan was working—his dad and Marta liked each other. She studied his face to determine when the bomb hit.

"Today. Sherri's upstairs in the guest room."

"Really, Dad?"

Mac nodded.

The scream from upstairs jolted Marta to her feet. Mac was up the stairs and next to her before she could run, holding her arm firmly. Rob didn't know what to think or do.

Mac spoke calmly, all the time holding Marta close, wanting to reassure her that Sherri wasn't hurt or in danger. "I think she found your snakes, Rob. Why don't you go see?"

"Are you sure?" Marta wanted to run along behind Rob.

"I'm sure. Her scream came from his room."

"Mac." Marta tried to pull away.

"It's okay."

"I'm sorry, Mac. I've got to be sure."

Mac released her arm. Marta ran to the door of Rob's room.

"You feed them these mice?" She quickly realized her daughter spoke in a normal tone.

"Sure, that's what they eat."

She tiptoed away. At the top of the stairs Mac took her hand in his and they descended together. He was gracious enough not to say "I told you so."

WITH MAC'S ASSISTANCE all Marta's stuff was moved to her new room with just one trip up the stairs.

"That's all you have?" he asked as he stood there with nothing more to do.

Marta shrugged self-consciously. "Yeah, that's it. I don't need much for just a week. Would it be okay if I used one of your drawers?"

Mac walked over to the dresser, relieved to have something purposeful to do. "I emptied the three top ones last night. I wasn't sure how much room you would need."

"I'm sorry if this puts you out." Marta opened the suitcase full of lingerie, instead of the one with jeans, and quickly snapped it shut.

"No trouble. I just stacked my things in the armoire." He could tell he was making her nervous. It was making him nervous just thinking of her underwear in his drawers. "Maybe I should go start the barbecue."

"I'll be right down to help. This won't take long."

Marta quickly emptied her suitcases and hung up her clothes. She had no difficulty finding plenty of room in the spacious bathroom for all her favorite items. The door to the adjoining room was open, and she quietly stepped in there.

Mac apparently kept the room as a home office, with a beautiful antique oak, rolltop desk proudly taking up half of one wall, flanked by matching oak file cabinets. Another wall was full of glass-fronted bookcases, housing his medical books and journals. Marta checked the sofa and found it was a sleeper-type, and already made up. She replaced the cushions she'd moved. Everything was neat and tidy, right down to the straight fringe on the Oriental rug.

She went to see if Sherri needed anything and found her lying on her new bed, hugging Dixie.

"I came to help you unpack, sweetie," Marta said, sitting down on the bed beside them.

Dixie looked up as though she might be in trouble, but didn't budge anything other than her tail, which she wagged hopefully. Sherri buried her face deeper in the soft, golden fur.

"It looks like you might be all done, though. I don't know if Dixie's supposed to be on the bed." She saw Sherri's arm tighten around the dog. "Did you talk to Rob yet?"

"*He* still likes me."

Marta patted Sherri's back, but only briefly because she got shaken off for her effort. "Mac's starting the barbecue."

"Can Laurie come?"

"No."

Sherri lifted her face and yelled at her, "You said Laurie could come!"

"I said sometimes, and she can. Sometimes, but not this time. We just got here, Sherri. Let's start out like a family, because that's what we're going to be. Later on, you and Rob can both have guests, but this is just for the four of us."

"I'm not coming!" Sherri's face disappeared into Dixie's fur again.

"Well, maybe you'll change your mind later." Marta rose from the bed and walked to the door. "I'll call you when it's almost ready."

MAC CALLED both children for dinner when it was ready. Rob showed up with dirty hands and had to be sent to wash, and Sherri slammed her door loudly enough to be heard outside. Apparently she thought it wasn't loud enough, because it slammed again a few short seconds later.

"I hope nothing falls off the walls," Marta told Mac. "It seems that she learned to slam doors in the last twenty-four hours."

Mac shrugged. "Don't worry about it. Rob hasn't come to the table with dirty nails in over a year. I expect we'll have lots of these little rebellions for a while."

They waited for Rob to return before they dished up the food, and the three of them sat around the patio table.

"Isn't Sherri going to eat?" Rob asked, uncomfortable without his ally. He wanted someone to share his misery with him, someone who was also partially responsible.

"Maybe later," Marta answered.

Mac and Marta were determined that dinner wouldn't be quiet and uncomfortable. They couldn't discuss the kids with Rob there, and Rob wasn't very talkative, but they found plenty of neutral subjects. Rob rushed through his meal and started to leave quickly.

"Come back in fifteen minutes so we can do the dishes," Mac said, interrupting his departure.

"The dishes?" He sounded as if he'd never done them before.

Mac nodded. "Yes, you know. Those things we clean up every night after we eat."

"Why do I have to help? She's here."

"She?" Mac's tone was cold. "Don't be rude, Rob. Her name is Marta, and you know that."

Marta was getting uncomfortable. It was one thing to deal with her own daughter's rebellion, but it was quite another to sit there and be the subject of Rob's. She felt distinctly unwanted.

"If she's here, how come I have to do the dishes?"

"We always do the dishes."

"But she's moving in here like a mom or something. She should do them."

"I think you can do them alone tonight."

"But, Dad—"

"No buts about it."

"But, Dad—"

"Rob..." Mac sounded threatening enough for Rob to turn with a big groan and stomp into the house.

"I'm sorry, Marta. He didn't learn that from me."

She wanted to lighten the mood. Sherri's belligerence must have hurt Mac, too, like Rob's hurt her, but he had shrugged it off. They were going to have to do a lot of that, she thought. "What? The groaning or the stomping?" she asked with a smile, trying to convince Mac it was okay.

He finally matched her with a grin. "The chauvinism."

"Good grief, Mac, if I didn't know that by now, I'd have to be blind."

"Just checking."

Rob did the dishes alone that evening, but not without his boom box. He carted it down from his bedroom just for the occasion, and Marta could testify to the fact that the volume control worked just fine and could easily register on the Richter scale.

Mac didn't even tell Rob to turn it down. When he and Marta walked into the house, he just shut it off.

"Hey, Dad—"

"It's too loud."

"I need it. I don't have anyone to talk to, you know," he said resentfully.

"Aren't you afraid you'll deafen your snakes with it?" Marta asked, trying to break some of the tension, trying to reason with him.

"Snakes can't hear." If he could have added "you dummy" and gotten away with it, Marta was sure he would have.

"That's enough, Rob," Mac warned.

No sooner had the two adults left the kitchen than the blasting began again. Mac disappeared and returned with the boom box under one arm. "I have to go do rounds. You want me to drop you somewhere?"

"No, thanks. I think I'd better stay here. I have something to do."

KELLY'S ANSWERING MACHINE came on the line with a brief message about Tupperware parties, and Marta stayed on the line through the familiar recitation before leaving her message. "Kelly, this is Marta. You won't be able to reach me for a while. Remember that doctor I met? The one I got flowers from? And sent balloons to? Well, I just moved in with him. Sherri, too, of course. She adores him."

She thought about leaving the number for Kelly, but preferred to drive her sister nuts. "Anyway, you'll love him when you meet him—"

"Marta, wait. Hold on! I'm here!" Kelly practically yelled into the phone while she turned off her machine. "When can I meet him?"

"Kelly, hi," Marta said, ignoring the question. Make her suffer. "How are you? I didn't know you were there."

"Yeah, yeah, hi yourself, kiddo. When do I get to meet this hunk?"

"Hunk?"

"Sherri says he's a nine on a scale of one to ten. And you moved in with him? Way to go, sister!"

Marta couldn't believe it. You'd think she'd just won the lottery, not moved in with a man. "Thanks. Just put it right there, Mary. Thank you."

"Who's Mary?" Kelly demanded to know.

"Oh, the housekeeper," Marta lied. "I think it's Mary. There're so many people around here, I'm not sure. Maybe Mary's the cook."

"The cook?"

"No, no, she's Mary all right. The cook is Mrs. Something. I'll have to ask again. I'm not used to all this luxury. Kelly, you wouldn't believe this palace I'm living in. There are servants coming out of the woodwork. Just think, I'll never have to clean house again."

"When can I come over?"

Marta thought she was laying this on thick enough that Kelly probably wanted to move in, too. "Well, let me get Sherri settled in first. I'll let you know."

"Promise?"

"Oh, yeah, I promise."

"Has he popped the question yet?"

"I'm here, aren't I?"

"You're getting married?"

Marta could picture Kelly dancing around on the other end of the line. "Well, he hasn't actually asked me yet. But I'll send you an invitation when he does."

MARTA WAS IN BED reading a novel when she heard Mac drive around back and park.

He came upstairs carrying a tray, saw her lying awake in his bed, and broke into a big grin. "Isn't this nice?" he said more to himself than her. "I could get used to this. How about a snack?"

Marta set her book aside and smoothed a place for the tray. "Sounds good. I guess I didn't eat enough dinner with all the tension. How were rounds?"

"Normal." Mac didn't discuss them further. He didn't want to talk shop. "You can start if you're hungry," he said as he set the tray carefully on the water bed. "I'm going to 'slip into something more comfortable.'" He waggled his eyebrows.

Mac pulled gray sweat shorts and a short-sleeved sweatshirt out of his armoire before going into the bathroom to change. He returned to sit cross-legged on the bed facing Marta over the snack tray. "Ah, you waited," he said with pleasure.

"I couldn't open the wine bottle."

They had cheese and crackers and wine. Marta was touched that Mac remembered she liked spritzers and had brought up a can of soda on the tray, too.

"How'd it go after I left?"

"They were quiet as mice. I didn't even have to tell them when it was bedtime."

"That's good."

"Good? That's scary. I checked on them twice after they were asleep just to be sure they hadn't climbed out the windows and run away."

Mac sighed and rubbed his neck, clearly tired and not unaffected by the tension in the household. "I'm off on Wednesday. Is it at all possible for you to take a day of vacation?"

"I'll have to check on it."

Mac nodded. He understood Marta didn't have as much freedom as he did, with either time or money. "I just thought that after two more days of tantrums, maybe we could have a day to ourselves? Lunch without boom boxes or doors slamming?" He enjoyed Marta's company and wanted to give her an opportunity to enjoy his, without crabby kids interfering and ruining it all.

Marta nodded in agreement. After the last twenty-four hours, that would almost be heaven. "By then we should be able to discuss our progress and how soon we can put them out of their misery."

"Or maybe we could just do what we want to do," Mac suggested gently, "and forget the kids for a few hours."

Marta looked over her wineglass and into his eyes. "Maybe. Mac, I've been wondering. Are you ever going to tell Rob that we ganged up on them, or just let them always think they blew it?"

"If we tell them we plotted against them, they might turn right around and do the same to us. Again. But if we don't tell them, they'll probably just think it's better not to start something."

"That's kind of what I was thinking. I'm not sure, though."

"Well, it's not etched in stone. Let me know if you do decide to tell Sherri, so I can tell Rob at the same time. Done?" he asked as he removed the tray and set it on the bedside table.

Marta nodded, wondering how they were going to handle this. His sofa sleeper was made up in the other room, waiting for him, but here he was on her bed, the tray no longer separating them. She said nothing as he leaned forward until he was on his knees, his hands on either side of her for support, grazing her hips. The water bed rocked and then stabilized. She tipped up her glass to stall him.

Mac smiled and waited patiently. "I want to kiss you good-night."

"Mmm, yes, I figured that out."

Mac let her keep her glass as security as he leaned forward those last few inches and made contact. Her lips were cool and moist and fruity from the wine.

Marta felt everything everywhere at once: his lips pressed gently on hers; the warmth from his body through the sheet even though he was a foot above her; the pressure of his wrists against her hip bones; his knee bumping hers as he straddled her legs; the gentle rocking of the bed.

"Mac."

His other knee crossed over her legs, too. He was leaving the bed. He paused for another kiss. "I know. Good night." He traced her bottom lip with the pad of his thumb. "Sleep tight."

Mac looked back once and tossed her another kiss as he left her room via the bathroom and closed the door behind him.

Marta let out the breath she had been holding. She was starting to realize that maybe, just maybe, fairy tales could come true, if one wished hard enough. And she doubted if it would take two weeks to tell. She was certainly attracted to Mac. She just didn't know if she could live with him and all he represented... or if he really wanted her to.

Chapter Eight

Monday morning wasn't easy for Mac. He stood in the bathroom doorway at the crack of dawn, watching Marta sleep in his bed. He'd pictured in his mind how she'd look. The reality was better.

She slept comfortably, at ease with the world, secure. She slept toward the middle of the bed. If he crawled in with her the way he wanted to, they would be close. He could gather her in his arms, and if she wanted to she could just fall back to sleep while he held her like that.

Yeah, when donkeys fly, he told himself, wishing again that she enjoyed this relationship as much as he did. He closed his eyes so he wouldn't see her anymore, but found that didn't work, either. He just saw more.

Frustrated, he opened his eyes, prepared to make himself get ready for work and get out of there. It was then that he saw Sarge. At least he thought it was Sarge. The two snakes were difficult to tell apart, and he hadn't expected either one to be slithering across his instep.

"Looking for a warm spot, fella?" he asked the snake as he carried it into Rob's room and placed it in the aquarium next to its companion. "Thank goodness your roommate's still in here."

Mac looked down at his sleeping son and knew he would have to have a talk with him that evening. Snakes were easy to catch, but the intent had been unkind. If Rob decided to let the mice loose, Mac would have to put down traps. He had expected some resistance on Rob's part, but there were limits to what he'd put up with.

"BREAKFAST!" Marta yelled up the stairs at seven o'clock Monday morning for the fourth time. "Rob! Sherri!"

Sherri flew down the stairs fully dressed, carrying her tote bag, and disappeared into the kitchen without a good-morning for her mother.

Marta sighed resignedly. Sherri was hurt, resentful, shocked. Sunday was finally over, and she had hardly stepped out of her room. Monday didn't look much better, from Sherri's point of view. As far as Marta was concerned, all was going as planned.

Marta went upstairs to roust Rob out of his bed so he could catch the school bus. She knocked, then opened the door when she didn't get an answer.

"You can't come in here. You're not my mother." He sat, fully dressed on the foot of his bed, staring at the snakes in the aquarium.

"I know, Rob," she replied sympathetically, wanting to sit beside him and put a comforting arm around his hunched shoulders. "And you're not my son, nor Sherri's brother. But right now you're the only way she can get to school. She doesn't know what bus to catch or anything."

He got slowly to his feet. "I'll help her. I'm sure she doesn't want to hang around here all day." Rob knew that Sherri and he would both have more fun in school than they would by staying home and suffering with this new "family" the two of them had created.

Marta stood aside and let him pass through the door. Rob pointedly waited for her to step out of his way so he could close his door practically in her face. His way of saying "keep out."

"She'll need to know which bus to take this afternoon, too," Marta reminded him. "I'll see you when I get home from work."

DOUBLE-PARKED in front of a two-story brick building on a through street, Marta and Summers opened the rear doors of the ambulance and extracted a long backboard and the jump kit. A man had fallen down the basement stairs. Marta cursed softly as they entered the apartment foyer and found themselves in another poorly maintained building with no lights in the hall.

"Hello!" Marta called out. "Anybody here?"

"Down here."

As their eyes adjusted to the dim interior, they noticed that the floor was laid with dark tiles, and the walls of the narrow hallway were covered with dark brown paneling. The stairs were at the back of the hall, and at the bottom lay a man. A lone light bulb dangled off to the side.

Summers started down the stairs, then turned to warn Marta that the railing was unreliable. It hung there loosely.

Marta tugged at the back of her partner's jacket. He had the long backboard in his hands. "Let me go ahead and test the stairs."

They changed places, and Marta descended the dimly lit stairs first, testing each step as she went. There was no sense taking any chances in a building that obviously received little or no maintenance. She introduced herself and Summers to the man lying on the concrete floor.

"Where are you hurt?" she queried.

"My back. I twisted it when I started to fall, and then the railing came loose. Down here." He tried to point to his lower back, grimacing in pain from the movement.

"Okay, just hold still. Try to relax. I'm going to do a quick check for broken bones and bleeding before we attempt to move you. I'll start with your head."

While Marta checked him from head to toe and Summers prepared the straps on the backboard, the man told them more about his accidental fall.

He had been trying to replace the battery in the smoke alarm located high on the wall inside the stairwell. He'd had to stretch in order to reach it and had lost his balance and grabbed for the railing. The railing had given way and he'd fallen.

"You own this building?" Summers asked.

"No, I rent here. I was just trying to help out, you know? Some realty company owns it. A lot they care about keeping it up," he scoffed. "Their manager hasn't done anything in two years."

Two other men showed up to help, one of whom had called for the ambulance. Summers positioned them and instructed them in what to do when Marta gave the signal to lift the patient onto the backboard.

"I know it's not comfortable," Marta explained, "but we need you to lie still on this board to prevent any further injury to your back while we get you to the emergency room."

Then they strapped him on securely, in order to keep him from shifting on the uneven ascent they would be making on the stairs.

One of the two neighbor men tried to take Marta's end of the stretcher as they started up the stairs, but she firmly refused and handed him the jump kit to carry instead.

"Anything we can do?" one neighbor asked at the last minute before Summers closed the back doors of the ambulance.

"Yeah. Call the management company and get the name of their insurance company," the patient requested through lips tightly compressed in pain. "They're gonna need it."

"Is that the same company you called last week?" Summers asked Marta softly as they waited with the patient in room four. They had a couple of minutes to spare before the handoff.

Marta's mind was on Mac. With Dr. Fletcher out for a while, Mac had taken up some of the slack in the ER. She hoped she'd see him, to say good-morning. He had been gone when she got up.

She nodded absently. "The manager sounded like a nice enough guy, thanked me for letting him know about the bad wiring before he had a fire on his hands and said he appreciated my concern."

"Hawk was telling me he and Johnson had a call to a similar building. Same thing. Nice outside, rundown inside, apartments for rent. They had to go back out and get flashlights to find their way through the hall."

"Do you remember if their call was for an accident?"

"Yeah. A guy tripped over some loose carpeting in the hall outside his apartment. He gashed his head on the door frame and was a little out of it. To top it all off, Hawk tripped over the same loose carpet on his way in."

"Oh, great," Marta complained. "Like we don't have enough to worry about as it is. Is there someone we can call about these things? I mean, there must be city ordinances requiring adequate lighting and sturdy railings that are being violated here. Maybe Mac knows who to call, he's a landlord."

"I know a guy in city hall. He eats slumlords for breakfast. I'll call him."

Marta agreed. This realty company obviously was negligent, not just letting one apartment slip through the maintenance net by oversight. Whole buildings were going downhill and dangerously so. It was bad that innocent renters were being injured, and even worse that those who came to help in unfamiliar buildings were also subjected to dangerous conditions. Nonexistent lighting, loose carpeting, dangling stair rails, all those were on-site hazards that could be eliminated. Worse were the dangers that hadn't been identified yet.

AS THEY WERE LEAVING after the handoff, Mac walked up behind them. Without a word he put his arm around Marta and ushered her into an empty treatment room, pushing the door shut. He'd been thinking of her all morning, ever since he had tiptoed quietly around at dawn, getting dressed and leaving her there, alone, in his bed.

"Mac, I was hoping I'd see you!"

"Me, too."

Marta thought he looked wonderful. White lab coats obviously suited him, setting off his tan, making his smile seem brighter.

"I wanted to say good-m—"

Mac covered her lips with his, effectively cutting off anything she could possibly say. His back was against the door. No one would barge in.

Marta was surprised at his affectionate display and completely relieved. If he was this happy to see her, and the kids weren't around, then this must be a positive sign.

She went with the moment and relaxed, returning his kiss for all she was worth.

"Wow," he said when he released her. "I must be a helluva doctor."

"Why's that?"

"Two minutes alone with you in this treatment room and I'm feeling like a million bucks." He'd thought this would be fun, but it was much headier stuff than he'd anticipated. It would be even better if he knew whether she enjoyed it as much as he had.

Marta laughed lightly, nervous about her reaction to Mac's kissing. She wondered if she'd overdone it. "I'd say that makes me pretty potent medicine, Doctor."

"I'm ready for another dose."

"Summers is waiting." She hoped Mac didn't care.

"He's the one who doesn't talk much, right?"

She nodded.

"Good," he said as he smiled down at her.

Marta met him halfway, rising onto her toes as she wrapped her arms around his neck, glad that she didn't wear lipstick to work, careful not to run her fingers through his hair and ruffle it. He was, after all, on duty and might have to go tearing out of the room at any second.

"I missed you this morning," she said when she had time to take a breath. If she'd known he was going to be so happy to see her, she'd have missed him more.

Mac kissed her eyelids. "Not as much as I missed you." He thought of her closed eyes and soft smile as she'd slept in his bed.

"At least you got to see me when you passed through."

Mac groaned. "I remember. You were all alone in that great big bed." Her hair had been mussed from sleep, and he wished he'd been responsible for its disarray. He kissed her one last time, then held himself back. "Let's make a deal."

"What?" Marta stalled him with a soft parting kiss.

"I'll quit torturing you if you quit torturing me."

"You mean right now?"

He nodded, and as he slackened his hug, Marta stepped back. She reached up and straightened his tie. It was a little thing to do, but it allowed her to touch him some more.

"On one condition," she agreed.

"Anything."

She pulled on his tie to get his full attention. "You don't even know what it is yet."

"I don't care. Anything. What is it?"

"Are you going to kiss me like this every morning?" She hoped so. Maybe if he did he wouldn't remember this was all supposed to be just a prank.

"Lady, I'll kiss you like this every morning and every time you come into the ER."

Marta laughed softly with elation and pulled away as Mac bent for more, saying, "I'd better get out of here." She relented and planted a quick one on his lips before ducking out the door.

MAC WAS HOME in time for dinner with Marta and the children. Rob and Sherri sat at the table shuffling their food.

"Here," Marta said as she put a vitamin in front of Mac. One look at Sherri and Marta decided a few days without wouldn't kill her. She wouldn't press the issue, but she set one in front of her just so she would know she wasn't forgotten.

"For me?" Mac asked.

"Sure. I take care of my family." She set one in front of Rob, who pointedly ignored it.

"Oh. Okay." Mac swallowed it. "How come I only get one? You get six."

"I thought I oughtn't push my luck," Marta said with some relief. "I know how difficult change can be."

"Well, bring them on. I suppose you've researched this carefully and know just what I need?" He knew she had, but he wanted to make the point clear to the children that vitamins were like medicine, and you didn't just take them indiscriminately.

"Absolutely, and you don't need all six. This one's extra iron; you don't need it."

Mac studied his vitamins, then looked at his son. "How about it, Rob?"

Rob looked at Marta, wondering if he had a choice. "No thanks, Dad. I made it this far without any." He didn't sound too happy about having a "new mother" now.

"I care about all of you," Marta explained, understanding that Rob was unhappy with the situation that he and Sherri had created. That was, after all, the objective.

"Yeah, right. May I be excused, Dad?"

"You know the rules. No dinner—no snacks."

"I'm not very hungry."

"Neither am I," Sherri finally spoke.

Mac excused them and sent them upstairs for the evening.

"That was nice of you," Mac said.

"He's a nice boy."

"I know. But I had no idea teaching them a lesson would be so hard on us," Mac said with a groan. "How about if the two of us go out to a movie tonight? I know four people who could all use a break."

"Sure. You go tell them while I clean up."

"I'll help you."

Marta laughed. "Uh-uh. No, you don't. I spent this morning with them, remember? It's your turn to go talk to the brick walls."

"Yes, dear," he agreed with a smile. But he didn't race upstairs.

Mac found both kids in Rob's room.

"How come you get so many pets and I don't get any?" Sherri was asking.

"I guess 'cause this is my house."

"You should share."

"Okay."

"Really?"

"Sure. How many mice do you want?"

"Mi-ice," she whined. "I don't want any of your dumb old mice."

Mac chose that moment to step inside.

"Oh, hi, Dad."

"Hi, kids. I just came up to let you know Marta and I are going out for a movie. We'll be at the Galleria if you need us."

"Sure, Dad." Rob wouldn't look at him, as if that way Mac would realize he was unimportant and go away.

"Sherri, I'll leave the number by the kitchen phone," Mac told her. "And I'm sure you know all about 911."

"No kidding."

"You want me to show you where we keep the videos, in case you get your homework done?"

"No, Dr. Mac."

Mac sighed quietly. So they were back to titles again. In a way she was very much like her mother.

"And Rob?"

Rob waited to acknowledge, but felt pressed into it when his father didn't take up the slack. "Yes, Dad?"

"I found your snake this morning."

No reply.

"Sherri, would you mind if I talked to Rob alone for a minute?"

Sherri said nothing, just looked up at Mac, shook her head solemnly and left the room.

"You know, son, if we keep living creatures as pets, we have a responsibility to protect them. There are a lot of hazards for a snake that gets loose in unfamiliar territory. Like a big old house, for instance."

"I guess I left the lid off by mistake."

"We also have a responsibility to our guests, to see that they don't get hurt or frightened by anything."

"Sure, Dad. I know, Dad."

Mac believed that about as much as he believed Rob had left the lid off by accident.

"I'm glad it wasn't the mice. Mice chew insulation off the electrical wires in the walls. That causes a lot of house fires. If the mice get loose, we'll have to put down traps."

Rob looked at his dad and chewed his lip.

"Well, we'll see you guys in a couple of hours. Be good. Do your homework."

"WHAT'S WITH YOUR MOM and vitamins all the time?" Rob asked Sherri when she returned immediately after Mac left the room.

Sherri was torn between bickering with Rob, who wasn't very happy to have her here, and being mad at her mother, who had made her come here against her will. She shrugged.

"I mean, I'm eleven years old already and healthy. I don't need vitamins. If I did my dad would know it. He's a doctor." He said it as if that was the answer to everything, and then he wondered why he was defending his dad. He preferred to think it was his dad's fault Marta and Sherri had moved in.

"Oh, yeah?" Sherri retorted. "Wanna know what my mom says about doctors?"

"Wanna know what I think of your mother?"

"At least she doesn't keep mice in her room!" Sherri said, pushing her way out of Rob's room and slamming his door. "I wish I'd never met you, Rob Macke!"

"And stay out!" he yelled. He got paper and a marker and made a sign for his door. "Disturb and die."

MAC TOOK MARTA to an adventure movie with a romantic subplot. When he stretched his arm along the back of her seat she cuddled closer, and when they left they held hands.

"Good movie," Mac said as they walked to the car. "Did you like it?"

Marta gave his hand a squeeze and smiled up at him. "I sure did. Especially the company."

Mac unlocked and opened her door, but kept her from getting in by pulling her close to him. "Me, too." He dipped his head down for a quick, light kiss, and Marta savored it.

"Too bad we have to go home and listen to the kids." She sighed and got in the car. "But I guess we do."

"What do you think will be waiting for us when we get home?" Mac asked when he got in on his side.

"Slamming doors?"

"Blasting music."

"Crabby children." She groaned.

"Want to stop for a banana split?"

Marta smiled. "How do you feel about being chased out of your own house by two children?"

"We weren't chased, we retreated. Every good general knows when to take a break. Besides, this way you know they'll get a snack while we're gone, so we don't have to worry that they're hungry. Maybe I'll get double chocolate to make me feel better."

"Me, too. Let's go to the place in the mall."

Marta held Mac's hand again as they walked into the ice-cream shop and waited in line to order before finding a table.

"Hey, Mac!" Marta heard a man call his name, and waited for Mac to acknowledge it.

"He's new at the hospital," Mac said quietly to Marta. "Do you mind if we join him?"

"No, it's fine."

John Lafferty introduced himself to Marta and introduced his wife Julie to both of them. The men started in on shop talk, even though Mac tried to steer John in a different direction.

"I'm so glad to meet someone my own age," Julie confided to Marta. "We just moved here, and it seems like everyone John introduces me to is...well...established, shall we say? Have you been married long?"

Marta smiled at Mac, who was temporarily oblivious to the woman. "Oh, we're not married."

Mac heard her, and to show it he slipped his arm around her shoulders and gave her a hug and a big smile. "Just dating," he added.

"Dating, hmm?" John asked. "Didn't we used to do something like that?" he teased his wife.

"Yes, dear. Twelve years ago, before the twins."

Marta and Mac both talked at once, had to laugh and start over.

"Do they meddle?" Mac asked.

John and Julie laughed together. "Do they!"

"Give them an inch and they'll take a mile," Julie warned.

It was then that Marta forgot she was socializing with a doctor. No, two doctors.

"What do you do to make them stop?" Mac asked.

"Take away the phone," John answered.

"Give them more chores," Julie replied.

"Neither works," they said together and laughed.

"We're interested, because we each have an eleven-year-old," Marta said. "They're starting to gang up on us."

"Together we stand and all that," John said. "Hang in there. If you come up with the perfect deterrent, and market it, you'll be millionaires."

"We're working on it," Mac admitted.

"Yeah, we thought if we gave them more than they asked for—you know, all the drawbacks they never thought of—maybe we'd come out on top," Marta explained. "Things like more time together as a family and less privacy."

"More sharing their own parents and less personal attention," Mac added.

"Hmm, that might work," John agreed.

"I don't know. How's it working so far?" Julie asked.

Mac shrugged, and Marta threw up her hands in frustration. "Who knows? Right now they're in the slamming-the-door phase."

John smiled. "Sounds like it's working to me. If they're avoiding you, they're not meddling."

"Just so they learn," Marta said with great hope.

The two couples spent another hour discussing children, preteens especially, school, work, endless hours and lack of free time. Time flew, and Marta was surprised to realize that she suddenly had two new friends.

"My gosh, look at the time, Mac. We'd better get back and see if the house is still standing."

"Oh, so do we," Julie said as she slipped into her sweater and looped her purse strap over her shoulder.

"Yeah, I've got to be in early tomorrow to cover for Dr. Fletcher again," John said. "I sure hope he gets those legal problems straightened out soon."

"He will," Mac replied. "He's a good man. And you'll get to pick up a few new patients while you're in the ER."

They promised to do it again sometime, said their goodbyes, and Marta and Mac headed straight home.

Chapter Nine

The children's bedrooms were dark, and they both appeared to be asleep. The adults moved quietly into Marta's room and closed the door.

"You can have the bathroom first," Mac offered.

Last night had been their first night, but Mac had gone out to do rounds and not returned until Marta was in bed. Everything seemed so much more intimate with Mac on the other side of the door as she slowly changed into a nightgown and robe. She couldn't stall forever. Mac had to get through the bathroom to his own room.

He stood by the closet, bare-chested. Her eyes followed the contours of the powerful muscles rippling beneath his tanned skin as he silently crossed the carpet and closed the bathroom door behind him.

She let out her breath, slipped out of the robe and in between the warm sheets.

"Sorry," Mac said quietly as he tiptoed back over to the closet, wearing just his loosely-belted robe, to hang up his clothes. "Want some wine again tonight?" he whispered.

"No thanks. I meant to ask you last night—how come you have a water bed?"

"My patients kept asking me if they should take so-and-so's advice and get a water bed for their bad backs. I thought I should research it."

"And?"

"And I tell them to find a motel with one and try it out before spending the money," he said with a laugh.

"Don't you like it?"

"Let's just say I miss it." He sat on the edge nearest her left hip.

Mac wanted to be close to Marta again. They had had fun drinking a little wine and snacking on cheese and crackers last night before he went to sleep in his own bed in the adjacent room. Almost like camping and sleeping in the same tent. They were building a wonderful friendship, a great basis for what he wanted to follow.

"I can sleep in the other room," she was quick to offer. It was, after all, his water bed.

"Don't you like it?"

"Are you kidding? I never had a bed with warm sheets on a chilly night before." She snuggled in deeper.

"Then your ex-husband was sadly lacking," he murmured as he bent slowly forward. He wanted to have the right to snuggle with her. And he wanted to see just what was snuggling under those sheets.

Marta didn't want to think about her ex-husband. Her awareness of the fragrance of Mac and his soap and toothpaste grew stronger as he leaned slowly closer, then receded as his warm lips closed softly over her open ones and completely disappeared as his touch increased.

"I would never let you get into a bed with chilly sheets," he spoke quietly between kisses, his voice almost husky. "Never." He continued raining kisses from one corner of her lips to the other, teasing her, making her want more.

The bed sank in the region of her back as he pressed his elbow into the mattress on the far side of her body, supporting some of the weight of his masculine body, letting the rest of it lie across her ribs.

Marta felt herself growing warmer, and it had nothing to do with sheets or water beds. "Mac," she breathed on a sigh. He covered her lips so she didn't want to speak more. But she knew that she should. Her hands lifted to his head, wanting to push him back so she could talk, but her fingers got lost in the softness of his hair.

Mac's breath escaped on a moan as he felt the tingle of her fingers in his hair. He lifted himself to lie next to her on the bed. "Mind if I stay here for a little while?"

Marta studied his eyes and knew he wasn't asking for more than she was willing to give. She answered him with a kiss, which he readily accepted.

Mac drew her closer to him, as close as possible with the silky sheet encasing her body beneath it. He circled his arms around her, pushing the sheet down until he could get his arms under her back. He pulled her closer until he could feel the mounds of her breasts pressing against his bare chest. His lips burned a path down the smooth skin of her neck.

"You have the softest skin," he murmured between kisses.

Marta thought much the same of his lips, but was unable to say the words.

Mac lifted his head until his lips were mere inches above hers. His hand lay still on her ribcage, his fingers only centimeters away from proof that sending him away would be difficult.

"I'm glad you're here," he whispered. He wished he knew whether she felt the same.

"So am I, Mac." She smiled. She was more glad than he knew. More than she'd expected, and that scared her a little. "Maybe we'd better say good-night."

"Is something wrong?" He was concerned. Perhaps she was as overpowered by the currents between them as he was. He was falling in love with this woman, and he wanted her when she was ready. He wanted her to talk to him about her feelings.

"I don't feel right about this, Mac. Maybe it has something to do with our kids being so close by and hating us already." She stopped herself from rattling on. "I'm sorry."

Mac slowly pulled the sheet back up and moved his hand to safer territory, then lowered himself and kissed her warmly again. She was careful to keep her hands off his body while she luxuriated in the feeling that he cared enough for her to let her wait.

She felt chilled by the withdrawal of his body heat when he lifted himself off her, belted his robe and gently closed the door on his way out through the bathroom. She seriously considered going to him in the other room. He was special, and she felt so very lucky, and she knew if he came back tonight she would welcome him with open arms. Fortunately, she thought, Mac was honorable and would respect her stated wishes. He wouldn't return tonight, and she wouldn't have to make the decision.

"AUNT KELLY, I need help," Sherri said over the phone after school Tuesday.

"What is it, sweetie?" Kelly sounded alarmed.

"Well, it's about Mom and Mac."

"Aw, isn't it working out?"

Sherri shrugged and twisted the phone cord. "I don't know."

"Tell her," Rob said with an encouraging poke at her shoulder.

"Well, the housekeeper was here today. She changes the sheets and stuff."

"Yes, I can imagine what stuff. You lucky devil you."

"Well, she changed the sheets on the sofa bed in Mac's other room, too."

"Office," Rob corrected.

"Yeah, his office. It's right next to his bedroom."

"That's her job, Sherri."

"Rob says his dad never uses it."

Kelly was quiet for a minute. "What are you asking me, Sherri?"

"I . . . we think maybe Mac's sleeping in the office."

"Did they have a fight already? I'll have to talk some sense into that—"

"No," Sherri interrupted. "They're getting along fine, I think. So why would Mac sleep in the office, Aunt Kelly?"

Sherri could hear her aunt sigh over the wire. "I don't know, pumpkin. You're not crying, are you?"

"No," Sherri said with a laugh. "Rob just said we should spill something on the sofa so his dad has to sleep with Mom."

"Maybe you should be more subtle."

"What's that?"

"Sneaky."

"Oh." Sherri brightened. "You think it's okay, then?"

"Hey, you've come this far, kid. Don't quit when you've got a good thing going. Don't tell your mom you called, okay?"

"Okay. Thanks, Aunt Kelly. You're the greatest."

"Just make sure I'm invited to the wedding."

Eleven Year Match 159

Rob and Sherri still weren't quite sure what their parents were up to, but they knew all wasn't as it seemed. It made them remember why they'd banded together in the first place. Gone was the misery they'd shared when they thought the situation they'd created had gotten out of hand. Their parents had tricked them. This meant war!

TUESDAY EVENING Marta arrived home to find Rob and Sherri nose to nose in his room, spread out on the floor with cookies, milk, school books, discarded tennis shoes and a small pad of paper that Rob quickly stuffed under his chest as he lay there, trying to look innocent.

"Hi, kids."

"Hi, Mom," Sherri said brightly. "Did you have a good day at work?"

"Yes," she replied, suspicious about this sudden attitude change.

"That's good."

"We're doing our homework," Rob announced. Marta said hello to him, too. "They really piled it on," he hinted.

"Oh, okay. I'll just go... see about dinner."

"The housekeeper was here today. Dinner's in the refrigerator, not in the freezer. All you have to do is microwave it for fifteen minutes."

"Thanks, Rob."

Rob and Sherri exchanged grins as Marta left them alone.

Marta stripped and showered in the spotlessly clean bathroom, then decided "what the heck" and ran a hot bubble bath and flicked on the whirlpool jets. As vacations went, this one was nice in that she didn't have much cleaning to do and little cooking. It was miserable when the kids were grumpy, but that was the plan.

Now that they had cheered up, it was probably time to pull out that list of things for her and Sherri to do, just as they would have to if they were really moving.

"Enjoying yourself?"

The whir of the motor had prevented her from hearing Mac until he spoke. She cracked open one eye, then closed it again, knowing she was decently covered by bubbles. "I'm having my vacation. The kids are happy, I'm happy, dinner will practically cook itself. Your housekeeper even set the table. The beds are made, the bathroom's spotless. What more can I say? She even found a sock you dropped the other night."

He chuckled. "I never was very good about that. My ex-wife couldn't get over the fact that I couldn't manage to get everything into the laundry chute in our bathroom."

Mac sat back on the closed toilet, one ankle crossed over the other thigh. Could she have felt uncomfortable with him last night because she thought he used to be with his wife in that room? "We lived out in West County," he said conversationally. Now she knew.

"Did you say the kids are happy?" he asked suddenly.

She nodded, eyes closed again, head back on a soft folded towel. She remembered Rob's furtive actions, and her eyes flew open and found Mac's. "They're up to something, too."

"What?"

"I don't know, but I can feel it. I think they're plotting. They were working over a list when I saw them in Rob's room."

"I guess I'll go say hi—on tiptoe."

Mac crept quietly up to Rob's open door. "May I hold one?" he heard Sherri ask.

"Sure. Just curl it through your hand, like this. And see, if he wants to move, you can just guide him onto your other hand."

"Hi, kids. Is this the same young lady who screamed on Sunday?" Mac teased Sherri as he stepped into the room.

She smiled up at him. "Look, Dr. Mac. He doesn't even mind my cast." The red- yellow- and black-ringed snake looked as happy as Mac imagined a snake could look.

"Good. As long as you don't, either, we're all happy."

"Are you kidding? Look, I even covered your drawing with clear nail polish so it wouldn't get dirty." Sherri lifted the two-foot-long reptile where its body lay over the drawing.

Mac looked. The cast was still clean all over and around the cartoon in an uneven border made by the invisible polish. "I'm flattered, Sherri. No one ever bothered to preserve my work before. Except my mother, of course."

"Did she have a cast?"

"No, silly," Rob said with a laugh. "He means kid things. Like ashtrays and finger paintings and stuff."

"Oh, my mom saves that, too. Do you, Dr. Mac?"

"I wouldn't part with it."

"He even has some of my stuff in his office," Rob boasted.

"Could I see your office sometime?" Sherri looked at Mac hopefully.

"Sure, honey. If you really want to, I won't even make you wait until your cast comes off."

"Neat. Thanks, Dr. Mac. Can I still call you Mac?" Sherri's attention quickly returned to the snake who had decided to go up her arm instead of down.

"You sure can," Mac said with a great big smile as he patted her on the back. Peace at last.

Mac wandered back into his room to change. Sherri had warmed up to him just now the same way she had when they had first met. Apparently all was forgiven for making her move away from her best friend. Rob, too, no longer seemed angry. A few days of "Home Sweet Home," and maybe Marta and Sherri wouldn't want to move back out.

TAP, TAP.

It was 10:00 p.m. All good-nights had been said, and the children tucked in. Marta had just lain her head on the pillow and Mac was doing some reading in his office.

Tap, tap.

Marta lifted her head. "Who is it?" she asked quietly, not convinced she had really heard anything.

"It's me, Mom. Can I come in?"

"May I," Marta corrected. "Just a minute."

Marta was covered in a perfectly decent dorm shirt, so she zipped into Mac's room without a robe.

"What?" He looked up in surprise from where he sat in a chair reading a medical journal, his feet propped up on the foot of the bed.

"Sherri's at the bedroom door. I thought you ought to come back for a few minutes so it wouldn't look funny."

"Sure." As he rose smoothly from his chair, looking Marta over from head to toe with a smile as he did so, she returned to the comfort of the water bed and let Mac open the door to Sherri.

"Mom? Oh, hi, Dr. Mac. I mean Mac. I forgot to tell Mom something." She walked right in without any further invitation to tell Marta that she didn't need a lunch packed tomorrow because she liked what they were serving at school, and then left just as quickly.

"I guess she just needed some reassurance," Marta explained to Mac as he returned to his room.

Knock, knock.

It was 11:00 p.m. and Marta had been sound asleep for forty-five minutes. "Mmm?" She rolled over and went back to sleep.

Knock, knock.

"What?" she forced out the word.

"Can I talk to Dad?"

"Just a minute." Marta pushed the covers back and rolled out of the water bed, then stumbled through the bathroom and into Mac's room, covering her eyes because of the glaring light still on in there. She propped herself up against the bathroom door frame.

Mac tossed his journal down onto the bed and held out his arms to her. "I was hoping you'd come back."

She shook her head. "It's Rob. He wants to talk to you." Mac paused and planted a kiss on her sleepy lips on his way back to the master bedroom. "You look too neat," she said in explanation as she unbuttoned a couple of buttons on his shirt and pulled the shirttail loose from his waistband. "Now you're ready."

"Well, in that case," he said as he unbuckled his belt and pulled it through the loops with a snap, then tossed it onto a chair.

Marta plopped back into bed and rolled over, falling asleep before she could even hear what Rob had to say.

Tap, tap.

It was midnight, and Marta wasn't even fazed by the tapping at the bedroom door. She didn't awaken until she heard Mac walk into the room and open the door.

"She's sound asleep, Sherri. Can't it wait until morning?" Mac spoke quietly.

"No, I might forget." The next thing Marta knew, the bed was sinking and sloshing under Sherri's weight. "Mom. Mom." She made her whisper sound urgent enough that Marta pried open one eye. "Our class is going bowling tomorrow. I need five dollars."

"Mmm. Tell me in the morning."

"I might forget. I need five dollars or I can't bowl."

"Bowl? What class is that?"

"Gym, Mom. Can I get it out of your purse?"

"Here, Sherri." Mac dug his wallet out of his back pocket and handed her a bill. "Now, get some sleep, will you? It's after midnight," he complained.

He had just closed the door behind her and tossed his wallet onto the dresser when the knocking started. Marta reached for a pillow to put over her head, but it didn't help.

"I suppose you need five dollars, too."

"Gee, no, Dad. But I'll take it." Rob didn't even sound sleepy.

"Aren't you going bowling, too?"

"Who's going bowling? It's the middle of the night."

Mac took a deep breath for patience. "Sherri's gym class is going bowling tomorrow."

"Lu-cky. Think you can write me a note to let me in girl's gym, Dad? Just for tomorrow, of course."

"Rob, what did you want?"

"Oh." He paused. "I forgot, Dad."

Marta opened her eyes to see Mac hang his head in frustration.

"Good night, Rob."

"Good night, Dad."

"Rob?"

"Yes, Dad?"

"If you remember what you wanted, save it until tomorrow. Okay?"

"What if it's important?"

Mac sighed. "Okay, okay. If it's important, you can come back. But if I'm sound asleep and don't answer this door, and you wake me, the answer will be no."

"Okay, Dad."

Mac stumbled around the room muttering under his breath until Marta started giggling.

"Reassurance, my butt. Those kids are up to something," he grumbled. When he unzipped his pants and dropped them to the floor, Marta rolled over. She was wide awake now. He continued muttering as he opened and closed drawer after drawer.

Marta sat up. Mac was moving about in the room lit by moonlight, searching for something. He wore only dark briefs, the color indistinguishable in the dimness. "What are you looking for?"

"Pajama bottoms. I used to have some somewhere. I figure Sherri will be the next one at the door, and I wouldn't want to shock her. Ah, these'll do." He pulled them out of the drawer with one hand and stripped his briefs off with the other. "Oh, sorry," Mac apologized as he looked at her and turned his back to pull on what looked like sweat shorts. "I'm not used to having company."

"Either that or you have no modesty whatsoever."

"Actually I'm a flasher," he teased as he pulled back the covers on the far side of the bed and scooted in.

"What are you doing?" Marta was still sitting as she scooted as far away from his body as possible.

"Marta, this is a king-size bed. You don't have to sleep on the other rail, there's plenty of room. I'm getting tired of playing games, going from room to room every time one of our children knocks on the door."

Mac lay down, grabbed his pillow and hugged it to his chest, closed his eyes and appeared to be asleep.

Tap, tap.

"What?" Marta hollered in response. "Come in!" she crabbed.

Sherri opened the door and peeked in, then smiled at the two of them in bed together. "Never mind. It can wait until morning, I guess. Sorry." She backed out and closed the door firmly behind her.

Marta frowned. "Mac?" She didn't receive any answer but a light snore. Sitting there watching him sleep seemed a dumb thing to do as tired as she was, and she didn't want to leave the warmth and comfort of the water bed. One of the kids could be back anytime, as it seemed they had a plan to drive her insane by depriving her of a good night's sleep.

Silently, trying to move as little as possible so as not to waken Mac, she lay back down and curled into a fetal position with her back to him.

MAC CLEARED his throat again, louder this time. Then again. Marta rolled over and opened her eyes. Sunlight streamed into the room and across the carpet.

She jumped into a sitting position. "What time is it? The kids'll be late for school!"

"Never fear," he soothed as he handed her a glass of orange juice. "They're gone." He dropped his robe on the covers and climbed back into bed still wearing his gray sweat shorts. "I found a note on the alarm clock this morning."

Marta sipped the juice gratefully. Then panicked. "Have they run away?"

Eleven Year Match 167

"Are you kidding? They kept us awake last night so that we would be sure to sleep in on our day off. One of them sneaked in here, turned off the alarm—my bet's on Rob—left this note," he said, waving it in the air until she snatched it from his hand, "and got themselves off to school."

"Dear Mom and Dad," Marta read aloud. "Sorry we've been so mean. Have a nice morning together. We'll get breakfast and go to school on time. Love, Rob and Sherri."

"They really are good kids, aren't they?" Mac said, with a note of praise in his voice.

Marta nodded. "I know. Meddling seems like such a big thing at the time, but it's not much compared to what I know other kids are doing."

"Yeah, but it sure seems like a lot when we're the ones on the receiving end," Mac agreed. "And they're such intelligent kids."

Marta stared at him as she woke up a little more and suspected Mac was up to something. "Good kids? Intelligent? After keeping us hopping around in here half the night, you're praising them?"

Mac shrugged. "Maybe they're smarter than we give them credit for. Maybe they were right in the first place."

"Excuse me?"

"Well, sometimes people—kids, too—get a clearer perspective on things when we give them a fair chance." Marta crossed her arms over her chest and waited for him to continue. "I mean, take your dislike for doctors, for instance. You were ready to hate me right away when you knew I was a doctor, but Sherri knew deep down that I'm an okay kind of guy. The point I'm getting to is—we do like each other. So why teach them a lesson? It'd be like cutting off our noses to spite our faces."

Marta finished her juice and set the glass on the night stand. "So?"

"I'd like to change our original plan." Mac scooted closer to Marta.

"Yeah? Like how? Move to my house so they don't enjoy it so much?"

"No." He was in the middle of the bed now. "Maybe call the movers. For real. Stay here with me."

"Mac..."

"Marta, I'm falling in love with you. Let's give us a chance."

"Not this way, Mac. It'll be harder on everyone if you and I can't make it and I have to move us out in a few weeks, or months."

Mac scooted over the remaining distance, slipping down on the mattress until his head was near her ribs. "You're what I want, Marta." He kissed the tight skin over her lower ribs through the soft fabric of the dorm shirt. "I don't want to check into motels and get up in the middle of the night and go home." He put his right arm around her hips.

Thinking over what he said wasn't easy while he was nuzzling her. He lifted the hem of her dorm shirt and stroked the bare skin over her stomach with his warm lips. His hands splayed over her lower back and hips, as far down as the mattress would allow.

She had come to care for Mac a great deal. He was everything she wanted—caring, loving, tender, demonstrative, humorous, patient with her daughter, and with her.

With great ease, Mac used those strong arms of his to pull her hips forward and slide her down under him. Her shirt rode up farther during the maneuver, and he followed its path upward with soft, gentle kisses. He cupped his hands around her breasts, pushing her shirt up even farther, baring her feminine curves to his sight.

Marta was lost in a world of touch. His fingers electrified her skin, creating heat wherever they touched, manipulated, roamed. And lower, where he hadn't touched her, she could feel the heat there, too.

She murmured his name on a sigh, and he moved upward, farther upward until his lips found hers. With his bare torso covering the exposed flesh of hers, he separated her thighs with his knee and slid the bulk of his solid leg between her more slender ones, pressing it against her.

Marta thought about nothing except how right it was to be here, in Mac's arms, under him. Without thinking, she moved her hands over his hard muscles, giving pleasure in return, encouraging Mac to proceed, assuring him that she felt what he felt.

His hand slowly followed a path down her ribs, across her waist, smoothed over her abdomen and under the low waistband on her silky panties. Her skin quivered as his fingers followed the elastic around to the side, then pulled it slowly downward, over her hips, over her thighs, slipping them off under the covers, followed by his own.

Reaching upward again, he discarded her dorm shirt before she even knew she had lifted her arms to assist.

"Wait," she whispered, holding on to the very end of her shirt. "Mac, please."

"What, sweetheart? What is it?"

"I . . . I haven't had much luck with sex, Mac. Not in a long time."

He smiled. "Relax, then. We'll take our time." His lips returned to planting small, gentle kisses slowly, all around on her lips, neck and throat. "We'll take as long as you like." He dropped lower to press his lips against the less yielding but not less sensitive skin covering her shoulders and collarbones.

He explored lower, finding her vulnerable areas and tracing their surfaces, probing, separating, teasing a purring sound from deep in her throat before lifting himself and settling between her legs.

"You are so beautiful like this," he said as he smiled down into her eyes. He fanned her hair out across the pillow and settled himself closer. "I knew you would be, Marta. I've thought about you like this ever since I realized I was falling in love with you."

Marta couldn't verbalize her response. His hardness was pressing against her, taking her breath away with the spasms that ran through her body. She tensed with a jolt when she realized they had never discussed birth control.

"Relax." Mac whispered, sensing her turmoil. As if reading her thoughts, he leaned over to the bedside table and opened the drawer. "I want you to know I'm not the kind of guy who keeps these in stock," he said, making use of the protection he'd provided.

Marta smiled.

"Everything's okay then?"

Her answer was to draw him back down to her.

His lips returned to the softness of hers, captivating, drawing her deeper into the well of desire as he moved against her. When her lips broke free of his, when she started to lose control and let her body move by instinct alone, then he entered her and let them both ride the thunderous waves. Over and over, the spasms of pleasure captured them, drawing them into the next world, milking them of all strength before releasing them to lie, one tangled with the other, in wonderment.

"YOU DIDN'T SAY what you thought of my new plan," Mac announced as they sat catty-corner from each other at the oak dining table. He was holding her hand while they ate grilled sandwiches.

Marta dabbed at crumbs on her lips with a cloth napkin. His new plan had been to give up their prank and have her move in for real. She had answered with love. "Since we didn't do any talking, I thought I was very explicit. And if you say I'm blushing, I'll move out tonight."

"But I love it when you do." He squeezed her hand. "What if I didn't completely understand?" he asked with a wicked grin.

"Well," she replied with a coy smile, "I would like to go over it again. Just to make sure we completely understand, of course."

He grinned wider. "Of course. Mind if we finish here first? I need my strength. Just in case you have a lot of questions, and we have to go over it again and again." He took another bite of sandwich and washed it down. "And again."

She laughed. "I should be so lucky."

He pushed back his chair and scooped her out of hers with one arm behind her back and the other under her knees, holding her against his chest as they left the kitchen and started up the stairs.

"*I* should be so lucky," he said as he lay her on the bed.

"You already are." She pulled him down on top of her. "Couldn't you tell you were getting a sex-starved woman to help you with this new plan of yours?"

"Sex-starved?" He raised his eyebrows. "No kidding? I knew we were made for each other. I'll bet I can get my clothes off before you."

"No." She placed her hands on his to stop him. "I'll bet I can get your clothes off before you can get mine off."

"You're on," he accepted as he grabbed her playfully.

"SEVEN, EIGHT, NINE." Marta grudgingly counted out the spaces determined by her roll of the dice. She could see she was destined to land on a space that would cost her more in rent than she had accumulated during the whole game.

"Two thousand dollars!" Mac ordered triumphantly.

Marta glared at him.

"Please." He smiled.

"Mac, I've already landed there twice. Shouldn't the third time be free?"

"Free!" He uttered the word to sound dirty. "Free?"

"Oh, all right. Boy, if you run your apartments like this, Rob *will* end up a tycoon." She started to mortgage her property.

"Well, I don't charge two thousand dollars. But every time I drive by one of the buildings, I can't help but think the manager has them looking so nice that I probably should raise the rent. I mean, this guy must spend all his time painting and watering and cutting the lawn. He even trims along the sidewalks!"

"Oh, shut up and help me figure this out."

"Just give up, Marta. You're beaten. Admit it. The pro has won."

"I had no idea you were such a tyrant, Dr. Macke. I can't wait to get back to work tomorrow. Picking up broken bodies on the street will be more fun."

"Ah, remember you know the best orthopedic surgeon in St. Louis." Mac started to disassemble the game.

"That would be a conflict of interest, I think." She covered his hands with hers to stop him from taking her property. "How about if I promised you the next two orthopedic cases? Could I have a free ride this time?"

"Free ride, yes." He leaned across the board and kissed her passionately. "Free rent, no," he said as he grinned wickedly and scooped up all her property.

The phone rang and Marta tossed her few remaining bills of play money over his head. "I'll get it."

"Uh-uh. In this family, losers put the games away."

In this family. Marta mused over that as Mac left the room to answer the phone. *This family* had a nice sound to it. She was dying to tell Sherri they were going to try to become a family of four—a real trial marriage. But to tell Sherri what she already thought she knew would be admitting that she had been deceiving her daughter all along.

Sherri was obviously happy with the arrangement. She had quit pestering them last night after seeing them in bed together; as if she had known somehow that Mac was sleeping in the adjoining room. Shrugging her shoulders, she vowed to ask Sherri about it sometime in the distant future. Chances were both kids had known. Time and again she was surprised at the perception of children.

"That was Rob," Mac announced as he returned to the room to find Marta daydreaming over the scattered remnants of their board game. "He and Sherri are going to make a stop on their way home, so they'll be a little late."

Dixie strolled into the room and picked up a motel gently in her mouth. Mac cleared his throat to get her attention, held out his hand, and she neatly dropped it where he indicated.

"I don't believe it," Marta complained. "Even your dog is helping you collect."

"Oh, was this yours?" Mac asked ever so innocently.

"Yes, two moves ago, before you became a tyrant."

"Tycoon."

"Tyrant."

Mac laughed at her playfully and kissed her soundly before helping to put away the game. He returned to the room with a pad of drawing paper.

"I remember this cheered you up on the river." He sat on the couch and began quickly drawing.

Marta sat pouting on the carpet. When a few minutes had passed without him saying anything, just drawing, her curiosity finally got the better of her and she slowly worked her way to his side.

He had drawn a vicious-looking Dixie collecting the rent money for a very innocent-looking landlord.

"Tyrant!" she accused as she proceeded to find out whether he was ticklish.

Chapter Ten

Knock. Knock.

Marta opened her eyes from her reclining position in the whirlpool bubble bath. "Who is it?" she asked in a mellow voice. She could really get into this vacation thing.

The knob turned slowly, and the door opened just wide enough for a hand to sneak in and tape a note to the wall then disappear again.

"What is going on?" she asked no one in particular, then roused herself enough to move closer to the door without getting out of the bath. By squinting her eyes a little she could tell it was a cartoon, not a note, but still couldn't see it well enough to know what it was. It looked as if someone had wrapped her daughter up in a rope. "Sherri giving you trouble, Mac?"

Trying to relax back into her mellow mood was impossible once she realized Mac might really have his hands full dealing with her daughter, and she reluctantly left the warm water and wrapped herself in a bright blue bath sheet. Studying the picture more closely, she discovered that the rope wrapped around her daughter had a head and two eyes. Frowning, she opened the door and strolled into the master bedroom.

Another caricature was taped to the closet door, and she studied it as she got dressed in jeans and a pink sweater. This picture depicted Rob's two snakes in their aquariums, easily identified by their colorful rings, flanked by a third snake, about ten feet long and overflowing its own glass enclosure. It sported a bow on its head and a big grin.

"Mac?" she called out as she left the bedroom and entered the upstairs hall. There was no answer, but the corner of something new in Sherri's room caught her eye.

"Oh, no," she groaned as she walked into the room and stared at the largest aquarium she had ever seen. Taped to the glass was a drawing of a snake big enough to hold Dixie captive in a corner. "Mac!"

Marta flew down the staircase in search of Sherri or Mac. Giggles from the direction of the kitchen drew her that way.

Sherri was sitting in the middle of the room on a chair, with a snake wrapped across her shoulders and hanging down one arm. It was much shorter than any of the drawings had depicted.

"Oh, thank God," she said with a relieved sigh.

"Hi, Mom. Isn't he awesome?" Sherri popped out of the chair and proceeded to introduce the snake to her mother, eyeball to eyeball.

"Just lovely, I'm sure." Marta held out her hands to keep the reptile from tasting her face and edged her way around the room to where Mac was cooking at the stove. "What's going on here?"

"It's a present from Rob," Sherri answered. "We went to the pet store after school because he wanted to buy me a snake for my very own, and there was a guy there trying to sell this one on con... con..." She looked to Rob, sitting on the counter eating pretzels, for help.

"Consignment," he answered for her. "It's a boa constrictor," he informed Marta. "I have too many mice, anyway, so it won't cost anything to feed it. And the cage came with it."

"And my room is plenty big enough," Sherri chimed in. "You always said you wished I could have a pet, but our house was just too small for anything. Isn't it neat we moved here?"

"And it loves being handled," Rob added. "It's not grouchy or anything about being moved."

"Should you have a constrictor that close to your neck?" Marta asked her trusting daughter.

"Mo-om," she whined.

Rob hopped down off the counter. "Dinner's almost ready, Sherri. Let's go settle her in her new home."

The two children disappeared like magic before Marta could form a lecture in her brain and deliver it. It would have been a short lecture anyway: don't let the snake wrap around your neck; don't sleep with it; don't come screaming to me when it swallows a mouse face first and leaves the tail sticking out of its mouth.

"Well?" Mac prompted.

Marta slowly let herself down into the chair Sherri had vacated.

"Did my pictures do what they were supposed to?"

Marta smiled. "You mean prepare me for a monster so a three-foot snake seemed mild in comparison?"

Mac put a lid on the pot he'd been stirring and leaned back against the counter, with his arms crossed over his chest. "Something like that. I particularly liked the one with Dixie cowering in the corner."

"I'm sure that snake was really too expensive for Rob to buy as a gift."

Mac shrugged. "It's his way of letting Sherri know she's welcome here. Let it go. He can afford it."

Marta sighed, and Dixie crept silently from around the corner and lay her head in her lap. When Marta started to pet her, she tried climbing up onto her. "I think Dixie feels left out," she said as she hugged her soft golden friend.

"Really?" Mac took a cookie out of the cookie jar. "Whoops," he said as he dropped it onto the floor.

Dixie almost fell over herself in her hurry to retrieve the food before a human could clean it up. She trotted off with the bounty in her mouth to eat it in the privacy of another room.

Marta smiled coyly. "What about me? I was enjoying the attention. Now I feel left out."

"Never," Mac said as he pulled her gently to her feet and into his arms. "I just wanted you to myself."

He was able to rest his chin on top of her soft hair as he held her wrapped in the circle of his arms. She felt warm from her bath and smelled of bubbles, and he thought he'd like to send her a dozen roses at work tomorrow.

"I guess it's time to eat," he whispered moments later.

"Okay. I'll get the kids." Marta reluctantly loosened herself from his hug and went in search of the children, hoping they still had all their fingers and noses intact.

On her way up the stairs she could hear them talking quietly in Sherri's room, sharing this new experience better than most siblings would, and she was happy.

THE SMOKE HUNG thicker than usual in the EMT lounge, and Marta felt compelled to wave her hands to blow some of it aside. "Is there a fire in here?" she asked as she checked the wastebasket.

"Hawk's doctor told him to quit smoking, so he's getting it out of his system," Johnson informed her. He and Hawk were playing gin again.

"At our expense," Summers complained.

Marta tossed her Tupperware lunch box into the refrigerator and grabbed a doughnut out of the bakery box. "You know, Hawk, you're killing us with that smoke, too."

"Yeah, yeah," he said as he discarded a cigarette, completely unperturbed by her complaints.

Marta picked up the folded newspaper from the table beside Johnson and waved some of the smoke toward the open window, then sat down over there to eat and read in the fresh air.

"Have you read this?" she asked everyone a few minutes later.

"No, not all of it," Johnson answered.

"What is it?" Hawk asked.

"That old doctor—what's his name?—Fletcher, or something. Anyway, he's being sued for malpractice," Johnson answered.

"Geez, man! Don't you know better than to leave articles like that lying around?" Hawk complained. "She'll be going on about this for hours."

"We know this guy," Marta said aloud. She turned in her chair and spoke to Summers, not noticing whether he was paying attention. "Mac knows him, too."

Marta wondered what Mac knew about the situation. Had he been working with Fletcher on the day in question? Did he know about the suit? Was Fletcher guilty as charged?

"Howard! Summers!"

"Thank you, Lord," said Hawk.

Marta jumped up to get the data on the call as Summers tossed down his journal and hurried to the ambulance.

"Where to?" he asked when she hopped in.

She read him the address, followed by "Sick baby."

"Guess who manages it," he answered with a grunt.

"Who?"

"The same management company that runs all these buildings we're having trouble with."

"How do you know that?"

"That friend I mentioned—we've been doing some research. All the buildings this guy manages seem to be owned by one realty company. There aren't that many. We've just been unfortunate enough to visit most of them lately. He's digging now to find out who's behind the realty company."

"I'd like to see the building the owner's living in," Marta said.

They rode in silence the rest of the way. Marta was more concerned with the article about Dr. Fletcher at present than the realty company.

"We're here."

They could hear crying on their way up the neat front concrete walkway, and it got louder as they climbed the clean stairs to the wide porch. There were two doors, one beside the other. Marta banged on the left.

A teenage girl opened the door, the crying toddler on her hip and two other quiet children standing behind her.

"This is the one." She indicated the little girl she was holding. When Summers reached out to be friendly, the teenager gladly thrust the child into his hands. "She won't stop crying, ever since I got up."

"Are you the mother?" Marta queried.

"No, this is my sister. My mom has to work."

"How old are you?"

"Thirteen. She's two."

Marta asked several questions about symptoms while Summers did a quick survey of his own. The phone rang and the teenager disappeared.

"What have you found?" Marta asked her partner.

"One weak baby. Her gums are a little blue. She smells like she's been vomiting. No signs of diarrhea, though. She's old enough to get around. I'll check the kitchen."

"I'll get the bathroom." Marta was checking for poisons, cleansers or medications that the baby might have ingested. Plants were the leading cause of poisoning in children, but there were none in the drab apartment. On her way to the bathroom Marta tried unsuccessfully to get the teenager off the phone in the hall.

The bathroom wasn't very clean, but there were no diarrhea diapers in the trash can and no bottles of medicine within a child's reach. Cleansers were on the floor in the closet, behind a door that was almost warped shut, but there were no signs of them having been disturbed.

She looked into two bedrooms off the hallway on her way back to the living room. A crib was visible in the one on the left, pushed up next to the wall where it barely fit by the door. The door frame and the wall bore signs of an active baby.

"Can you believe this?" Summers asked as he strolled into the bedroom with the toddler on one hip and a baby bottle in the other hand. "Those little kids say this bottle of chocolate milk is hers." He indicated the patient who was eyeing the bottle hopefully.

Marta took the bottle from him, opened and smelled it. "It's not chocolate. I can't remember the name of the stuff, but doctors prescribe it for kids who are constipated. Babies, actually. She's too big for this."

"Maybe she's been constipated for a long time."

"You mean chronic? And the mother just never bothered to follow up on it? Could be." Marta looked at the damaged wall again. "Are her gums bluish, or is there actually a blue line?"

Summers struggled with his one free hand to lift the little girl's lip just enough to see, while she struggled to twist her head away at every opportunity. Marta held up the bottle.

"Want your bottle?" she bribed. "Let Uncle John see your pretty teeth." It worked.

"Blue line," they said in unison as they observed a classic symptom of lead poisoning.

"You take her," Summers said as he handed the toddler to Marta and pulled his knife from his pocket. "I'll get a sample of this paint for the lab."

"I didn't know they even made lead paint anymore."

"This top coat probably isn't. But the stuff under it could be. She could be getting it somewhere else, too." He snapped his knife shut and stuffed the tissue with paint chips into his shirt pocket. "Let's go."

"We'd like to take her to the hospital," Marta tried to tell the teenager. She had to repeat herself twice.

"All right! I'll tell Mom when she gets home." She was clearly annoyed at the interruption and turned back to her conversation on the telephone.

"Can you believe this?" Marta looked at Summers helplessly.

"Real reliable sitter, isn't she?" he said sarcastically.

"See what you can find out from the other kids. I'll stick to this girl like glue—that'll get her off the phone so I can call the mother."

Marta's strategy worked and they were able to leave five minutes later, knowing the child's mother would meet them at the hospital.

"At least this building doesn't have those awful dark halls like the other ones," Marta said on their way out.

"No, just poison on the walls," Summers muttered.

MARTA REREAD the newspaper article about Dr. Fletcher on the way back to the office. All her old prejudices were coming back to haunt her. She hated it, but she immediately assumed that, innocent or guilty, every other doctor in the city would be behind Fletch one-hundred percent. When she thought about it, she knew she was going too far.

Mac had been trying over the past few weeks to get her to know his colleagues as human beings, not the enemy. It had been working. Until now. Now she wasn't sure.

"You're going to worry that newspaper to death," Summers finally said.

Marta looked down and saw that she had indeed been playing with the paper while she was thinking. She had to run her hands along her work pants several times to remove the ink from her fingers.

"So, what's the problem? Is Mac involved?"

"No. At least, I don't think so. I guess he could always be called for a deposition or something." She was starting to worry more. This line of thinking hit closer to home. If called, would Mac be evasive and not incriminate Fletcher for the sole reason that they were colleagues? She couldn't believe it of him.

No sooner had they returned than they were sent out on another call. Marta had hoped to be able to call Mac, but didn't even have time to pick up the phone. She knew she needed to talk to him. Soon. Before her imagination got the better of her.

"YOU DIDN'T LOCK my door, did you?" Mrs. Simpson asked for the third time from where she lay strapped securely to the stretcher.

"No, ma'am," Marta replied again, with a reassuring pat on the elderly woman's hand. "I left it unlocked, just like you told me."

"Good. Otherwise my granddaughter won't be able to get in. I watch her after school, you see, until her mother gets off work."

Marta climbed into the ambulance and secured the stretcher. A neighbor had been drafted for baby-sitting duty in Mrs. Simpson's upcoming absence. "Ready to go," she informed Summers.

"And tell that nice young man not to turn on that awful siren. I don't want all my neighbors thinking I left here with a heart attack or something."

"Summers..." Marta started to pass the message up front to her partner. She was telling him for Mrs. Simpson's peace of mind only, because Marta knew her partner well and knew he never missed a thing. Probably because he always listened and seldom spoke.

"Yes, ma'am," he announced loud and clear for the patient's benefit.

"Do you have children?" Mrs. Simpson asked.

"A daughter," Marta answered. "One eleven-year-old bundle of energy." Two, if she counted Rob, which she suddenly realized she did. She didn't mention him because Mrs. Simpson might then ask questions about the husband she didn't have, and Marta didn't want to get into a discussion on extended-family life in America today.

"Who watches her after school? Does she have a grandmother? I hope so, dear. I don't think baby-sitters are very reliable." Her tone left no room for disagreement, had anyone been so inclined.

"I have to agree with you there," Marta said, avoiding the question. She took the woman's outstretched hand and held it during the short ride. "Sometimes I think baby-sitters need baby-sitters."

Marta smiled, pleased that Mrs. Simpson's mind was on Sherri's after-school arrangements instead of on her own broken ankle. If Mrs. Simpson wanted to listen to Marta rattle on about her daughter, then Marta didn't mind, either. It would keep her mind off Dr. Fletcher and the malpractice suit until they reached the hospital.

Mac was working at his office today, so she knew she had no chance of bumping into him in the ER and asking about Dr. Fletcher. She wished she could, because she wanted to know how he was going to handle the situation.

"We're here, Mrs. Simpson," Summers interrupted their conversation ten minutes later.

"Oh, my. Already? We didn't run any red lights, did we? I've seen ambulances do that, you know."

"No," Marta said with a smile. "We didn't run any red lights. Summers is a very good driver." He took weird routes sometimes, but he was good, and he was careful. "Now, fold your arms like this while we move you," Marta said as she demonstrated.

"Room four, guys," the triage nurse directed them quickly.

They completed the transfer to the examining table and a teenage volunteer bounced in to take vital signs.

"How's it going here today?" Marta asked.

"Are you kidding? Dr. Fletcher's on duty, and everyone's walking around like this is a morgue."

Summers grabbed the girl by the arm and propelled her in front of him—out of the examining room and out of earshot of the patient.

"Who's Dr. Fletcher?" Mrs. Simpson asked warily.

A dozen different answers raced through Marta's mind, but she spoke none of them. A lawsuit did not equal guilt. However, she wondered if she would want Dr. Fletcher treating Sherri in the ER just now. She had to admit, she would feel better if he didn't.

"Is he going to fix my ankle?"

Marta forced a smile and patted Mrs. Simpson's hand reassuringly. Innocent until proven guilty, she reminded herself over and over. "I'm sure he will, Mrs. Simpson."

She felt like a traitor, as though she had covered for a doctor who might be guilty. But he very well might not be, and she couldn't bring herself to ruin his reputation or a patient's confidence in him. She wanted to remain neutral, but she knew it would be a fine line to walk.

MAC SAW SUMMERS in the main corridor and knew that Marta was here with a patient. He had hoped to explain about Dr. Fletcher himself, later this evening at home, but Fletch had called an hour ago and asked Mac to take over for him in the ER. He had done so willingly, arriving about ten minutes ago. He knew Fletch was a good man and that he was taking this suit personally. And hard.

"What room?" he asked the nearest nurse.

"Four. It's an ankle injury."

"Hello, I'm Dr. Macke," Mac said to Mrs. Simpson when he entered the room, letting the door swing shut behind him. He shot a special smile Marta's way.

"I thought I was going to get Dr. Fletcher."

Eleven Year Match

"Dr. Macke's very good, Mrs. Simpson," Marta said as she patted the woman's hand. Seeing Mac was a big surprise, and her face lit up. "He even set my daughter's arm."

"We'll get you over to X-ray in just a few minutes," Mac explained to his patient. "Mrs. Howard, may I see you in the hall?"

Mrs. Howard? Marta followed Mac through the door.

"You can call me Marta in front—" Her words were cut off as Mac urged her into an empty examining room just one door away.

Thinking that Mac was in a hurry to spirit her away and kiss her in secret, Marta was very surprised at his next words.

"It's nice to see you today, but I wish the circumstances were a little different." His clipped tone did not support the fact that he'd said he was glad to see her.

"Mac, what are you upset about?" Marta had never seen him like this, not even when he was mad at Rob for something. This was way beyond mad.

"That look of relief on your face when I walked into the examining room instead of Dr. Fletcher." If a man could growl, Marta thought, Mac was doing a fine job of it.

She knew he was right. She had felt relief. "So, don't get mad at me just because one of your friends is in trouble."

"He's not in trouble, that's the problem. Just because somebody decides to sue him doesn't mean that he did something wrong. Anybody can sue anybody."

Marta was astonished, then wondered why. What had she expected? She should have known that another doctor would not remain neutral. She braced her hands on her hips. "You're getting mighty defensive, Mac."

"Me? You've already convicted the guy!"

She shook her head slowly. "I knew this wouldn't work." With a sinking feeling she realized it had all been too good to be true—a fairy tale.

"What?"

"Us. We're too different, Mac. You immediately assume the guy's innocent."

"You immediately assume he's guilty."

"I haven't assumed that at all. I'm trying to keep an open mind. It's you who's choosing sides already, and putting me in the wrong."

"Marta—"

"Never mind, Mac. The lesson's over anyway. The kids are starting to enjoy themselves. Maybe Sherri and I should move out this weekend."

Mac looked at her in astonishment. He had expected her to be closed-minded about Fletch. He had expected her to be mad at him for speaking up in defense of Fletch, even though everyone was supposed to be innocent until proven guilty. What he hadn't expected was for her to jump all the way to moving out this weekend. He wanted to discuss this.

The nurse poked her head in the door. "Code Blue on the way in! Two minutes!"

Mac dashed out of the room toward the phone that would link him with the ambulance.

Chapter Eleven

It was Marta's turn to shuffle her dinner around on her plate, and Rob and Sherri noticed immediately.

"Is everything all right, Mom?" Sherri asked, sending a worried glance over to Rob.

"Hmm?" Marta's mind was on Mac, and it was difficult to switch gears. She had just been thinking about the pros and cons of their relationship, trying to keep a list of each straight without writing it down.

"Is everything all right?"

"Oh." Marta smiled. "I guess my mind's somewhere else."

The kids looked momentarily relieved by her smile, but shot worried looks at each other again when Marta immediately returned to her former state.

Mac was a wonderful father. He had been wonderful to Sherri. He had been wonderful to her. The pro list was looking great, she thought. Even in his profession he didn't overprescribe, and he worked well under pressure. He respected her expertise. Vitamins hadn't scared him— he even had Rob trying them. Natural healing remedies weren't anathema to him.

"I give up. You try," Sherri said.

"Marta."

"Yes, Rob?"

"You aren't mad about Madonna, are you?"

"Madonna?"

"I know I should have asked you first, but I really wanted to get Sherri a snake of her own, and the guy was there, and he wanted to sell it right then. I checked it out real careful. She looks healthy."

Marta smiled to reassure Rob. "Oh, its name is Madonna, is it? No, I'm not upset with you, Rob. Or you, Sherri. I just have something on my mind. Work. You know."

Rob breathed a sigh of relief. "I'm glad you're not mad. I wouldn't want you to move out on account of me."

Marta felt a shiver run the full length of her spine, and she refused to let her mind wander off again. She'd had no idea her preoccupation was scaring the kids. This was not part of the lesson, and she wasn't out to ruin anyone's self-esteem. "You like us being here?"

"Gosh, yes. I was upset at first. I mean, I wanted you to like my dad. And I even thought about you being my new mom and all. But it happened so fast. And now..." Rob suddenly got very busy with clearing the dishes and didn't finish.

"Now you're afraid I'll get mad at you and move out?" Marta asked him.

Rob nodded and didn't look at her. "It's really fun having Sherri for a sister. She's not a drag like my friends' little sisters."

Sherri took offense. "I'm nobody's 'little' sister. I'm the same age as you."

"He said he liked you," Marta pointed out, soothing Sherri's ruffled feathers. "And if I ever decide to move out, Rob, it won't be your fault." Marta walked over to

Rob and put her arm around him. "I love you just like my own son."

Sherri looked a little unsure.

Marta leaned over and kissed Sherri on top of her head and was glad to see her smile return. "Thanks for cleaning up, guys. I'll be in my room."

MAC'S WORK ran into the wee hours of the night because, after covering in the ER, he had to go to his office and finish there. He got very little work done with his mind on Fletch's problem, on wondering how the malpractice case would affect his and Marta's relationship. Mac *knew* Fletch was innocent of any negligence, but he didn't and couldn't know whether Fletch had made a mistake. As for Marta, if ever a trial marriage was about to be tested, this was it.

Marta had always been up-front with him regarding how she felt about doctors in general, and he admired that. Lately, meeting some of his colleagues, she had begun to mellow. She had let down her guard. Mac supposed a malpractice suit against anyone in St. Louis probably would have fueled her animosity again, but for it to be someone she and he both knew, someone she had to work with, that might be asking too much.

He was worried. Hell, he thought, he was **scared**. She might not listen to reason.

He slammed down the journal he had been staring at on the desk, the sound jarring him into action. He might as well go home and face the piper. He wasn't accomplishing anything at the office.

MARTA WAITED UP for Mac. There was no way she could have slept. On one hand she felt hollow inside, as though Mac was already defending his colleague before all the facts were in. He had seemed so defensive about her happiness to see him instead of Fletch in the ER.

On the other hand Mac was a good and kind man. He was honest, forthright and sincere. And if Mac stuck up for Fletch, Marta hoped it would be because he believed him innocent.

Mac showed up at eleven, a tray of chocolate chip cookies, wine and soda in his hand.

"Peace?" he asked, hesitating in the doorway. "I noticed your light was still on."

"I've been waiting for you." She schooled her voice carefully, not wanting to sound either defensive or offensive.

"I remember you told me once you're always asleep by ten." He set the tray on the bed, then tossed his coat onto a chair, followed by his tie.

Marta admired Mac. He always remembered the little things, making her feel like an important part of his life. He knew and understood, without being told, that she was making an effort to meet him halfway.

"There's plenty of room here," she said as she poured him a glass of wine.

"I'm sorry I'm so late. There was more work to do, but I just couldn't concentrate. We need to talk." He propped two pillows up against the headboard to cushion his back.

"Mmm, I know the feeling. I've been going in circles all evening. I'm afraid I scared Rob."

"He's been yelled at before. He'll get over it."

Marta gave a small grunt. "Yelled? I'm afraid I was scarier than that. I was quiet, off in my own world, thinking. He thought I was mad at him about Madonna—the snake," she added.

"Oh." Mac's attention seemed to be on his cookie. "Are you?"

Eleven Year Match

"No." Marta sighed. "He was afraid I was going to move out because of him. I can't tell you how bad that made me feel." Marta's only explanation for her eyes getting teary was that she was tired and stressed out, and she loved Rob.

"Well, this is all new to him. Me, too. I'm scared you're going to move out because of me."

"Yeah, me, too. It sounded like the best thing this afternoon"

Hope welled up inside Mac. She was no longer standing in front of him, hands on hips, declaring that they were too different, and that she would be gone this weekend. Perhaps she would listen to reason.

"You know how you said anybody can sue anybody?"

"Yes." She *had* listened to him.

"It made me think, mostly because I have been concerned about people suing me someday."

"You think about that?" He was a little surprised.

"Every year when I pay my insurance premiums. I mean, my profession almost invites it. And I started wondering if everyone would gossip about me if that were to happen. Would they assume the worst? Even people who know me?"

"Not me."

Marta smiled. "Of course not you. I wouldn't assume the worst if someone sued you, either."

"Why not?"

"Because I know you. I trust you. I know you're a good doctor, and you would never be negligent."

"Accidents happen."

"Is that what happened with Fletch?"

"Fletch is also a good doctor, and he would never be negligent."

"So it was an accident?"

"No, they think he was negligent."

"And you're going to back him up?" She hoped she wasn't sounding like a shrew.

"Let me ask you something. If Summers got sued tomorrow, how would you feel?"

Marta was taken aback. "Summers? He'd never do anything wrong."

"You can state that unequivocally? No doubts? No second thoughts?"

"Of course I can. Summers is—" she couldn't think of all the right words to describe her efficient, ethical partner "—Summers. He's tops, Mac."

"That's a lot like I feel about Fletch."

They looked at each other for a long time. Marta would never know for sure whether Fletch was guilty or not, but she would know, did know, that if Mac backed his friend, it would be because he believed in him. Not because he was a colleague, but because he was a good doctor.

"Do you trust me, Marta?"

"Yes. I do."

"Then trust me on this."

"I have no choice, as long as you realize I trust you because you're honorable, not because I love you."

"That is why you love me."

"**That**'s my line. Shut up and eat your snack."

Mac smiled a relieved smile. "Snack? This is my dinner."

Marta took the tray from between them and set it on the night table. Mac thought she was going to cuddle, and he felt warm inside already.

"I didn't eat much dinner, myself. I make great omelets." She hopped out of bed.

"Omelets?"

Marta saw his crushed look. "Don't you like omelets? You cook scrambled eggs all the time. What's the difference?"

"The difference is," he said as his hand snaked out and grabbed her wrist, "I thought we were going to kiss and make up."

"I'm hungry."

"Me, too." He waggled his eyebrows.

"Oh, quit that Groucho Marx routine, Mac," she said with a laugh. "I'm serious. I have to eat. I'll kiss now and make up later, all right?"

Marta bent down to kiss Mac and didn't resist when he tumbled her onto his lap. "Promise?"

"Yes."

MAC CRAWLED IN on her side of their water bed that night, sneezing.

"Are you allergic to something I put in that omelet?" Marta asked. "Mushrooms, cheese, peppers..."

"I'm not allergic to anything."

"I hope you don't have a cold. I wouldn't want the kids to catch anything," she said, moving away from him.

"To heck with the kids. Where are you going, woman? I need some TLC." He sneezed again.

"You need some vitamins."

"I need you." Mac moved quickly and pounced on Marta before she could move farther away. She didn't really want to move, anyway.

"Mac, cut it out. The kids might come in. If they have colds—"

"If they do, they'll knock. Besides, I locked the door." Mac was inching the sheet down over Marta's breasts, surprised to find her without her dorm shirt.

"Oh, you did, did you?"

"Yes, I did." He inched it lower, just barely exposing a peak, teasing a response.

"What did you have in mind?"

"I hear that when a person catches a cold, he should be warmed up."

"Oh?"

"I hear body heat is a good way to do that."

He covered her silken skin with his lips, moistening it with his tongue, and Marta slid down lower into the bed.

"Remember the first time we did this?" he asked.

"Mmm-hmm." She showed him she remembered where he liked to be held.

"You said you hadn't had much luck with sex, for a very long time."

Marta could barely think with the way he was tasting her. "Forever," she admitted. "You were the first, Mac, in the most important way. You were the first to really love me."

Marta's words were a revelation to him, and Mac's heart caught in his throat. "That's because I really love you."

"I love you, too, Mac."

He sneezed against her breast and they both started laughing.

"Mac?"

"Hmm?"

"Cut that out and love me some more."

MARTA WAS IN THE BATHTUB, immersed in soothing warm, bubbly water. There was a can of soda on the tile rim, next to a plate with cheese, crackers and six vitamins. She had gotten into this bathtub routine thinking it was only for a week or so, and now she was hooked.

"So! This is what goes on when I'm slaving away at the office," Mac said, entering the humid bathroom, pulling his tie loose as he sat down on the step to the tub.

Marta smiled the satisfied smile of a cat who has just swallowed a canary. "Welcome home," she said, raising her soda in a toast.

"You, too," he said meaningfully, leaning over to accept the kiss she offered. "Actually," he said as he rose and started stripping off his clothes, "I was just on my way up here because Rob said there was some woman in my tub, and I figured I'd better get her out of here before you showed up."

"Oh, really?" She was more interested in the fact that he was locking the bathroom door.

"Yes, really. But it's awfully nice of you to provide refreshments." He took a sip of her drink and a bite of her cheese.

"I aim to please," she said with a grin.

"Good." He stepped out of his snug red briefs and tested the water with his left foot before moaning in pleasure as he sank into the soothing flow of warm water, facing her and leaning back against his end of the giant tub.

"Good?"

"Yes. Good." He smiled a wicked smile as he slipped his errant foot between her thighs.

"Mac, stop!" she said with a giggle and tried to squirm away. "We're in a tub, for heaven's sake." She captured a foot in each hand to get him to behave, then decided maybe that wasn't what she wanted.

"So?"

"Don't you know how many accidents happen in tubs?"

"No!" He gasped theatrically. "You mean other people are doing this all over the city?!"

"No," she barely managed to say through her laughter as one of his feet escaped and nestled in place again.

"I happen to know we won't have an accident."

"Why?"

"Well, look," he reasoned as he pointed to her vitamins lying on the tile. "Have you ever responded to an accident in a bathroom where the victim had vitamins lying in plain sight?"

"No."

"Well, then," he announced as though it were the most logical conclusion in the world. "People who take vitamins in the bathtub don't have accidents."

"You're going to have an accident if you keep coming up with theories like that."

"Oh, really?" He moved forward, grasping her hands and letting his very talented foot do what it may.

"Yes, really."

Mac slid his hands around behind her and pulled her hips forward, sliding her along in the tub until she sat just in front of him, her legs straddling his, her breasts brushing his chest. "Show me."

"Here? Mac, we can't do this here. There's not enough room."

"There's plenty of room."

"Oh, sure. And where's the scuba gear so I don't drown in my moment of ecstasy?"

Mac laughed at her playfully and hugged her close, liking the feel of her hard nipples against his chest. "Not necessary," he whispered against her lips. "Let me show you."

At times like this, she never wanted to be without Mac again.

"GAME TIME!" Mac announced after dinner.

"Monopoly!" Rob declared.

"Not if you play like your father," Marta complained.

"What did you play at your house?" Mac asked diplomatically.

"Uno," Sherri answered.

Rob pretended to stick his finger down his throat. "No strategy."

"If you want strategy, you should play Risk," Sherri retorted. "But we didn't bring it."

"We've got one, but we never even opened it."

"We do?" Mac asked.

"Yeah. *Grandma* gave it to us at Christmas."

Apparently, the way Rob said it, Grandma's games had been bad news in the past.

"Never played it?" Marta had hopes of beating Mac at a game this time. Mercilessly.

"But, Mom, they won't know the rules," Sherri reasoned.

"Nor the strategy," Marta said with a smile. "Let's teach them."

The kids ran off to find the game.

"What kind of look is that I see on your face?" Mac asked, standing just inches in front of Marta.

She tried to look very innocent. "Just happiness that we're going to play a game together, as a family."

"Uh-uh. Why do I get the feeling I'm about to get the pants beaten off me?"

"Mac!" Marta tried to look shocked. "Not in front of the children."

"You know what I meant. Although, I like the way you think." He stepped closer, until they were chest to chest.

Marta tipped her head up to keep her eye on him. "This is another one of those property-type games, Mac. Only, instead of buying blocks and building houses and apartments, we get armies and try to take over the world."

"You sound too excited about this game."

"Mom! We're ready!" Sherri called from the other room.

Marta kissed Mac lightly and quickly. "It's not the game getting me excited." She turned and left the kitchen.

"Then we'd better get going so we can finish the game early," Mac agreed as he followed her to the family room.

"MAC, I'LL GO against you in Irkutsk," Marta said as she shook the dice in her hand. Mac was turning out to be a formidable opponent, though Rob was already out of the game.

Dixie lay on the carpet near them, waiting for an errant die to be tossed her way. As yet she had not been included in the game and had been looking left out until Rob lay back and rested his head on her.

"Come on, Marta. You can do it," he cheered.

Mac rolled and lost, and Rob cheered again.

"Remember who pays your allowance," Mac shot his way.

Rob laughed.

Marta had offered Rob her spot in the game when he lost early, but he had declined. Apparently he was used to losing his fair share of the time and wasn't upset by it. He preferred to stay close and study Marta's and Sherri's strategies, which were different and both effective.

"Sherri, I'll go against you in Northern Europe," Marta challenged next.

Marta lost eighteen of the next twenty times she got to roll the dice and was the next one out of the game.

"Hey, Rob, how about we go make some banana splits?" she suggested.

"With hot fudge?"

"Do you have some?"

"Sure!"

"Then hot fudge it is. Orders, anyone?"

Sherri and Mac were both specific in what they wanted and went on playing without spectators.

"That's a pretty neat game," Rob said as they worked together in the kitchen. "Grandma usually picks real losers. like Scrabble."

"I love Scrabble."

"I hate it. It's like spelling class."

Marta didn't want to tell him that Risk was like geography class—he might learn to dislike it on principle.

"You sure you want three scoops of ice cream?" Marta asked. "You ate a pretty big dinner."

"Hey, I'm a growing boy. Look, my jeans are getting too short."

Marta did look. "Didn't your dad buy you new ones when school started?"

"These are them."

Marta sighed. "Why do kids always grow *after* we buy new clothes?"

Rob grinned wickedly. "So we get more new ones, of course."

"Of course." Marta dished up three scoops, as requested.

"So, can I have some new jeans?"

"May you," she corrected automatically.

"Yeah, may I?"

"I guess I should talk to Mac about it before I answer. But if he says yes, would you like me to take you shopping?"

"Yeah, I'd like that." Rob picked up two of the desserts and headed for the other room, completely unfazed by this new step in their relationship.

"Yeah, so would I," Marta said to herself, and smiled.

MAC FLIPPED OFF the ten o'clock news with the remote button and looked down at Marta cuddled against his side in their bed.

"You still awake?" he whispered.

"Mmm-hmm. I wanted to talk to you about something." Marta shifted a little to wake up more. She was nervous. They had said they loved each other, but what if Mac didn't want a permanent roommate? Nothing had been said about her extending her vacation.

Mac scooted down in bed, taking Marta with him. "It must be pretty important." Mac was nervous. It was a half hour past her usual bedtime, and she was still awake and had something to discuss with him. Had she changed her mind about trusting him?

Marta nodded against his shoulder and cuddled closer. "I like it here."

"I like having you here. I'd like you to stay, but I'll understand..." He was willing to give her more time, if need be. If she wanted to move out and continue dating, well, he'd make the best of it.

Marta looked at him closely. "You'd like me to stay?"

"Yes. And it has nothing to do with the kids. I love them both," he added hastily, "but I want you to stay because I love you."

Marta thought he kind of wanted some reassurance, to be certain that was exactly how she felt, too. "I love you, too, Mac. And that's why I'd like to stay." Her hand rubbed over his chest nervously. Did he mean permanently, or just a little longer?

Mac let out the breath he had been holding. "That's a relief! I was afraid you were going to say you wanted to move back to your house and start dating again. And I didn't know where we'd fit it into our schedules and still have time for the kids."

Marta laughed softly. "What were you going to say you'd understand?"

"Oh, nothing."

"No, tell me," she insisted.

"Oh, okay, if you're going to drag it out of me."

She poked him in the ribs.

"Hey, cut that out. I was just going to say I'd understand if you needed more time to think about it."

"How much more time?"

"No, no fair. You already said you wanted to stay."

"I'm just curious."

Mac rolled over, halfway on top of her. "About twenty seconds."

"I don't need it."

"What do you need?"

"You."

MAC WOKE MARTA UP ten minutes early. "Tell me I wasn't dreaming." He sat on the side of the bed, fully dressed for work, tie and all.

"What time is it?"

"Six-twenty."

Marta yawned and stretched. "What?"

"Was I dreaming, or are you staying?"

"I'm staying." Marta was not a night person, and she knew she hadn't gotten all the answers last night that she should have. She was awake now and thinking more clearly. "But as long as we're on the subject, could we define that a little better?"

Several answers flew through Mac's mind, one of which he was afraid she would reject on the basis of the fact that they hadn't known each other all that long. He stood up to give himself more time to select an answer he was sure she would agree to.

"I mean," Marta continued as she sat up and pushed her hair out of her eyes, "did you want me to extend my stay a week, or make it longer?"

Mac opened his mouth to answer.

"Now, be honest," she warned as she looked up at him. "If you only meant another week and want to talk about it again, then say so." She wasn't about to foist herself on someone because he had said something in a moment of weakness that he would later regret.

Mac smiled. "I meant permanently. What did you mean?"

Marta's smile matched his. "Gosh," she said as she looked around the room. "I only intended to come here for a week or two."

Mac chuckled and inadvertently caught her attention.

"What's so funny?" she demanded.

He shrugged. "Nothing."

She got out of bed and playfully slugged him with a pillow. "Talk or die."

"Now you sound like a pirate." He backed away a step.

She pursued. "It must be catching, but you're still not talking."

Mac looped his arms around her and pulled her in to his chest, the pillow squashed between them. "Let's just say when I talked you into this in the first place, I had hopes that we would kind of hit it off, so to speak."

"You did, did you?"

"Mmm-hmm."

"You're very tricky, Dr. Macke."

"You're very desirable, Mrs. Howard." Mac tossed the pillow aside and pulled her as close as possible for a good-morning kiss. "But," he said, moving away reluctantly, "duty calls. See you tonight."

Chapter Twelve

"I am so sick of this rain," Marta said with a groan as she gingerly slipped out of her raincoat. "I haven't been dry in three days." She plugged her blow dryer into the nearest outlet and proceeded to drown out all answering conversation as she bent over at the waist and brushed her hair upside down in front of the warm air flow.

"I said..." Johnson said loudly when she turned the appliance off two minutes later. "I said, Howard, that you got another delivery this morning."

Marta smiled brightly, reminded of Mac again as she looked around for her rose.

"We put it in water since you didn't get back right away," Hawk explained why the bud was stuck into the neck of a Pepsi bottle sitting on the scarred table.

Johnson snorted. "Yeah. Besides, we couldn't wait to see the latest update on your sex life."

"You are totally disgusting, Johnson. Your theory about red roses versus white ones is totally unfounded."

"Sure. Then how come he sent you white ones before you moved in with him two weeks ago, and now it's red, every day, day after day."

"Oh, I give up." Marta threw up her hands in defeat. "You're right, Johnson. It's because I 'put out' every night," she threw his own disgusting lingo back at him, "and I'm so damn good he wants everyone to know."

"Take it easy, Howard," Hawk soothed as he drew a card from the pile of the everlasting gin game.

Johnson started to gloat, but jumped in his chair as he received a swift kick to the shin under the table from his opponent.

"I'm sorry, guys. Chalk it up to the rain, okay?" Marta walked over to Summers's couch, grasped the hem of his pant legs, swung his feet off the sofa and onto the floor and sat herself down in the newly vacated space.

Summers struggled to sit up from his awkward position. "Trouble in paradise?" he asked warily.

Marta let her head rest on the back of the couch, sighed and smiled. "No. I can't believe how well things are going, as a matter of fact. Who would think you could take four people, toss them into one house, stir in at least four pets, and come up with paradise? I'm in love, Sherri's in heaven." She looked over at Summers and whispered conspiratorially, "Can you believe she asked me yesterday when she can introduce Rob as her brother?"

"You're getting married?" Hawk laid down his cards.

"Remind me to tell your wife you're not hard of hearing, Hawk. Nothing's been said. Let's just say I wouldn't be surprised if the topic came up."

"Hawkings! Johnson!"

The two men jumped up from the table, leaving their cards where they lay, dragging the last puffs from their cigarettes as they consulted with their supervisor and the street guide. With a final grind of the butts in the ashtray before slipping into their wet raincoats, the team disappeared out the door and thumped down the concrete stairs to the garage.

Rainy weather was miserable for ambulance crews. Water dripped down the vinyl coats and onto their pant legs, and more water splashed up onto their ankles from the ground wherever they rushed on their calls. The seats of the ambulance got wet, and if their coats slipped up when they sat down, their pants got wet up in the thigh area. Their collars got wet no matter how they tried to keep them dry. They wore their shirtsleeves rolled up to keep the cuffs dry, and the cold surface of the coat sleeves chilled them to the bone. They had all waterproofed their leather shoes, but even that worked for only so long. Three days was way beyond their limit.

More automobile accidents happened in rainy weather, so more calls were made out in the elements, rescuing patients, protecting them and trying to keep them, the blankets, padding and bandages dry. Calls came more frequently and seemed to last twice as long. Their tempers were shorter. So were those of their patients and the motorists who were delayed as a result of an accident.

"I HAVE NEVER known you to pace before," Marta told Summers as she filed the last of their reports for the day. She paused and leaned on the open file drawer, following his every step with a worried frown. "As a matter of fact, I've never known you to do anything other than hold that couch down."

"That's because there's usually a severe lack of oxygen in this room." He continued wearing a path from the main door to the supervisor's office door. "We should have heard something from them by now."

Marta closed the file drawer and stepped deliberately into Summers's path, hands on her hips and ready to do battle. "You've been pacing for half an hour, and fifteen minutes ago you checked with the supervisor about something. Now, what gives?"

Summers began pacing in a path perpendicular to the one he had been wearing in the floor. "They went to a Robson building... for an accident. Robson Realty is the company that owns those poorly managed buildings."

"Oh," Marta almost groaned. It was dark and dreary outside, and none of those apartment buildings that she'd been in so far had hall lights. Most of them had unsafe carpets or stairways. "What's he doing about it?"

"He planned to call the police if he hadn't heard from them—" Summers consulted his watch "—about five minutes ago."

He continued pacing, waiting for the phone to ring in the other room, while Marta sat at the table and shuffled the cards in preparation for a game of solitaire. When the phone rang, her fingers slipped and the cards flew all over the table, some spilling onto the floor. They both left their places to hurry across the lounge to the office door and listen in on the conversation.

The supervisor didn't say much into the receiver before hanging up. He ran his hand through his thinning hair. "That was the police. They're on the scene." He rose slowly and walked over to the door where Marta and Summers stood quietly waiting. "They've been on the scene for an hour now. So have two fire departments and their rescue squads."

"What about Hawk and Johnson?" Marta heard Summers say. She seemed to be unable to form words herself.

The supervisor slipped his hands into his pant pockets and shook his head. "The man I talked to just now didn't know. He said there's a lot of people in their apartments because of the bad weather—"

"Let's go!" Summers practically shouted at Marta. He grabbed his raincoat and ran. She turned and followed suit.

For the first time since she had been riding with Summers, she was completely thankful for his back-street shortcuts. He kept them out of snarled traffic, was able to detour around stalled cars and downed trees and delivered them safely and quickly to the congested accident scene.

There were two bright yellow fire trucks on the site, ladders extended into the dark afternoon sky, reaching third-story windows that were no longer crowned by a roof. Police barricades quickly opened for their ambulance and closed just as quickly behind them to keep out the public, who had ventured out in the inclement weather to see what the commotion was all about.

"There!" Marta exclaimed, pointing as she spotted the ambulance that had been manned by Hawk and Johnson. Under normal circumstances, the team would not have been on a scene for this length of time without notifying their supervisor.

"Damn!" Summers replied as he banged his fist on the steering wheel.

An ambulance crew in front of them had just closed their rear doors and was preparing to pull away from the curb. Marta unbuckled her seat belt and let it fly back as she threw open her door and jumped out, yelling to the crew in front of her as she ran to their vehicle. They halted momentarily, just long enough to answer negatively to her query as to whether their patient was an EMT.

Summers parked their ambulance out of the way of other emergency vehicles, ran over to Marta with the jump kit, and grabbed her by the arm. "Let's stay together," he shouted over the noise made by the large rumbling engines, shouting men and a large thunderclap. In case she had other thoughts, his grip on her wet sleeve remained firm and unyielding as they wove through the crowd of emergency personnel.

They each questioned several men on their way up the front sidewalk, asking about two missing EMTs, how extensive the damage was, how many persons were injured and had yet to be moved. When Marta finally found the fireman who was in charge, they were informed that one EMT had already been removed on a stretcher and rushed to the emergency room, and that one more was indoors, injured but still on the premises.

He went on to inform them in the few seconds allotted that it was an ambulance crew who had called them, stating they needed a ladder truck in order to remove persons from a building with an unstable roof and a questionable stairway.

"As you can see, they were right about the unstable roof," he concluded as he was interrupted by his radio. He turned away to answer it.

"Let's go," Summers said quietly. "I've got the jump kit."

"I put a flashlight in there."

Debris from the crumbling walls and ceiling above littered the stairway. The carpet was soaked and felt squishy beneath her feet. The wooden balustrade lay on the tiles of the first-floor hallway, where it had landed after the wet wood had pulled loose from its moorings. Marta couldn't let Summers get more than a few feet ahead of her because the interior was in darkness and they had only one flashlight.

At the top of the narrow and dark stairs, they had to hurry across the landing to avoid the imminent fall of plaster hanging from what was supposed to be the ceiling.

"You okay?" he asked as Marta almost ran over him in her attempt to keep from being hit by debris.

"Yeah." She brushed wet plaster from her shoulders. "Keep going and don't stop. Maybe everything'll miss us."

They passed through a doorway, knowing where to go by listening to the voices of the other emergency personnel in the building. Paramedics were supervising the removal of a patient on a stretcher through the window. Part of the roof was hanging down into the apartment, leaning on the floor and sodden furniture. Rain was falling in through the hole, along with runoff from a higher part of the roof that was still intact.

"Boy, am I glad to see you," one of the paramedics said, recognizing them. "Your buddy is in the next apartment, doing the best he can do with one arm and ten kids."

"Ten?"

"There was a birthday. Hawk's trying to help the firemen get everybody out on the other ladder. We're okay here right now. Would you see what you can do in there?"

Another crash out in the hallway reminded them of the fact that they were in a very unstable building.

"You can go through the bedroom," the paramedic told them, pointing toward the back of the building. "The roof is actually lower nearer the stairwell, and it's been leaking for three days. I wouldn't trust it not to go anytime."

Marta and Summers entered the bedroom to find part of its back wall had crumbled, allowing them to see into the back apartment where Hawk was sitting on the floor facing a group of children, one hanging on his right arm.

"Wave bye-bye," he was telling his little group. "Billy, it'll be your turn next." He turned to follow the children's stares and saw his coworkers. A weak grin broke out on his face.

Hawk didn't look well to Marta. His color in the dim light looked bad, and his grin seemed forced and drawn with pain. "Hawk?" Marta asked, to get him to look at her directly. She didn't like what she saw and did a quick survey while Summers distracted him by palpating the arm the child had been hanging on.

"I'll go see if I can find some dry blankets," she said quietly to her partner. Hawk was exhibiting early signs of shock, and it was of the utmost importance to get him warm.

Marta carefully explored the rooms available to her, avoiding any areas where the ceiling was dripping or hanging suspiciously low, knowing that tons of water, plaster and wood could be waiting to cascade down on her. She found two blankets wrapped in a plastic trash bag on the top shelf of a closet and pulled them out quickly.

Upon her return she found Summers splinting Hawk's right arm to his upper body.

"What happened?" she asked as she draped one blanket across his lap and around his lower back.

"Part of the ceiling fell on Johnson and me," Hawk replied through lips thinned in pain. "He was hit pretty hard in the upper back and knocked down. The paramedics took him out on a backboard before the ladders got here."

Hawk fell silent as Summers finished splinting his fractured arm, and Marta took the second blanket and covered him snugly from his chin down to the floor.

"Which one of you is Billy?" Marta asked the huddle of children as she saw the fireman return to the window via the outdoor ladder.

Billy was too shy to raise his hand, but three other boys pointed him out immediately.

"Okay, come on. Hawk said it's your turn." She held out her hand and smiled reassuringly at the seven-year-old. "Let's go over to the window and see if the other children are waving at you."

Billy timidly rested his hand in hers, but hung back increasingly as they approached the window. When Marta turned to coax him closer, he latched onto her body in a death grip, his legs wrapped around her waist and his arms tightly holding onto her neck.

"Look, son, your friends are down there waiting for you," the fireman spoke encouragingly to the youngster. "Tommy said to tell you it's better than *He-Man*."

Tommy's opinion obviously didn't carry much weight with the scared little boy Marta was carrying.

The fireman gently tried to pry Billy loose from Marta, but gave up when the boy's quiet whimpers threatened to escalate into full-blown, ear-piercing screams.

"We don't want to upset the others," the fireman said quietly to Marta as he glanced over at the remaining children still huddled around Hawk and Summers. "It looks like you'll have to take him down."

"Say what?"

"Keep calm," he cautioned. "Remember all those things you were going to tell Billy about how much fun this will be, and about how his mommy is waiting for him down by the fire engine?" he spoke as though he was really talking to Billy. "Well, just tell yourself those same things while I help you out this window and onto the ladder."

"I think I understand how Billy feels now," she said through a sweet smile at the fireman. "Perhaps you would like to take one of the other brave boys down first so Billy could see it again?" She emphasized the word brave, hoping that there would be a volunteer. There wasn't.

"Nice try," the fireman said as he smiled a real smile back at her. "But now it's time to cut the bull and get going. Let's show these kids how to follow the rule about always obeying the nice fireman."

The hand which grasped her arm firmly was warm and strong. At his insistence she moved toward the window and through it, one leg at a time, until she was sitting on the sill. Then she stepped onto the safety of the ladder. Her movements were hampered by the sixty-pound child stuck to her like glue, but made easier by the strength and guidance of the fireman.

Marta refrained from looking down as she made her way toward the ground. She could feel the change in Billy as they approached terra firma and he began looking this way and that, searching for his mother and his friends. He began wiggling, then waving, then calling out to the others who had gone before him. Marta felt like a mother ape up in a tree with a very active and clinging youngster.

At the bottom another fireman quickly moved beside her to lift Billy down, who was soon swallowed up by his exuberant friends and relieved mother.

"You did great!" the fireman told Marta as he gave her a hearty pat on the back. "Want to go back up?"

She looked up from her relatively safe position toward the dark third-story window. Her partner, her friend and several children were still inside, and minutes counted. "Can we bring down two at a time?"

"You bet."

She nodded. "Let's go."

"Give me a second," he yelled over the general noise of the area.

Marta glanced around from her position still slightly above the crowd. The other fire truck and ladder and firemen were still removing injured adults through the window in the front of the building. Ambulances were waiting to take over from the rescue squad when the patients were safely on the ground. Police were controlling the public, announcing over loudspeakers to keep the area clear for emergency vehicles and cautioning everyone to stay out of the building.

A movement near the entrance caught her attention. The tan all-weather coat was out of place in a sea of uniform raincoats. Marta felt his form was familiar, but still gasped when he turned and she stared into Mac's face. Her shock was like an electric charge straight through her as he looked up and saw her.

She could see his lips forming her name in surprise as he ran over to her, but couldn't hear him until he stood in front of her.

"What are you doing here?" she asked, surprised that he would be dealing in emergency medicine on location.

"How bad is it?" he asked simultaneously. He ignored her question and repeated his. "How bad is it?"

"It's terrible, Mac. The whole roof could cave in anytime—the stairs are impassable now. These ladders are the only way in or out.

"Mac, what are you doing here?" she asked again as she realized he was not tending the injured.

"One of the tenants called me. He said if I wanted to see my building one more time before it washed down the storm sewer, then I better get over here—fast."

"Your building? Which one?"

Eleven Year Match

"Are you kidding?" he asked as he looked at her in amazement. "This one!" He turned, then, and looked around for the tenant who had called him on the phone.

Marta stared at the back of his head. "You own this building?" she repeated in disbelief.

An elderly couple approached Mac. "Well, well, Rob's son. And what would your fine father think of his building now?" the gentleman asked loudly.

"Mr. Donegal," Mac said, reaching out to touch the man's shoulder. "Thank God you're okay."

"Your father rented to me fifty years, he did. Always kept the place up, too. It's a good thing he didn't live to see it all come to this. Indeed."

"Mr. Donegal, I don't know what to say."

"You own this building?" Marta repeated. "Who's Robson Realty?"

"I am," Mac admitted as he faced her. "Rob's son. Remember?"

Rob's son, Mr. Donegal had called him. Robson Realty. Mac had kept the name simple for his elderly tenants who'd known him by that name for over thirty years.

"In the old days there was a name for the likes of you renting to the likes of me," Mr. Donegal continued.

"Slumlord," Marta thoughtlessly said out loud.

"What?" Mac turned back to her. "Marta, how can you say that? I have eight other buildings—"

"Probably no better than this one," Mr. Donegal said with disgust.

"I have a building manager—"

"Slumlord," Mr. Donegal agreed, and spat on the ground for emphasis. "Your building manager, he's nothing but a crook, taking our money for two years and letting the roof fall down around our ears. Your fine father would be rolling over in his grave!"

Marta listened as the elderly gentleman railed at Mac. She watched as another injured adult was brought down the ladder and lifted into a waiting ambulance. She felt her heart break as she realized she had been living with the man who was responsible for several injured people over the last few months alone. Needless injuries, possibly permanently damaging, in the case of the man who had fallen down the unsafe staircase and the baby with lead poisoning.

"Time to go." The fireman had returned for Marta and indicated she should ascend first.

"Marta, don't go back in there!" Mac reached up for her, but she slipped out of his grasp.

"I have to. It's my job—" she wiped a tear off her cheek "—cleaning up after accidents caused by people like you."

"Like me? Marta, you sound as though I don't care."

"Do you? Do you?" She hurled the accusation down at him as she began her ascent. "Every building you own is like this one!"

She saw Mac look around in disbelief, but could no longer hear him yelling back to her as she rose higher and all the noises below blended together.

Her attention quickly shifted to the next two children, waiting up above to ride down with her and the fireman.

"How's Hawk?" she asked the fireman when he passed another seven-year-old boy to her.

"Weaker. They're taking him down on the other ladder now. Your partner's going to take another child down then the two of you can take Hawk to the hospital in your ambulance. I've already called down on the radio. I can handle the last boy."

Marta was first to reach the ground and immediately passed the little boy to his mother.

Eleven Year Match 219

"What do you mean all of my buildings are like this one?" Mac demanded, falling into step with her as she jogged over to her ambulance through the light rainfall.

"Just what I said. They should all be condemned!" she shouted at him across the vehicle as she wrenched open the driver's door with unnecessary force.

"And what makes you the judge?" he demanded again as he heaved himself into the passenger seat.

"Get out of my ambulance!"

"No!"

She accelerated quickly, throwing Mac back against the seat as she positioned the ambulance as near as possible to the second fire truck, waiting for Hawk to be unstrapped and moved to where Summers was waiting to open the rear doors.

"Dr. Macke," Summers said in surprise as he stepped into the rear of the ambulance. "Doing mobile orthopedics, now?"

"Meet Robson Realty," Marta snapped.

"I'm waiting for an answer to my question—what makes you the judge of my other buildings?"

"Accidents!" she shouted at him again. "Accidents, Mac. One after another. Electrical, structural, chemical, for pity's sake!" Marta was shaking physically, both from the cold and damp and from the tension. "I thought you were different," she sobbed on a final note. "I thought you cared for people."

"Dr. Macke, you'll have to step out now," Summers ordered.

Mac hesitated for only a second before complying with the request. Hawk was being loaded through the rear doors, and Mac exited through the passenger door and walked around back to observe.

"Dr. Macke, are you really Robson Realty?" Summers asked.

Mac nodded. "You don't have to make it sound dirty."

Summers let loose a punch that sent Mac sprawling backward into the bushes. Marta could see no more as her partner climbed quickly into the back and closed the doors. "Go!"

MAC WATCHED, horrified at what he had heard, as the ambulance pulled quickly away. He had tried to call his building manager as soon as he had received Mr. Donegal's call, but had not been able to reach him. He had difficulty trying to remain open-minded about what Marta had told him. How could all his buildings be in such bad condition, when he had a building manager who mailed him regular reports about all the maintenance that had been regularly performed? And paid for. He had even mailed Mac photographs of the renovations taking place in two of his buildings, as per schedule. Marta must be mistaken, but she seemed so sure.

Mac also had the niggling feeling that this building was one of the two that were supposed to be undergoing extensive renovations. But without his real estate files he couldn't swear to it. If so, this disaster was blatant testimony to the fact that Marta was right.

He rubbed his jaw, just beginning to feel the throb of pain from the punch. He wasn't sure whether Summers's response was job-related anger, or because he had made Marta cry. Either way, Mac would be more careful around that guy in the future.

He walked slowly to where his car was parked just inside the barricade. He'd been allowed in when he had identified himself as a physician. Everything was as under control here as it could be, and he buckled his seat belt and set out to see for himself what the situation was for his other tenants.

AT MIDNIGHT, Mac stumbled wearily out of his eighth and last apartment building. He had knocked on every tenant's door, some of whom he had never met, and after he'd identified himself to one new tenant, he'd had second thoughts about identifying himself to any more, though he'd done it anyway.

All the stories were the same. Even the old people who had rented from his father before him, and who were afraid to complain for fear of being thrown out, eventually came around to saying that conditions had worsened since he'd hired the new building manager two years ago. He was told that when some of the more vocal tenants had complained, they had been encouraged to move through questionable tactics.

Mac was devastated. His tenants thought the worst of him, his buildings were in sad and sometimes unsafe condition, and Marta had accused him of being a slumlord. And the worst of it was, she was right. He was a slumlord, albeit unknowingly.

Conditions had been so appalling in the third building he visited that he'd made arrangements with a nearby hotel to house his tenants there. He asked them to send him their bills for the duration until he could either find them accommodations they could afford, or until he could get things put right in their apartments.

He called his lawyer and got him out of bed, explaining about the insurance claims and lawsuits which would be following. His lawyer advised him of charges that might be filed against him and what he could do to protect himself. But Mac's first concern was his tenants.

Chapter Thirteen

Marta arrived at Mac's at two in the morning. She had checked on Johnson and stayed with Hawk in the hospital until he was asleep. The tension of the long day, dealing with Hawk's wife and facing her own betrayal by Mac had taken their toll. Exhausted, depressed, anguished, she had driven straight home without even changing into dry clothes.

She drove up the long driveway and around to the back of the house, afraid she would find Mac at home. She wasn't ready to face him yet and didn't know if she ever would be. It would be bad enough if she had to run into him in the hospital sometimes. If she saw him now, she didn't know if she could be held responsible for whatever she might say to him.

Mac's car wasn't there, and Marta was relieved. She parked close to the back door, went upstairs and threw everything she'd brought into suitcases and put them in the car. Next was Sherri's room. She didn't wake Sherri until she had all her clothes in the car, too.

"Come on, Sherri, wake up," she said as she gently shook her daughter. "Wake up, sweetie."

Sherri woke up. "Where are my jeans?" she asked sleepily.

"I put your clothes on the bed."

"Mo-om. I can't wear these to school."

"It's not time for school, sweetie. Just get dressed."

Sherri was too far gone to argue. She got dressed, then lay back down.

"Come on, sweetie," Marta said, rousing her again.

"Where we going?" she asked.

"Home."

Sherri balked. "This is home."

"I'll explain later. Let's go. The car's all warm. You can bring your pillow."

"We're leaving?" Sherri was close to tears.

"Yes. I'll come back later for all your stuffed animals."

"Madonna!"

Marta made a face. "I'll come back for her, too."

"No. I'm not going without her. Where's Mac?"

"He's out for the night." Marta wasn't sure about that, and she wanted to be gone before he returned.

"I guess the two of us can carry her." Sherri tossed her pillow back onto the bed, opting for the snake instead.

Once the snake was comfortably settled in its aquarium in Marta's back seat and Sherri was falling asleep in the front, Marta paused and looked at the house. Specifically, she looked at Rob's window. He lay inside, peacefully sleeping, unaware that when he woke up later, everything would once again be changed.

She glanced at Sherri, knowing she would be all right in the car. Hopefully Mac wouldn't arrive while Marta went up to Rob's room for a few minutes.

She looked down at him for a moment, then touched his hair gently. She remembered how he had been upset once before, afraid she would leave because of him.

"Oh, Rob, I'm so sorry," she whispered. "I'd give anything not to have had this happen."

He rolled over and opened his eyes. He mumbled.

"Rob, wake up a little bit, sweetie."

He nodded, but his eyes soon flickered closed again.

"Rob, I've got to tell you something. Sherri and I are going."

"Where?" he asked with a sigh as he rolled back onto his side and tucked one hand under his cheek.

"Back to our house."

He pushed the sheet down. "Okay."

Marta was just about to give him a little shake and tell him again when he sat up. "What are you doing?"

"I'll come, too."

Marta didn't know whether to laugh because he was asleep and didn't know what he was saying, or cry because he wanted to go with her. He obviously didn't understand she wasn't coming back. She gently pushed him back down and covered him. "You stay here, sweetie. I love you, but you belong with your dad."

Rob nodded, but barely. He was soon fast asleep.

"Bye," Marta whispered and kissed him on his forehead. "I love you."

She brushed her tears aside, found a paper and pen and wrote those last words down for Rob. It was all she could give him now.

"GO TO BED," Marta told Sherri after they placed Madonna's aquarium on her new desk.

"I don't like it here," Sherri complained. "I want to go back to Mac's."

Sherri had started complaining as soon as Marta woke her up at home. She no longer looked sleepy, but Marta was exhausted.

"We'll talk about it in the morning."

"It is morning."

"It's three o'clock, Sherri, and I've been up since six-thirty yesterday. I've got to get some sleep before I collapse. Don't wake me before ten. Better yet, don't wake me at all."

"Mo-om."

"Good night," she said sternly. "We'll talk when I get up."

"But, Mo-om."

Marta saw that Sherri was holding back tears, and she was close to them herself. "Oh, sweetie, I love you." She sat on the bed and held her. "Everything'll be all right."

"Promise?"

"Yes, I promise. I love you, and I'll take care of you. Now, let me get some sleep, and I'll explain everything later."

MAC ARRIVED at home in the early hours of the morning to find Rob asleep in the master bedroom, curled around Dixie. Marta and Sherri and most of their belongings were gone. He collapsed on the bed next to his son, hoping he could get twenty-four hours' sleep before waking up and finding out this nightmare was real.

"Mo-OM."

The phone rang again, and for the first time Marta regretted her decision to have it installed next to her bed instead of in the kitchen. She pulled a pillow over her head, but it didn't help.

"I said don't answer it, Sherri."

"It might be for me."

Not likely. All Sherri's friends had her new number at Mac's house, or "Dr. Mac" as they all referred to him.

Besides, they were in school, and Marta hadn't gotten up in time this morning to get Sherri ready. On the other hand, several people could be phoning to talk to Marta, but right now she wasn't in the mood to deal with any of them.

Hawk could be calling to say how he was doing and give her an update on Johnson. She had checked his emergency room X-ray report the night before, and while Johnson was in a great deal of pain and would not be working for quite some time, at least there were no spinal fractures.

Summers could be calling to speak with her about his having punched out her lover. He had been his usual quiet self after the fracas last night, and she had been too upset with Mac and shocked by Summers to say anything.

Linda, her neighbor, could be calling to see why Marta had moved back into her little house after spending what Marta had told her were the best two weeks of her life at Mac's. And Marta certainly wasn't up to explaining that she had fallen in love with the lowest kind of scum on Earth—the kind that didn't care if their negligence caused injury to others. Sherri would undoubtedly see Laurie later and tell her part of the story—that her mother had lost her mind.

Her supervisor could be calling back to find out how she was doing after her very long night. He had instructed her to take the day off, mostly because she was too exhausted to work safely, but she was expected back tomorrow.

But the caller would most likely be Mac. And she couldn't talk to him yet. The wound was too new. Mac had taught her to believe in him and then had ripped her heart out without anesthesia to dull the pain.

When she could no longer stand the ringing of the phone, she lifted the receiver and slammed it down again. When the connection was broken, she removed the receiver from its cradle and stuffed it into the drawer of her bedside table.

MARTA AWOKE to the sound of cartoons and checked the clock. Two-thirty in the afternoon. She should have felt well rested, but she didn't. She had slept a long time, but the sleep hadn't been all that great.

"Hi, Mom," Sherri said quietly when Marta collapsed onto the couch in the living room. She tucked a pillow under her head and an afghan over her bare feet.

"Hi, sweetie."

Sherri looked as though she was afraid to say anything, and Marta held out her hand.

"Do you feel better?" Sherri asked as she scrunched up on the couch behind Marta's knees, her legs over her mom's.

"I guess. I'll bet you have a million questions for me."

Sherri shrugged, reluctant to begin. "Are we going back?"

"No."

"Did Mac do something bad?"

"Oh, boy," Marta said. "I'm not too sure how to answer that one."

"Did... did he hurt you?"

"Not where it shows. In here," she tapped over her heart. "Mac would never hurt me physically, Sherri. Nor you."

"So I can still talk to him?"

Marta thought a moment. It probably would be better that way. Sherri could talk to him a couple times on the phone, then gradually lose interest. "Sure, sweetie."

"What did he do, Mom?"

Marta wished Sherri were this persistent in science class. "You know Mac owns some apartment buildings, don't you?"

"Yeah, I guess so."

"Well," she chose her words carefully, "he didn't take very good care of them." She wondered why she was being so delicate. He damn well let them fall down around people's ears! But, she reasoned, she couldn't let Sherri go to school and tell others that Rob's father was a slumlord. That would only hurt Rob, and Marta wanted to make this as easy on both the kids as possible. "There were a lot of accidents that shouldn't have ever happened."

"Did you go there?"

"Yes, with Summers. And last night Hawk and Johnson were both hurt in one of Mac's buildings."

"How?"

"The roof caved in during the rainstorm. It fell on them."

Sherri's eyes were wide. "Are they all right?"

"They're both in the hospital, but they'll be okay. Hawk has a broken arm, and—"

"Like me?"

Marta smiled. Tragedy wasn't part of an eleven-year-old's vocabulary. They could relate to cuts, bruises, even broken bones. But Sherri was naive about what could happen when a rain-filled ceiling caved in on a human. "Yes, like you. He was very brave like you, too."

Marta wanted to tell Sherri more. She wanted to tell her her heart was broken, and she might be a pain to live with for a while. She wanted to tell her that she and Mac had been in love and had planned to make the move permanent, so she would understand better. But now that would hurt Sherri more than it would help Marta.

When she got really depressed, she wanted to yell at Sherri and blame her for starting this whole mess, but Sherri didn't need any more hassles. She was suffering her own stress without her stuffed animals, being moved in the middle of the night and having to put up with a mother who cried a lot.

"KELLY, this is Marta. I'm back in my—"

"Hello! Marta, I'm here," Kelly said as she picked up during the message. "So, when's the wedding?"

"There won't be any damn wedding!"

"Whoa, what're you yelling at me for?"

"Because I can't yell at Sherri, and you're just as much to blame for this as she is."

"Back up and explain that, would you? I'm lost."

"You were in on that little cupid maneuver to get Mac and me together on the river, remember?"

"Oh, you figured that out, huh?"

"It really wasn't too difficult," Marta said with a sneer.

"It worked."

"Maybe next time—and there better never be a next time, by the way—you'll research your subject a little better first."

"A real loser, huh?"

"Try reading the morning papers, little sister. He'll be lucky if someone doesn't shoot him before they lock him up."

"Marta, what happened?"

Marta started crying.

"Marta, honey, what's wrong?" Kelly urged.

"He didn't care, Kelly." She sniffed. "He let his apartments get rundown and unsafe, and people got hurt every week, and he didn't care."

"Are you sure?"

"Read the damn paper, Kelly! I was there! Two of my colleagues are in the hospital."

"Okay, okay. Calm down."

"I don't want to calm down. I want people to quit meddling in my life."

"Okay, you got it. Golly, Marta, you're scaring me. You want me to come over?"

"No! Not until I'm not mad at you anymore."

Kelly knew better than to ask when that might be, but she vowed to stay in touch with Sherri, just so she could be sure everything was all right.

THREE WEEKS. No, three weeks and three days to be exact. The worst twenty-four days in history.

Marta plodded through her job every day, and every time she splinted a fracture she saw Mac's face. She could picture him drawing a caricature of how the bone got broken, the same way he had caricaturized Sherri's fall from the low beam.

Four more days and she was supposed to keep an appointment at Mac's office to remove Sherri's cast. That was the only reason three weeks and three days hadn't stretched into eternity. Hell was approaching, and that sped things up a bit.

She debated changing doctors, but Sherri loved and trusted Mac, and orthopedists did not like doing someone else's work under these conditions. When a patient's mother got mad, for whatever reason, everyone started slinking around for fear of hearing the word *lawsuit*. Be-

Eleven Year Match

sides, Marta had to admit, Mac was a good doctor and she trusted his expertise.

Mac quit calling after the first week. Marta had finally stooped low enough to let Sherri answer the phone and tell Mac any damn thing she pleased. And Sherri was made to understand that Marta didn't want to see or talk to him, ever. She had no idea what their conversation had been like, and she didn't want to know.

Personal confrontations were not Marta's forte. She dreaded them, hated them, got sick worrying about them. Just the thought of the upcoming visit to remove Sherri's cast had her stomach too upset to keep more than a minimal amount of food down, just barely enough to keep her alive and moving through each day.

"I'm coming!" she called out as the doorbell rang again. She peeked through the peephole she had had installed so she could avoid Mac if he showed up on her doorstep. If he recognized her car in the drive, well, so be it.

"Rob," she gasped as she saw him through the little hole, standing between two stuffed gym bags.

She threw open the door without hesitation, holding out her arms when she saw his wan face. He hugged her tightly. "I didn't know where else to go," he admitted in a muffled voice against her shoulder.

"Why don't you come into the kitchen and tell me all about it?" Marta invited, helping Rob bring in his bags. They were followed by a strawberry-golden, tail-wagging blur that Marta tried to greet with a pat on its way past her legs.

Dixie occupied herself by sniffing every stick of furniture in the small, unfamiliar house, while Marta ushered Rob into her kitchen and sat him at the table, providing cookies and milk without being asked.

"Sorry they're not homemade," she said ruefully, "but I haven't felt much like baking."

She sat across the small table from Rob, watching him nibble a cookie, and tried not to intimidate him by staring.

"You said you didn't know where to go," she said, opening the conversation. "Is there something wrong?"

"It's Dad." He took a drink of milk, then started nibbling again.

Marta gave in and asked. "Is he okay? I mean, he's not hurt or sick or anything, is he?"

"No, he's just busy." Rob started eating again, and Marta waited him out. "I never see him anymore, Marta. He sent me to my grandma's last week, but I don't like it there. She asks too many questions, and she never gives me vitamins like you do."

Marta could imagine the questions. "Too busy for you, Rob? He loves you."

"Not anymore. He spends all his time with his apartments. He's either there, or at his office or the hospital. Can I stay here, Marta? You stayed with us," he said in a rush to qualify his request.

She didn't want to push him just now for more information, knowing that children liked to be able to give it out at their own pace, feeling that that way they have a little bit of control over their own lives.

She patted his hand. "I don't know what to say, Rob," she admitted. "It's certainly okay with me if it's all right with your father, but I have no idea how to approach him." She wanted to add that she didn't even want to talk to him about it, but the look of hope on Rob's young, tear-stained face prevented her comment.

"You could call him," he offered brightly. "He's at the hospital. They'll page him for you."

Marta sighed and got up to pace the kitchen. She stopped to nibble on a cookie and pour more milk. "He does love you, Rob. You have to know that."

"I guess," he said glumly.

"Don't guess—you have to know it. Even if he says you can stay here, it's only temporary. He loves you, and he would never let you go."

"He sent me to Grandma's."

"That's different. Your grandma is family, and I'm sure it wasn't a permanent arrangement."

Rob shrugged, not willing to admit that everything she said was true. But he was still one very depressed little boy who needed support. "Will you talk to Dad if I call?"

Marta thought it over carefully but quickly. "You call him, Rob, and you tell him what you need. And then I'll talk to him to let him know it's okay with me if you stay here for a while."

She didn't even have to show Rob where the phone was. Sherri must have told him. Dixie kept her company in the kitchen, begging for a cookie while Rob waited for his father to be paged.

"I'll get her, Dad. Marta! Marta!"

Marta walked down the hallway to her bedroom, dreading every step that brought her nearer to talking to Mac on the phone. When she started to reach for the receiver that Rob was holding out to her, she had to pause first and wipe her sweaty palm on her jeans.

"Hello, Mac." She spoke quietly, knowing he would take it from there. She could always hang up if he was rude.

"Rob says he's all packed and wants to stay with you for a while," Mac said brusquely. "He says you said it was all right."

"Only if it's okay with you," she answered as she quickly glanced at Rob, hoping he had told his father that he had shown up on her doorstep, not that she had offered where she had no business offering.

"Will you promise to call me if you need anything? For him, I mean." He was brief and to the point.

"Yes. For him."

"Okay, then." The phone went dead as he hung up.

Marta held the receiver for a moment more, wishing he hadn't been so impersonal, while at the same time knowing that was how she wanted it. That was how it had to be.

The receiver was her last link to Mac. As she hung it up this time, she knew she would think of him every time she used the phone for the rest of her life. She just wasn't sure whether the feelings he stirred would be anger, regret or love.

"Okay, Rob," she said as she composed herself and smiled at the young boy looking so unsure of himself. "Let's get you settled in before Sherri comes home from school. I'm sure you two will have lots to talk about."

Marta and Rob made up the sleeper sofa in the living room, then folded it back out of the way for the rest of the afternoon and evening. She showed him where his towels would be kept in the bathroom, explained about laundry and meals and got a list of what he and Dixie would need from the grocery store.

"You didn't bring your snakes, did you?" she asked anxiously as she eyed his gym bags lying by the front door where she had left them.

"No," he reassured her with a smile. "Grandma's got them."

"Lucky Grandma. Perhaps you should call and tell her where you are so she won't worry when she finds out you cut school today."

Eleven Year Match

"Dad said he'd handle that because if I call Grandma, she'll be over here bothering you with twenty questions."

"Did he say that?"

Rob nodded, and Marta wondered why Mac would care. It must be that he didn't want his mother-in-law complicating Rob's life further at this point. The poor boy obviously had been shuffled around quite a bit in the past three weeks, and prior to that had his life rearranged when Marta and Sherri had moved in bag and baggage.

"She never stops asking questions," Rob complained. "Why is Dad always working late? Why didn't he know his manager was sending him false reports? Why is he paying the hotel bill for those tenants? Why did you move—" he stopped in the middle of repeating his grandmother's personal question.

Marta turned away and fumbled with picking up the gym bags. "Rob, I didn't know your grandmother knew about me."

He shrugged and looked at the floor. "I guess I must've mentioned it," he said quietly.

"I'm sorry, Rob," Marta said as a tear slipped down her cheek. "I never wanted this to hurt you."

"It's okay." He reached out and took the bags from her. "Don't cry, Marta. I'm sorry, too. Dad told me not to make you cry."

Marta couldn't believe it. Why did Mac still care? She had left him as abruptly as possible so he wouldn't have any doubts about how low a scumbag she thought he was. He should be annoyed, angry, ticked off, hurt, but not worried about how she felt. He wasn't playing fair.

"Please don't cry, Marta," Rob said in a small voice.

Marta brushed her hand across her cheeks to wipe away another tear that betrayed her. She didn't like crying in front of others, but this house was so darn small that she had hardly any other options. "I'm going to go take a shower. Make yourself at home," she said over her shoulder on her way out of the room.

MAC HUNG UP the phone at the nurses' desk and went back to work, but his mind wasn't completely and fully on the job at hand, though he managed to answer all the patients' questions well enough to make them happy.

He'd had mixed feelings talking to Marta on the phone. He'd had to keep it short and to the point, or he might have said things she didn't want to hear yet, or wasn't ready to hear.

"You're off in another world," Fletch said, interrupting Mac's deep thoughts. "More problems?"

"Yeah, wouldn't you know it?"

"Did you hire that detective?"

"Yes. Thank you! He uncovered evidence of several fraud schemes in two other states, so far. I wish I'd had him check the guy out before I hired him on as manager."

"Didn't you get references?"

Mac emitted a harsh laugh. "It seems con men travel in packs. I don't want to burden you with my problems, though, Fletch. You've been through the ringer already."

"And I'd still be there if it hadn't been for that investigator. Can you believe what lengths some people will go to? The stories they make up! Why, that lady could make a living writing horror stories with an imagination like hers.

"But I'm out of the fire, now, and I've got a sympathetic ear if you want to tell me more."

"No, that's okay."

"Mmm-hmm. Remember, I'm the one who told you she doesn't like doctors."

"Well, if you think she didn't like them before, look out now. I can hardly forgive myself for letting someone look after my responsibilities, so I can't very well expect her to forgive me."

"You're a good man, Mac. Deep down you know that."

"Right. That's why Rob moved in with Marta today."

Fletch's eyebrows rose, but he waited for Mac to go on.

"I sent him to his grandmother's. I've been busy with renovations, you know."

"I know. I've been seeing some of your patients, remember?"

"Anyway, I guess Rob got to feeling left out or unloved or something."

"And he moved in with Marta?"

Mac nodded.

"She took him in?"

"Does that surprise you?"

Fletch's gaze wandered. "No, not really. But, Mac, if she hated you, she'd never take in your son. Then she'd have to see you and talk to you."

"It won't be for long. Everything'll be finished in a few days, and I'll take Rob home."

Mac knew Marta would never be able to forgive him. He almost couldn't believe that she had willingly taken in Rob. But then, she was a generous sort of woman. She wouldn't stop loving Rob just because of him.

"THAT'S NEAT, Dad," Rob said into the phone. "Are all your tenants going to move back in?"

Marta turned off the water in the kitchen sink, where she was cleaning up after dinner. Normally she wouldn't have been able to hear his conversation over the noise, but she suspected he wanted her to. And she wanted to.

She was still confused about Mac. If he had been at fault, would he be working so hard now that his own son didn't get to see enough of him? They had conspired together to trick the kids and teach them a lesson. Had he been tricking her, too? Or had she tricked herself?

Marta wiped away the tear which refused to obey her command not to fall. She was sad tonight, as she was every night when Mac called and talked to the kids. They seemed so happy, and she regretted that their family hadn't been able to stay together.

"Oh, what a tangled web we weave," she mumbled to herself and resolved never to try to trick Sherri again, even if she did deserve it. She had only ended up fooling herself.

Rob's voice floated down the hall. "Yeah, it's great here, Dad. I miss you, but Marta's really nice.... Yeah, I keep all my stuff picked up." He laughed. "I have to, or we wouldn't be able to see the TV.... No, I don't hog the bathroom, not like Sherri. Are all girls like that, Dad? Ow!" he exclaimed, apparently on the receiving end of Sherri's displeasure.

"No, Dad. I know I'm not supposed to hit girls back."

"Hi, Mac. It's my turn," Sherri said, also louder than normal. "I miss you.... Nah, he's okay. He's better than my friends' brothers...."

Marta wiped away another tear.

Chapter Fourteen

Marta sat on the orange vinyl couch next to Summers, her feet propped up on one of the scarred wooden chairs which she had pulled over to the couch weeks ago for just that purpose.

"Is there any chance I'm going to get my couch back?" Summers asked.

"What's the matter? Are you afraid not enough blood is getting to your brain in that position?"

"No, I'm just tired of sharing my couch with a testy partner," he snapped back.

Marta sighed regretfully. "I'm sorry." She apologized for the hundredth time in less than four weeks. She thought about how rough things were at home, sharing a four-room house with two children, an active dog, a large snake and a load of regret. But she didn't want to mention it. "I never thought I'd hear myself say it, but I miss Johnson. And Hawk, of course, but I knew I liked him."

"How about Mac? Do you miss him, too?"

"Every time I look at his son," she admitted. "And every time I breathe. And every time I blink." She sniffled a little, feeling as close to weepy as always these days.

"How much weight have you lost?"

Marta swiped at a tear before it could escape. "What kind of gentleman are you, Summers?" She sniffled again. "You're supposed to remark about what a great diet I must be on, and my superb willpower."

"You didn't need a diet," he argued. "You keep losing weight, and you won't be strong enough to lift a stretcher. I thought that little drive we took last night would have helped. You've just gone from anger and self-pity to guilt."

"No kidding. And I have you to thank for all that," she complained dryly.

"I can't imagine why Rob stays at your house. It won't surprise me a bit if you go home one day and find that he and Sherri have moved back in with Mac."

"I hope they take the snake."

Summers was right and she knew it. But it was like some perverse little gremlin had taken possession of her body. Rob had been talking with Mac nightly on the phone. It cheered the boy up immensely to have his dad's undivided attention, even if only for a short time. Then Sherri had begun talking with Mac for a few minutes, too, before Rob hung up. It was a small house, and Marta couldn't help hearing the children discuss Mac's progress with the apartment buildings.

And then Summers had gotten so fed up with her that he had taken her for a drive after work yesterday to show her what was going on at the Robson Realty apartment buildings. Since the buildings had always been spotlessly kept on the outside, they had walked through two of them before Marta begged off seeing any more.

Everything paintable boasted fresh, light-colored paint, lightening the dark hallways and stairwells. Light bulbs filled every light fixture, railings were intact and sturdy, carpets had been removed or replaced, depending on the floor beneath. One foyer now had a refurbished black and white tile floor that had previously been covered, and it lent an air of elegance to the entry.

A big blow came when Marta checked the outlet by the bathroom and discovered a ground fault interrupter had been installed by the sink, as she had told Mac a mother hen would do.

The final straw had been when Marta wondered aloud where the tenants were during the construction. She was informed by Summers that the tenants had been found other accommodations at Mac's expense, until remodeling was completed, and were due to move back in this weekend.

She had been wrong. She knew it now, but that stupid little gremlin wouldn't let her admit it to anyone else. She had stormed back to Summers's car, demanded to end the tour and had snapped at him whenever he spoke since.

Tearing herself apart was a painful ordeal. She had thought she would like to die when she learned she loved the scumbag, but this was worse. She hadn't loved him enough. Everything that had been his fault was now hers. She hadn't had enough love or trust. She wasn't big enough to admit her mistake. It was her fault that they weren't one big happy family, living together, thinking of marriage and the future.

Knowing she would have to live with this much pain the rest of her life plunged her deeper into self-pity. Summers badgered her at lunch to eat, managing to humiliate her into swallowing a dozen French fries, knowing that was possibly all she would eat all day.

"What time is Sherri's appointment tomorrow?" Summers asked over his lunch, secretly hoping she and Mac would make up. Then she would cheer up and he could have his couch back to himself.

"Ten o'clock."

The lounge seemed dismal without Hawk and Johnson. They had been replaced temporarily by a nonsmoking team of EMTs, and Marta hadn't even been energetic enough to be grateful for the fresh air. She missed Johnson and Hawk's bickering over who owed who how many cigarettes, and she missed their incessant card games. She even missed Johnson's raunchy, perverted sense of humor and his jabs at her sex life.

The new EMT team had tried to fit in, as all new employees do anywhere. But they had quickly given up in the face of Marta's sharp tongue and Summers's normal restraint. That was something else for her to feel guilty and morose about.

Would it never end? she wondered. She couldn't even remember feeling this bad after her divorce.

AT FIRST, Mac thought, he had been angry, hurt and furious with Marta. He'd tried to convince himself that if she had so little faith in him, then he was probably better off without her in his life. He managed it for about two days.

Then, after reviewing what she knew about him from the short time they had known each other, he realized just what she had thought. She devoted her life to helping others, picking up the pieces after accidents, doing the best she was able with the injuries she was called on to handle. She saw terrible things every day—the worst. A person in her position had a right to have the safety-oriented quirks she possessed.

She had fallen in love with him in spite of the fact that she disliked doctors, so she wasn't totally closed-minded. And then she discovered he was the sole owner of buildings where she had been treating an inordinate number of

Eleven Year Match

accidental injuries lately. Accidents which could have been prevented and would have been, if he had known how things were deteriorating.

He gathered together all the reports he had received over the months from his property manager, all the canceled checks that proved, he had thought, he had been on top of things. He had photographs showing the improvements he was making in the buildings, statements from inspectors approving the work.

He had all this and more, and he'd still spent a sleepless night wondering if it would be enough. Sure, he probably should be furious with her for not giving him a chance to explain at the time. But, damn it, he loved her and he didn't want to risk losing her because of his stupid pride. He could grovel this once.

MARTA HADN'T SLEPT all night before taking Sherri in to Mac's office to get her cast removed. Her head hurt, her back muscles were in knots from the tension of knowing she would see Mac this morning, and she didn't know what she would say or do. Much as she owed Mac an apology, she didn't see how it would do any good.

She hadn't dressed up for this appointment. She'd just thrown on jeans and a sweater and added a belt to tighten her surprisingly loose waistband. She'd been unable to keep any breakfast down, not that she had wanted any, anyway, but Sherri had fixed it for her.

"Mom, come on." Sherri was speaking to her, breaking into her thoughts. Marta looked at her blankly, then noticed a nurse waiting by the open door. "It's my turn."

Marta followed Sherri as the nurse led them to the small examination room and closed them in. Rob had disappeared in these hallowed halls immediately after their arrival. That was another problem. She and Mac would have to discuss when Rob would move back home, much as she hated to see him leave.

"Good morning," Mac announced as he entered quickly, white coattails flying in his wake. As his bulk filled the tiny room, Marta had difficulty getting enough oxygen. He briefly and impartially explained that he would have Sherri's arm X-rayed one more time, then remove the cast, and her mother was welcome to wait in the waiting room and read a magazine.

She was dismissed. Standing outside the examination room, and looking confused because she had gotten turned around in the narrow halls, she had to ask a nurse to take pity on her and lead her back to the waiting room.

The magazines lying on the shiny coffee table were mostly news oriented or gossipy. One had an advice column that made her even more morose. She could write more than a column about why to avoid dating a man with a child, a dog and two snakes, because the woman might end up inheriting some or all of the above. Rob missed his snakes and had mentioned them the last two evenings, wondering if they had enough mice to last, et cetera. She made a mental note to remember to offer to drive him over to his grandmother's to check on them after this ordeal was over. She thought about how to avoid implying in any way that she might be able to find room for them at her house.

"DON'T YOU STILL love her, Dad?" Rob asked Mac as he cut off Sherri's cast.

"Rob, I don't think—"

"You do, don't you?" Sherri pleaded.

Mac sighed. "Yes, kids, I do. But," he hastened to add as they were both in danger of splitting their faces with such wide smiles, "I don't think she has forgiven me."

"For what, Dad?" Rob asked, trying to reason with his father. "You said you didn't know what was going on—that your manager lied to you."

"That's no excuse. I should have checked into things myself from time to time. It was my responsibility."

As Mac bent to his work, Rob sent Sherri an encouraging look.

"Does that mean you don't love me anymore?" she asked.

Mac's head shot up. He looked at Sherri and then he kissed her on the forehead. "I'll always love you, Sherri. This has nothing to do with you and me."

"That's what Marta tells me, too," Rob complained as he slumped in a chair.

"She does?"

"Yeah. She says she loves me, and she loves you but knows you'll never forgive her for jumping to conclusions and bad-mouthing you, and—"

Mac broke into a grin and tuned out the rest. When he remembered how sneaky the two kids were, though, he frowned. Would they tell lies to both him and Marta to try to get each to believe the other was still in love? Or was there really hope?

"HE WANTS TO TALK to you, Mom." Sherri was standing in front of her mother in the waiting room. Marta glanced at her watch and was surprised to see that an hour had gone by.

She should have asked Sherri how she felt, how her arm was, but she could see the cast was off, and she dreaded seeing Mac alone. She procrastinated. "What does he want?"

"Well, he explained some exercises to me. Maybe he wants to talk to you about that."

Marta stood slowly, grasping her purse like a security blanket, wanting to flee through the door, but knowing she had a responsibility as a parent to see this through. She could go home and throw up later, and she wouldn't have to dread ever seeing Mac again because the cast was off and she wouldn't have to talk to him about anything but work. Meanwhile, there was no putting off the inevitable.

When she entered the room that the nurse directed her to, she found herself alone in a carpeted, paneled office with a large wooden desk and plants in front of the sunny window. She wasn't sure what to do, so she sat in a leather swivel chair that faced the desk, and waited.

Mac entered the room, closed the door and stood there leaning back against it. "Hello, Marta."

Marta felt herself go weak at his gentle tone and swiveled her chair to face him. His expression was not the granite-hard one she expected, but sympathetic, kind and sad.

She wiped at her eyes with a sweaty palm, trying to prevent the inevitable tears from being released to do their worst. Let him yell at her, call her names, hate her. Anything but this.

"I have some things I want to show you." He moved to sit behind his desk and picked up a file folder.

Marta gasped. "Sherri's arm's okay, isn't it? I mean, didn't it heal right?"

Mac reached across the desk and touched her hand reassuringly. "She's fine. This is something else I want you to see."

Marta pulled her hand back and put it in her lap with the other one, fidgeting. "What?"

"Canceled checks." Mac set a pile in front of her. "Photographs of work in progress." Another pile, this time splayed out for effect. "Managerial reports." A pile of neatly typed pages.

"I've been by some of your buildings. I've seen the work going on."

Mac shook his head. "You don't understand. These records are all from prior to that day when the roof collapsed. This is what had me believing that my manager was taking care of business."

Marta looked at her lap and spoke quietly. "I knew it."

"What?"

"I knew I couldn't be that wrong about you." She lifted her eyes and looked into his. "I knew you couldn't be a slumlord, no matter how bad things looked that night. I should have stayed and talked it out." She also knew that nothing she could say now would make up for not standing by him in one of his darkest hours.

Mac felt his heart beat faster. She'd admitted she had been too hasty. What else? Were the kids right? Again?

Marta was nervous when Mac didn't say anything. She spoke quickly, before she could lose her nerve. "I judged you unfairly, I didn't give you a chance to explain, I ran out on you. You name it, I did it. I don't deserve for you to be nice to me." She had ruined a beautiful relationship.

"It did hurt—your mistrust."

Marta couldn't stop the tear from escaping her eye. It was followed in short order by another. "I know."

"Even if I was duped by my manager, I know I was responsible. And I understand that you can't forgive me for that. I just wanted to show you all this so you would know I'm not really a slumlord."

"I know that. I . . . I've known it for some time now."

Mac put all the evidence back in the folder and closed it. "Can we be friends, Marta? Sherri still wants to come visit, and I know Rob is attached to you."

Marta felt dismissed and stood up. "Of course." She held out her hand.

"Well, this has been some lesson we've taught the kids, hasn't it?" Mac asked as he accepted her hand in friendship.

Marta smiled. It was the most she could manage under the circumstances. "I don't imagine they'll try matchmaking again for a while."

Mac's smile was easy. "Oh, don't count on it. When I was taking Sherri's cast off, they were already telling me stories about how you still felt about me."

Marta's smile disappeared.

"It's not true, then?"

With a deep breath, Marta looked away, then back at Mac. "I've always taught Sherri that lying is wrong. I won't lie to you, Mac, but I understand how you feel about me, and I'll get over you. I think I'd better go now."

Mac caught her arm as she reached the door. "Wait a minute. You're not over me?"

"Please, Mac, I know I wasn't fair to you, but don't rub it in. Just let me go."

"The kids were telling the truth?"

"Please, Mac—"

"Marta, I love you."

Her mouth dropped open. "After what I—"

"Yes. I understand the pressure you were under. I understand how it looked. Tell me I'm not making a fool of myself here."

Marta smiled through her tears. "Oh, Mac." She stepped into his embrace and wrapped her arms around his neck. "I love you, too. How can you ever forgive me?"

A knock sounded at the door. "Who is it?" Mac called out.

"Just us, Dad," she heard Rob answer as he opened the door. Marta couldn't stop her tears even as she calmed down. "Gee, Dad. You told me not to make her cry."

"I know, son. I'm doing my best to cheer her up." She could feel the rumble of his voice through his body.

"Did she forgive you? Huh, Marta? Did you?"

Marta didn't trust her voice and she nodded into Mac's shoulder, darting a small glance at Rob and Sherri, hoping the kids wouldn't hold her swollen, puffy face against her later as a weapon.

"Great! Did you ask her, Dad?"

"No..."

"You said you would! You told me and Sherri and everything."

"Ask me what?" Marta spoke into Mac's shoulder, muffling her words, not wanting him to see her tear-stained face.

"Look at me." She shook her head in refusal. "There, you see, Rob. I can't ask her if she won't look at me."

"Marta!" Rob whined. "Please," he begged.

"Mo-om."

One glance at their hopeful faces and Marta had to look at Mac. "What did you promise them?"

Mac smiled innocently. "Only that if I presented you with all the facts and you could see your way clear to forgiving me, that I would ask you to marry me."

Marta couldn't speak, standing there with what she knew was a shocked expression on her face.

"Say yes!" Rob coached her in his excitement.

"No!" She pulled quickly out of Mac's arms and stepped back until she bumped the leather chair.

"No?" both males echoed.

"Mo-om!"

"Mac, how could you ask me to marry you after the way I treated you? I obviously don't know you well enough."

"But I want to call you Mom," Rob tried to reason with her with his preteen logic.

"I want to call him Dad," Sherri added. "And we could be brother and sister and everything!"

Through the door that the kids had left open, Marta could see a partial view of nurses and X-ray technicians gathering in the hall to listen, almost out of sight but not quite.

"Please, Marta," Rob continued whining. "He didn't know about the accidents—"

"Rob..." his father tried to warn him.

"He didn't mean for those people to get hurt. He's been working and working so hard—"

"That's enough, Rob." Mac was tired of standing there alone again and pulled Marta back to him, not taking her initial resistance for an answer, physically encouraging her to need him again by providing a haven in his arms.

"Don't you care if she doesn't want to marry us, Dad?"

Marta chuckled into Mac's hard, somewhat damp shoulder.

"We don't want to scare her, Rob. You have to give her time to think things over. Both you kids have to leave this office and give me time to tell her I love her."

"Oh."

Marta heard the door close.

Mac took Marta's face in his hands and gently made her look up at him, not caring that her eyes were red and puffy or that her skin was all blotchy from crying. To him she was the most beautiful woman in the world, and he needed her. He tried to convey his thoughts in his look and leaned down ever so slowly to join his warm lips to hers.

"Did you tell her yet, Dad?" filtered through the closed door.

Mac had to bite his lower lip to stop chuckling long enough to shoot a negative answer back through the door. "Marta—"

"Did you say yes, Mom?" Sherri asked.

"Oh, Mac." Marta threw her arms around Mac's neck and hugged him. "Put the kids out of their misery and tell them I said yes."

"Yes?"

"Huh, Dad?" Rob called through the door.

"I love you," he announced over the knocking at the door, hoping they would take the hint and give him a few more minutes. He continued in a normal voice, "And I understand. Everything."

"I am so sorry," she apologized, "that I jumped to conclusions. And I promise never to do it again."

"Not even if you find a long blond hair on my jacket?"

She shrugged and teased back, "With Dixie in the house, who could doubt you?"

The knocking started again. "Quick, set a date and we can tell the kids. Rob can start calling you Mom tonight if he wants."

"Gosh, but you're a pushy guy."

"I have to be. I almost let you get away from me once."

"All right. If you feel that way, what are you doing tomorrow?"

"Tomorrow? Are you sure?" He looked as though he would burst with happiness.

Marta shrugged playfully and smiled. "Sure. Why not?"

"Come in!" he yelled to his son before wrapping Marta in his arms again and covering her lips with his own. "We're getting married," he told Sherri enthusiastically, and she jumped up and down in excitement.

"Mom!" Rob held his arms open wide.

"Dad!" Sherri was equally dramatic with Mac, hugging him as well as she was able with a recently healed arm.

"Now that's settled I've got to get you all out of here so I can get some work done," Mac announced with a laugh as he ushered the three of them out of his office and into a hall filled with clapping nurses and technicians. He stood there and basked in the happiness of being with them.

"Come on, Mom, I'll help you pack," Rob announced loudly, obviously liking the sound of it. "You . . . and my sister," he said with a proud smile.

HARLEQUIN
A Calendar of Romance

Be a part of American Romance's year-long celebration of love and the holidays of 1992. Celebrate those special times each month with your favorite authors.

Next month, live out a St. Patrick's Day fantasy in

MARCH

S	M	T	W	T	F	S
1	2	3	4	5	6	7
8	9	10	11	12	13	14
15	16	17		20	21	
22	23					
29						

**#429 FLANNERY'S RAINBOW
by Julie Kistler**

Read all the books in *A Calendar of Romance,* coming to you one per month, all year, only in American Romance.

If you missed #421 HAPPY NEW YEAR, DARLING and #425 VALENTINE HEARTS AND FLOWERS and would like to order them, send your name, address and zip or postal code along with a check or money order for $3.29 plus 75¢ postage and handling ($1.00 in Canada) *for each book ordered,* payable to Harlequin Reader Service to:

In the U.S.
3010 Walden Avenue
P.O. Box 1325
Buffalo, NY 14269-1325

In Canada
P.O. Box 609
Fort Erie, Ontario
L2A 5X3

Please specify book title(s) with your order.
Canadian residents add applicable federal and provincial taxes.

COR3

My Valentine 1992

Celebrate the most romantic day of the year with MY VALENTINE 1992—a sexy new collection of four romantic stories written by our famous Temptation authors:

- GINA WILKINS
- KRISTINE ROLOFSON
- JOANN ROSS
- VICKI LEWIS THOMPSON

My Valentine 1992—an exquisite escape into a romantic and sensuous world.

Don't miss these sexy stories, available in February at your favorite retail outlet. Or order your copy now by sending your name, address, zip or postal code, along with a check or money order for $4.99 (please do not send cash) plus 75¢ postage and handling ($1.00 in Canada), payable to Harlequin Books to:

In the U.S.
3010 Walden Avenue
P.O. Box 1396
Buffalo, NY 14269-1396

In Canada
P.O. Box 609
Fort Erie, Ontario
L2A 5X3

Please specify book title with your order.
Canadian residents add applicable federal and provincial taxes.

Harlequin Books®

VAL-92-R

Harlequin Intrigue®

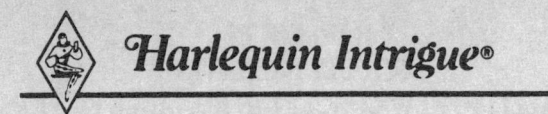

Trust No One...

When you are outwitting a cunning killer, confronting dark secrets or unmasking a devious imposter, it's hard to know whom to trust. Strong arms reach out to embrace you—but are they a safe harbor...or a tiger's den?

When you're on the run, do you dare to fall in love?

For heart-stopping suspense and heart-stirring romance, read Harlequin Intrigue. Two new titles each month.

HARLEQUIN INTRIGUE—where you can expect the unexpected.

INTRIGUE

HARLEQUIN PROUDLY PRESENTS
A DAZZLING NEW CONCEPT IN ROMANCE FICTION

TYLER

One small town—twelve terrific love stories

Welcome to Tyler, Wisconsin—a town full of people you'll enjoy getting to know, memorable friends and unforgettable lovers, and a long-buried secret that lurks beneath its serene surface....

JOIN US FOR A YEAR IN THE LIFE OF TYLER

Each book set in Tyler is a self-contained love story; together, the twelve novels stitch the fabric of a community.

LOSE YOUR HEART TO TYLER!

The excitement begins in March 1992, with WHIRLWIND, by Nancy Martin. When lively, brash Liza Baron arrives home unexpectedly, she moves into the old family lodge, where the silent and mysterious Cliff Forrester has been living in seclusion for years....

WATCH FOR ALL TWELVE BOOKS OF THE TYLER SERIES
Available wherever Harlequin books are sold

TYLER-G